PRACTICALLY
EVER AFTER

PRACTICALLY EVER AFTER

EVER AFTER • BOOK THREE

ISABEL BANDEIRA

Spencer Hill Press

Library of Congress Cataloging-in-Publication Data
Names: Bandeira, Isabel, author, illustrator.
Title: Practically ever after / Isabel Bandeira.
Description: First edition. | New York : Spencer Hill Press, [2019] |Series: Ever after ;
book 3 | Audience: Ages 13+. | Audience: Grades 7-9. | Summary: To high school senior
Grace, life is an equation where everything can be perfectly calculated to ensure maximum
success and the perfect future, including having the perfect girlfriend and being accepted
into a first-choice university, but life has a funny way of getting in the way of plans.
Identifiers: LCCN 2019028347 (print) | LCCN 2019028348 (ebook) | ISBN
9781633921092 (v. 3 ; trade paperback) | ISBN 9781633921108 (v. 3 ; epub)
Subjects: CYAC: High schools--Fiction. | Schools--Fiction. | Perfectionism (Personality
trait)--Fiction. | Dating (Social customs)--Fiction. | Lesbians--Fiction.
Classification: LCC PZ7.1.B3644 Pr 2019 (print) | LCC
PZ7.1.B3644 (ebook) | DDC [Fic]--dc23
LC record available at https://lccn.loc.gov/2019028347
LC ebook record available at https://lccn.loc.gov/2019028348

Published in the United States by Spencer Hill Press
www.SpencerHillPress.com

Distributed by Midpoint Trade Books, a Division of Independent Publishers Group
www.midpointtrade.com
www.ipgbook.com

This edition ISBN:
9781633921092 paperback
9781633921108 ebook

Printed in the United States of America

Design by Mark Karis
Cover by Jenny Zemanek

EVER AFTER SERIES

To the young dreamers who love physics, writing, math, and art growing up in a world that loves to tell people it's impossible to love both the arts and STEM:

The world needs your creative science and logical art. It needs your structure, and the beauty you bring to books, calculations, or anything you choose to create. You are more than a label or a "type." Don't let anyone ever make you believe you can't be all you're meant to be.

And with love to Mom and Dad, for instilling in me a love of words, a love of engineering, and a big dose of Bandeira stubbornness that has allowed me to chase both.

April–May

☐ Chapter 1

"Can you believe we only have two months left? I know I'm supposed to be excited, but it's just so weird to think we're almost done." Alec was the first to drop onto the grass and the rest of us followed. We weren't the only ones with that idea—all around us, other groups of Pine Central's finest seniors were in clumps on the football field, taking advantage of the time outside after our senior class panoramic portrait before any of the teachers decided it was time for us to head back to class.

Judging by the look on Mr. Hayashi's face when he tilted his head up to the sunshine, or how Ms. Lancaster had kicked off her flats to dig her toes into the grass, that wasn't going to be any time soon.

"Almost isn't weird, it's scary," Phoebe said, pushing her long brown hair out of her eyes. She had stuck her messenger bag under her butt to keep off the grass and was leaning on her boyfriend, Dev, to keep her balance. I didn't blame her—pink jeans and a white tunic top weren't exactly grass-stain friendly.

Em, on the other hand, was on her back, yellow cardigan discarded, bare feet propped on top of Phoebe's legs and ignoring any potential danger to her bright green tank top from the dirt. She waved one hand nonchalantly.

"Two months is still a long time." Em reached out as her boyfriend, Kris, passed, pulling him away from his conversation with a teacher and down onto the ground next to her. "Come socialize with people your own age," she said to him, ignoring the look of faux-annoyance he threw her way.

"Em's right," I said as I joined them. The morning sun still hadn't been up long enough to dry the dew, and I could feel it seeping through my jeans, but I could dry my butt with the bathroom hand-dryers later. "About all the time we still have, I mean. Besides, it isn't 'almost' until all our tests and projects are over," I pointed out. "I still have AP Physics this afternoon and you two," I pointed a long blade of grass at Phoebe and Dev, "have AP English on Wednesday."

My stomach churned at the thought. I really should have been memorizing equations in this extra time instead of hanging out on the football field, but I just couldn't drag myself to standing. I bit my cheek and mentally checked my schedule—if I hid out in the library at lunch, I could still get a little more studying in before the test.

"Don't remind me," Dev said. "I don't even know how to study for this one."

Kris nodded, a sympathetic look on his face. "I still have US government and Politics tomorrow. Thank God US History was last week, right, Em?" He shifted uncomfortably, like he'd rather be standing. The guy was probably worried about wrinkling his perfectly ironed slacks before the individual portraits. How our completely laid-back Em had ended up falling for someone like him was beyond us all.

"You are all a bunch of nerds," Alec said with a snort.

"Says the guy who built his own computer because he could 'stuff the heck out of this thing with more RAM and SSDs than stinkin' Pixar and Activision Blizzard combined,'" Em shot back.

"You remember everything, don't you?" He narrowed his eyes at her amused expression before heaving a fake sigh. "Okay, we're all a bunch of nerds." He made a show of pushing his thick, hipster-ish glasses back into place. I'd teased him about them earlier, but after an annoyed comment about how he wasn't trying to look cool, I bit back the urge to remind him again that he seemed to be loving his accessory.

Em looked from Alec to me and said, in a teasing tone, "Grace is the biggest nerd out of all of us. I only took AP History because my mom would have killed me otherwise. Well, that, and it's four less credits I have to pay for if I don't fail." On that last sentence, her tone grew heavier and Kris squeezed her hand, whispering something in her ear that seemed to comfort her. She visibly relaxed instead of going into an over-dramatic fit of "what-if's." Maybe he wasn't so bad for her, after all.

To break the cloud of test fear that had fallen over us, I took one of the clover flower crowns Phoebe had been twisting together while we were talking and put it on my head. "A kingdom of nerdiness and it looks like I'm the queen."

Phoebe's lips hovered between a smile and the slightest hint of a pout. "But seriously, everything's going to change soon. It really is scary," she said, her fingers wrapping tight around the other chain of clovers she was making, crushing the delicate flowers and all of our moods.

"Please. We're all going to be together for a long time. Nerd friendships don't have expiration dates." Em's words were so confident and directed right at her best friend. "It'll be fine, Fee."

"I thought you just tried to argue you weren't a nerd," Dev pointed out with a wide grin.

"Nerd and incredibly smart-non-nerds," Kris corrected with a confident grin. Technically, he wasn't really a part of our inner circle, but I tolerated his butting in for Em's sake.

I couldn't help but play devil's advocate, even though the thought of change added to the tightening feeling in my throat. "Our friendship might be fine, but you know the chances of high school romances surviving are pretty low, right? The statistics are against staying together."

Phoebe hmphed and settled deeper into Dev's arms. "You're just jaded. If people really love each other and it's meant to be, they can make it work. It's not impossible."

I shook my head. Phoebe lived in fairytales. "And the books you read always end while the characters are still teens. 'Happily ever after' usually doesn't make it through college."

Em looked from Phoebe to me, and back to Phoebe again. "If anyone can make it work, it'll be you and Dev and Grace and Leia. And I already know what I want to wear to both of your weddings, so don't screw it up." Ignoring Phoebe's now bright red face, Em barreled on, patting her boyfriend's knee. "Now, Kris and I..."

"Doomed from the start," he chimed in with a grin.

She scrunched up her nose and winked at him before continuing. "See, chances are my career splitting time between Broadway and Hollywood will be totally incompatible with Kris' time on campaign trails and hanging out in places like Kennebunkport and New Hampshire. We'll break up, despite our deep feelings for each other. Heartbreaking, but it'll be the best for our careers. Years will pass, and then, when he's President, I'll come to the White House and sing Happy Birthday to him. And then we'll start a torrid affair... even though neither of us would be married, so it really wouldn't be an affair..."

Now, that sounded like a twist on the familiar. "So: You're saying that you're Marilyn Monroe and Kris is an unmarried JFK?"

"Except it'll end up more like Meghan Markle and Prince Harry. She and I have a lot in common, like being actresses and fantastic at public appearances." Em nudged Kris. "You need to work on inheriting a throne."

I could tell Kris was trying his hardest not to break into a laugh. "Won't work. I'm for republics with elected heads of state. The monarchy is the antithesis of that."

Em heaved a dramatic sigh. "Then I guess we're doomed." She popped onto her knees to kiss him and the rest of our group started complaining about getting a room, Phoebe the loudest about PDA and detentions.

I covered my giggle by checking my phone. "And, with that, this nerd queen needs to go study so she can pass her exams and get the hell away from all of you next fall." I stood and wiped any stray grass off my Dulce and Gabriello jeans.

Alec popped up, swinging his backpack onto his back. "I'll come with you. There's no way I want to be a fifth wheel in this love-fest."

"And here I thought you were leaving because you're jealous."

Alec bumped me with his shoulder. "Nah, dating is overrated. You're right, it's not like most high school relationships survive, anyway." He glanced over at me and added, quickly, "You and Leia don't count in that, you know. You've been together practically forever."

"Yeah." I twisted my backpack strap around my fingers and ignored the leather as it dug into my skin. The tightness in my throat wouldn't let me say anything else and I chalked it up to pre-test nerves. Alec was right. Leia and I *had* been together forever—definitely above average for high school. What was a little distance to a relationship like ours?

☑

"So?" Leia's voice came over my phone at exactly 2:20, five minutes after the last bell and ten minutes before I had to cheer. I didn't even have to look at my screen to know it was her when my phone vibrated in my hand, just hit answer.

I dropped my physics notebook into my locker and slammed the door shut before leaning against it and smiling. Around me, crowds of students were rushing to catch busses or hanging out before a random after school activity, but I was in a happy bubble. Like everyone else was on mute.

"I think I did okay."

"Just okay? Or are you trying to be humble?" I could picture her arching her eyebrow in the adorable way she always did when she was teasing me.

"Cute, really cute. Mechanics was easy, but you know I don't like the electricity stuff. I think I messed up the Biot-Savart law." Phoebe came hurrying up the hallway, Em in tow, but I pointed at the phone and mouthed "Leia," and she nodded, slowing to a stop far enough away to give us some privacy. "I have to get at least a four." Penn State wouldn't even bother crediting me for less than that, which would have made getting ready for the test a giant waste of my time for the past few months.

"You were so ready for this. Your teacher knew you were

ready. Beeyo-Savant or whatever." She giggled at her own deliberate mispronunciation. "I know you kicked test butt. And, you know, no matter how you do on these two stupid tests, it doesn't take away from the fact that you're a math and science genius." Leia was my touchstone. Everyone else thought I always had it all together, but Leia saw through the unruffled face I showed the world. Just talking with her centered me.

"Plus, you like that physics stuff. What's the worst that can happen, you'd actually have to take it again at Penn State? What a terrible sacrifice." She drew out "terrible" in a way that nearly broke my sarcasm meter.

"Thanks being so comforting and for feeding my fragile ego."

"Anytime," she said, punctuating it with another laugh. Through the phone, I could hear a car horn and the sound of shuffling. "My mom's here, so I've gotta go. See you later?"

"I'll be home by 5 if they don't go into extra time. Do you want to go to the diner or hang out at my house?"

"Diner. I really need some disco fries after today." She didn't elaborate and I didn't push it. Leia would tell me about whatever was bothering her when she was ready.

I nodded at empty air. "Okay, diner it is. 5:30; I'll buy the fries."

"Oooh, big spender," she joked, then said, "I'll see you then. Love you."

"Love you more," I said, hanging up and smiling at my

phone for the few seconds before my friends could make it down the hallway. Leia always made things better.

Phoebe was the first to get to me, her fifties-style teal skirt flaring out as she stopped and dropped her bag next to the lockers. With a black three-quarter sleeve sweater and black ballet flats, my little style protégé actually looked very pulled together, like a stylistic mix of modern and classic, couture instead of costumey. I tugged at her sleeve.

"You changed out of your jeans."

She made a little twirl, ending in a model pose. "I had my 'Quietest' yearbook picture and all the club pictures. I didn't have my stylist okay it at lunch, but…"

"It looks cute. It's not exactly what I would have picked for pictures, but my little girl is growing up." I wiped away a fake tear and straightened the neckline of her sweater. I almost suggested adding a teal scarf as a finishing touch to perfectly balance the look but bit back my comment. Perfect was the enemy of good, as Leia liked to always remind me, and Phoebe couldn't exactly go back in time and re-take her pictures, anyway.

Em leaned on me, crossing her arms and stage-whispered, in a faux-conspiratorial tone, "Whoever voted her for 'Quietest' never got dragged to a book signing thing with her."

"An-y-way," Phoebe said, wrinkling her nose at Em, "you aced the exam, right?"

I looked from Phoebe's eager face to Em's smile and took a deep breath, straightening my spine into my most confident pose and pushing back all the doubts I'd shared with Leia. "Of course. Did you expect anything less?"

Em took my question at face value. "No. You're Pine Central's science genius, after all." She then added, "If you hadn't quit being a sciencelete to become a cheerleader, a team with you and Alec would have kicked ass."

"But the squad would have had one less person with acro and dance experience. We 'kicked ass,' too." I pulled my cheer duffle out of my locker and jammed my phone into the side pocket with the muskrat mascot logo. "Speaking of, I have to warm up to cheer our girls' soccer team on to victory in a little bit." I also needed to change *back* into my uniform, but that only took a minute. My hair was already up in a high ponytail with our school's red and orange ribbons thanks to the yearbook pictures earlier.

"Go. Cheer," Em said with a grin, pushing me in the direction of the gym and starting to walk with me. "We just wanted to see how you did. I've gotta go help break down the sets from the spring play and Phoebe promised she'd help."

"That's only because her boyfriend is in the theater club," I said, looking over at Phoebe, who shrugged at my teasing tone. "Bet you'll catch them making out in the costume closet." It was so easy to make Phoebe turn bright red, it wasn't even worth trying sometimes.

"Bet you not, because they're boring," Em said, then ducked the paper Phoebe swatted at her. "Still, it's better than my boyfriend, who won't even go even though his best friend *and* I are in the club. I'll take a reluctant bookworm."

"Aww, trouble in paradise with our illustrious class president?" I teased.

"That's impossible with Em, especially this close to the prom," Phoebe finally found her voice and shot back at Em.

"It's just the cross I have to bear from dating someone as hot as he is." Em fake-swooned, then recovered with a grin. "Look, the one thing I learned about dating is that you pick your battles. Cleaning up backstage and cleaning out the closets aren't worth a fight. Figuring out train schedules for next year between Columbia and Rutgers so we see each other all the time, totally worth it. I'm sure you and Leia have everything planned out, too, right?"

"Right." Because Penn State *wasn't* in the middle of nowhere Pennsylvania with practically no mass transit to it. It didn't help that she was going to Rowan, which was a good four hours away from my campus. We reached the gym and I pushed through the double doors, taking in the familiar smell of sneaker rubber, floor wax, and stale body odor. Even so, it calmed me, and I tossed over my shoulder, "Have fun tearing up London."

"It'll be *supercali*—" Em started to sing, stopping at a hall monitor's dirty look before rolling her eyes and turning in the direction of the theater. "Anyway, have fun cheering."

"Go, Muskrats!" Phoebe's voice echoed down the hallway, followed by a giggle, and, "I swear. Four years and I'm still not used to that."

I hurried across the gym floor and pushed into the

locker room, willing my mindset onto my next task. Cassie waved from where she was tying the red and orange laces on her cheer shoes and I sat down next to her, pulling out my long-sleeved shell. Time to be Grace the cheerleader.

☑Chapter 2

"You owe me an extra plate of disco fries for being late." Leia smiled up at me, waving a gravy-and-mozzarella-covered French fry as I slid into the booth's creaky vinyl seats. Carlo's Diner was already filling with the post-game high school crowd and the early-dinner-eating grey-haired crowd. As small as she was, though, I had no trouble finding her—it was impossible to miss the blue streak in her choppy, chin-length black hair peeking out over the top of our regular booth.

I stole the fry from her and popped it into my mouth before bending over to give her a quick kiss.

"Mmm, disco fry breath, my favorite," I said, plopping back into the seat and patting the ends of my hair to check if it had swung onto her plate in those few seconds. No gravy: I was safe. "Sorry, they actually went to penalty kicks before losing. Pine North is a tough team."

"I heard. They beat our girls team last week." Leia was still wearing her private school uniform, though she'd gotten rid of the little bowtie thing someone on their PTA had thought would look "adorable" with the blouse and had unbuttoned the top few buttons so the light blue top actually looked preppy-cute on her. The school had a really nice sweater dress option for the winter that looked straight out of a Ron Lauren catalog, but their spring/fall khaki skorts, blue-and-white saddle shoes, and ruched-sleeved blouse broke at least five fashion laws in one shot. "Of course, our cheerleaders pretty much suck compared to Pine Central's," she added with one of her cute suppressed smiles as she twirled another fry in the gravy-cheese mix.

"Not that you're biased."

Amusement sparkled in her eyes as she shook her head. "Not at all."

The waitress came over and I distractedly ordered more fries and some gluten-free empanadas they'd just added to the menu.

"So…" I took in the stress in her smile and the fact that she'd managed to polish off most of the fries on her own and leaned forward. "What's bothering you?"

She popped another fry in her mouth to avoid answering me. "Nothing these fries aren't curing," she finally said, then added, "I'm fine."

I steepled my fingers and arched my brow in quizmaster fashion. "Fine as in fine or fine as in 'I don't want to tell you about it' fine?"

"The second one." She pursed her lips at my expression and shook her head. "Promise you'll just listen and that you won't try to fix everything?"

"I don't try to fix everything."

"Mmmhmmm." She focused on getting the fry with the biggest glob of gravy and cheese rather than looking at me, her lips turning up a little in the corners.

"What's the point of hearing someone's problems if you can't offer advice?"

"You're such an engineer already," she teased. "They might as well just give you your diploma right now."

"And you're totally avoiding the question." I caught her eyes and, at her arched eyebrows, quickly added, "Which I won't try to fix. Unless you really need me to."

"Really, it's not a big deal. Just guess who got roped into early morning face-painting duty at my school carnival?"

I did a little mental check of the date and resisted the urge to grimace. Her school carnival was the day after Pine Central's prom, which meant she'd probably have to skip the post-prom sleepover at Cassie's parents' shore house.

"How early?" I asked slowly, trying not to let the disappointment show in my voice.

"9 a.m., right when the thing opens. Because, you know, you can't have pony rides without face painting and the Haddontowne Academy likes things 'bright and early.'"

Her last three words were in a high-pitched imitation of her school's principal, who apparently seemed to think she was a fairy godmother or something. "There's no way I'd make it down to Cape May and back and actually be conscious."

The waitress set down our food and I distractedly thanked her before saying, "I thought you asked for a night shift."

"I did, but Brooklyn decided she wanted that shift and since her parents just bought new smartboards for all the classrooms, guess who got bumped?"

"That worm did it on purpose. She knew about my prom and she wanted to ruin things for you, like she did for your prom." It really had been so *convenient* how her school had decided to institute a new "no non-Haddontowne student at the prom" rule the exact same year Leia was the only student planning on bringing someone from outside the school.

"We really don't know if she's the reason why I wasn't able to bring you. There are a lot of jerks at my school who probably complained. And you know the administration keeps saying it had to do with some drinking or something last year."

I wasn't going to argue with her again about that. Leia had taken the whole prom thing in stride, while I'd been riled up for a fight. "Can you switch with someone else? Talk to your principal about it? Heck, I'll talk to your principal if you want me to."

"You promised not to try to fix things." Leia tilted her head and frowned at me before finishing off the first basket of fries and grabbing one of the empanadas. "And I've already tried talking with everyone. Brooklyn has all her friends assigned for all the other face painting slots and big surprise, none of them can switch."

I felt my fingers curling tighter around my napkin and dropped my hands into my lap so she wouldn't see. "I'm going to shove a potato in her stupid BMW's exhaust. I hate spoiled rich kids."

The tiny smile at the corners of Leia's lips grew wider and she pointed at my bookbag. "So, how's the Laurie Witton holding up? And is that an Airmess scarf in your hair?"

I reached up and defensively patted the silk scarf I'd wrapped around my hair like a headband after my post-cheer shower. "I'm not spoiled, Miss Private Academy." Before she could point out that she was on scholarship and give me any more digs, I smiled back at her. "Look, I really don't care if she tolerates you or not, but I really don't understand why you let Brooklyn get away with everything."

"Because you really have to feel sorry for her. Her parents give her everything she wants, they manipulate the school and the teachers with their money, and she's never had to face failure because money keeps making problems just go away. Someday, when her safety net disappears and she actually has to experience the real world, it's going to hit her hard." Leia ran a hand through her hair, making the ends spike out even more around her ears. "You and I are different. We have real friends who care about us and parents who let us fail and succeed on our own terms. When things go bad—*when*, because this isn't a world of just sunshine and perfect rainbows—we'll be able to handle it. Maybe we'll even come out of bad things better off than before because of it. Who knows? We're really lucky like that."

"That's really deep. How did I manage to date someone so smart?"

A tiny, flirty smile played across her lips. "Dunno. I guess you're lucky like that, too."

I grinned, then nodded, thinking aloud about next steps. "Okay, we'll forget about the shore. I'll let Cassie and the rest of the squad know. Brooklyn is killing decades of Pine Central cheer tradition, you know."

"I'm sure they'll survive without me, but you can go if you want."

"You're kidding, right?" I shook my head, my lips pressing into a straight line. "No. We can go to that post-prom thing the student council is doing, instead. I'll get our tickets. We'll be home by one at the latest."

"That'll make my mom happier, anyway. You know she didn't like the whole shore house idea."

"Afraid it was going to be a massive cheerleader orgy?" I asked with a snort.

"You're not far off. You know she thinks cheerleading is the gateway to all things the stereotypical 'bad girls' do in high school." Leia rolled her eyes dramatically while scrunching her nose at me.

"She's just biased against elite athletes." I suppressed a smile and added, "Does your mom think I'm a bad girl influence? That I run around picking on math nerds in my free time?"

"Like you have free time," she said, a sarcastic note twisting with her teasing tone, then, as I deepened my pout, waved dismissively at me and added, "Oh, come on, you're probably the nerdiest cheerleader she's ever met."

"I'll take that as a compliment," I said in my most begrudging tone.

"You would. Speaking of cheer, any news from the tryouts?"

I really didn't need that reminder. I resisted the urge to check my email at that second, keeping my fingers busy by folding and unfolding my napkin, instead. I'd been waiting since March for Penn State to announce the list for next year's team, and this week, especially, had felt like a lifetime. "No. They didn't promise it would be up this week, though."

"Don't worry. You nailed the audition. They'd be silly not to take you." Her phone buzzed and she frowned as she flipped it over and glanced at the screen. "Sorry, that's Mom. She wants me home for dinner. 'Family meeting,'" she said, hooking her fingers in air quotes.

"Okay, Princess, go home before you turn into a pumpkin." I picked up the check, shoving away Leia's proffered ten-dollar bill, pulled a twenty out of my bag, and waved down the waitress.

She stuck her tongue out at me. "It's Ewoks and light-sabers, Princess. Which means that I'd turn into a Death Star. You should know that by now." At the waitress' confused look, she said, "Sorry, these people from Monaco just don't understand us Alderaanians." As the woman walked away, we muffled our giggles. Not too many people knew we'd both been named after princesses—in fact, our combined parents' weirdness was one of the first things we bonded over when we met. I was named after Princess Grace, who was from Philly, because my mom had this fairy-tale fantasy that I'd follow in her footsteps, while Leia was named after Princess Leia because her parents are *Star Wars* geeks. Even though I thought her name was infinitely cooler than mine, she liked to argue that she was just happy she didn't end up being named Amidala.

"Pumpkin, Death Star, totally the same thing. They're both sort-of round." We walked out of the diner and I put my hand on the small of her back to guide her down the steps and towards her car. My house was only two blocks away, but Leia lived on the other side of town, right where it edged Millbrook. A few more feet over and she would have been in rival school territory, private school or no.

"You're such a 'fake geek girl.' I should have known cheerleaders, especially blonde cheerleaders, were a total fail when it comes to getting mainstream pop-culture sci-fi references," she teased. Leia got to her little beat-up Hyundai and leaned against the door, looking up at me. Leia barely broke five feet and her hair and outfit only added to her pixie-like look, and even though I wasn't that tall, I eclipsed her, even in flats. In the glow of the setting sun, she really looked like she had just stepped out of a fairytale.

I laughed and stepped closer, slipping my arms around her waist. "That's why I have you. You're my geek cred." I bent down and she rose up on her tip-toes at the same time, our lips meeting at the midpoint. Just like our first kiss at my sixteenth birthday party, this one electrified me. Her arms went around my neck and her fingers tangled in my hair, playing with the knot on my scarf as she pulled me closer and deepened the kiss until I was the one pressing forward, practically trying to make the two of us meld into metal of the car door.

When we finally came up for air, Leia reached up and fixed the mess we'd made of my once-perfect hair while I tried not to look flustered. That wasn't our usual good-bye kiss. My fingers still tingled, hyper-sensitive as I straightened her blouse. I kissed the tip of her nose.

"What was that for?" I asked.

"For being understanding about the whole prom shore house thing."

"Right," I said with a grin, "Thanks for reminding me that I have to stock up on potatoes."

"Goose." She reached up for a quick kiss. "Leave Brooklyn's car alone."

"I can't promise, but," I held the door as she slipped into her car, "we'll still have an awesome prom. Prep-school maggot interference or not."

"I'll hold you to that." Leia shut the door and waved as she pulled away while I stood and watched until her car turned off Main Street. With a happy little sigh, I headed home. I definitely was going to make sure prom was perfect. I had to.

Perfect Prom Planning	To Do
☑ Buy Dress	☑ Get gardening outfit to help in Leia's garden
☑ Hair Appointment	☑ Turn on alerts for PSU cheer email
☑ Get tickets (ask Em to pick them up from student council office)	☑ Concept for Eng D&D class
☐ Rewatch "She's All That" and any other old movies Leia likes with prom scenes for ideas	☑ Senior Luncheon tickets
☐ Corsage (wrist or pin one? Both just in case?)	☐ History Paper
☐ Ask Em if prom presents are a thing?	☐ Graduation outfit (what looks good under those robe things?)
☐ Organize rides to/from prom	☐ Fix Post-prom situation
☐ ~~Pack shore bag~~ Post-prom tickets	☐ Saturday date ideas?
☐	☐ Buy potatoes???
	☐

☐ Chapter 3

I stared at the mentor availability calendar on the board, and with a frown, pulled my planner out of my backpack. A major perk of taking the independent study Engineering Drawing and Design class was that we actually got to work with grad student mentors from Schuylkill University on our final design projects, which was a great way to get a peek into college-level engineering. The downside, though, was trying to coordinate schedules, especially this time of year, when a lot of them were already deep into co-ops or internships and we were deep into finals.

"What time do you want?" I asked Alec as I scanned my already crammed week. He and I had both been partnered with a mechanical engineering grad student named Oliver, and always tried to schedule our times together. It was an incredibly logical compromise—not only did everyone save on gas and tolls, but, even though my and Alec's projects were different, a lot of things we needed help on were pretty much the same.

Alec didn't even bother to check his phone, only squinted at the list Mr. Newton had projected up on the smartboard. "How's Wednesday at 3?"

I didn't even need my planner for that. "No go. Cheer until 4."

He shrugged. "Okay, Oliver's also got time on Friday until 4."

I slid my finger along the rows of boxes on my planner until I got to Friday. I was supposed to help Leia with her volunteer program at that time, but as long as Alec, Oliver, and I met at the library, I'd be really late but could possibly still make it work. "Grab that one before Dave does."

"Grabbing." Alec said, hopping into the online class calendar.

Meanwhile, I inked the time into my planner, taking a minute to tap my pen hesitantly against the table before crossing out the original time next to "Leia's garden." She would understand. "Thanks." I glanced up to see our teacher making a beeline for us with a frown. "Newton incoming," I said under my breath, then flipped my notebook open to my last set of notes and concept sketches. Maybe I could distract him with design brilliance?

Alec, probably thinking the same thing, opened Creo on his screen and pulled up one of his incredibly cool but completely impractical designs in the 3-D modeling program.

Mr. Newton rounded our table to stand behind us and check out Alec's screen. He cleared his throat dramatically. "Good morning Grace, Alec."

"'Morning," Alec said without looking up from adding random rounds to what I guessed was some sort of gladiator chestplate.

"I think you two just broke your own record for blocking off Oliver's time in the class calendar," our teacher said, not even trying to hide the annoyance in his tone.

Alec gave one final click and rendered his model with a flourish of his mouse. "It's not our fault everyone else is slow today because they were up late last night binging *Technocracy*."

Mr. Newton didn't even crack a smile. "Speed aside, you both need to learn to negotiate schedules with your classmates. This is the second time you two have done this to them."

Technically, it was the third time we'd broken the unspoken rule of asking before scheduling with Oliver, but I wasn't going to correct him. It wasn't like Dave or Ilse actually had super busy schedules, anyway. Definitely not anywhere near mine. I gave him my most apologetic smile. "Sorry, we'll do better next week. It's my fault, my schedule is a mess." I angled my planner so he could see my perfectly detailed hourly layout, my entire life laid out in beautiful, unbroken, multicolored thirty-minute increments.

Mr. Newton made a disbelieving sound. "Next time you don't consult with Dave and Ilse and make sure they have a fair chance at scheduling, I'm docking class participation points from both of your final grades." He looked from Alec to me and seemed a little disappointed when we both just shrugged in response. "Now, have you both decided what your final projects will be? Deadline to submit your proposals is next Monday."

I nodded, holding up my notebook so he could see the crude sketches I'd made of a glove in isometric view. I wasn't perfect at art like Alec, but the idea I was trying to convey was recognizable. "I want to figure out a way to make a better version of the gloves some stroke rehab patients wear. My grandmother had to use one and complained about hers all the time. I thought maybe I could make something better than the one she had." When Mr. Newton had taken us on a short field trip to the university to meet Dr. Aubrey and her grad students, Oliver had shown us a robotic glove he had been working on for people with paralysis in their hands. The moment I saw the prototype in action, the ideas started percolating in my head. Not for a glove like his, but something that would help make things easier for people going through the same thing as my grandmother.

Mr. Newton took my notebook into his hands and studied it for a minute, nodding. "Good start. It'll be interesting to see how you work this out. Just don't bite off more than you can chew, as usual, okay?" He handed the notebook back, then turned to Alec. "I hope you're not making armor, because I don't know if I can justify accepting voice of customer from a comic book character again," he said, referring to Alec's last project. "It would be nice to see you do a project in this century and this universe, Alec."

"I know, but that was a really fun project to model." Alec gave his 3-D model one more spin before pulling out his sketchbook and opening it to a page full of doodles that were a million times better than my sketches. A few different thumbnail-style drawings filled the page in a way that defied all good documentation practice rules. Alec never had any trouble brainstorming concepts and usually had the most out-of-the-box ideas of everyone in the class. Instead of pointing to one of his rube-goldberg-esque designs that looked like something out of a DaVinci notebook, though, he'd circled something that looked a lot like a simple easel. "I'm thinking of designing an adjustable, ergonomic stand for my drawing tablet. My current kickstand sucks and I think I can make something better."

"That's surprisingly simple for you," Mr. Newton said.

"That's because I actually have to make it work," Alec said, taking back his sketchbook with a sheepish smile. "And you know I pretty much only took this class for the CAD and design, not the engineering."

I resisted the urge to snort. "You know you're not supposed to say that in front of the teacher right before starting your final project, right?"

Our teacher shook his head and cracked a smile. "It's not a surprise. Complexity isn't a requirement, but I do need to see a moving assembly. And you'll still have to go through the entire design process." He then looked pointedly over at me. "Remember, it's not about having the fanciest design, it's about showing you can develop an idea into a technically feasible prototype with plans for how you'd get to commercial launch. Simple is okay."

"Got it." I turned back to my computer screen and pulled up the project proposal I'd already started drafting. "I can do simple."

"Good. And remember to play nice with others, you two." Newton rapped his knuckles on our table before moving on to Dave, probably to lecture him about standing up to us.

"You're not going to make something simple." Alec knew me all too well. "It's, like, physically impossible for you, and I think you secretly love lording it over everyone else, too."

I didn't bother to contradict him, instead flashing him a confident grin. "If I want to be a real engineer, I won't succeed by taking the simple way out," I said, carefully typing "Stroke Rehabilitation Glove" into the project title space. "I can make it work." After some of the research I'd done over the weekend, I was positive my idea wasn't going to be too complicated to work out. There were only so many ways to design rehab gloves, after all.

"Oh, I believe you can." Alec said, turning back to his chestplate design. "Just save some of that energy for all your other finals."

"I'll be fine." I clicked the internet icon on my desktop

and started searching for pictures of other rehab gloves. "This is going to be fun."

"Ha, famous last words, Grace," he said.

"Not for me."

□

I was still running through my design ideas as I left class when a hand grabbed my arm and started pulling me through the hallway. I looked up to see Em grinning over her shoulder at me as she picked up her pace.

"Okay, you need to hear this and I want you to hear it directly from the source. This is the absolute best thing I've heard in days." Em practically dragged me down to Phoebe's locker, pushing through groups of people packing the hallway.

Phoebe's grey eyes grew huge when she saw us. Her gaze bounced between Em and me before she practically tried to stuff herself in the locker. "I told you, Em, I'm not going blonde," she said defensively from behind the half-open door. "First, Mom would kill me, second—"

"Relax, I was kidding." Em said, sharing an amused look with me. "Even though I think it might look pretty awesome on you. But we're not here about that."

"Oh, so..." she looked back over at me and I shrugged. There were times I just didn't get their best friend dynamic. "What's up?"

An evil little twinkle came into Em's expression. "Tell Grace where you're going to be staying this summer while you're in India."

Phoebe stopped using the locker door as a shield and closed it slowly, failing miserably at looking nonchalant as she leaned against the row of lockers. "Well, you know my parents weren't big fans of me spending every night for a month in the same house as my boyfriend even though we're going to be in completely different rooms and with his whole family," she started slowly. "So—"

Em jumped in before she could finish. "They're making her sleep in a convent."

Phoebe scrunched her nose as an annoyed look flashed across her features. "It's *not* a convent. It's an all-girls boarding school attached to a convent. And it's only a block away from his grandparents' place," she said pointedly.

Out of everything I'd guessed, there was no way I would have come up with that. At the semi-defiant look on Phoebe's face, I suppressed a laugh. "You're kidding."

"Dev's great aunt's sister-in-law is one of the Sisters who teach there. She was on a long call with my mom and his mom yesterday, working out all the details so I'd have somewhere to stay. They even found another convent school for me to stay at when we're in Delhi."

"Wow."

She crossed her arms defensively in front of her chest. Annoyed Phoebe was like a kitten who had been poked one too many times by a little kid. "It'll be fun. Classes might be in session, so I'll get to meet the girls who board there."

I quirked an eyebrow at her. "Your parents realize you're going to college next year, right?"

Phoebe blew air through her lips and rolled her eyes to the ceiling. "Look, the important thing is that, in about six weeks, I'm going to be standing under the Gateway to India with Dev."

"Probably chaperoned by his whole family. And yours, too, via videochat, if your parents have their way. I'm amazed your sister was allowed out enough to meet Petur, much less get engaged." Em turned to face me directly and Phoebe stuck her tongue out at Em from behind her back, "We can't let Phoebe and Dev miss out on prime romantic opportunities at the Taj Mahal or—" she waved her hand over her shoulder at Phoebe in a "fill me in" gesture.

Phoebe heaved a deep sigh and rolled her eyes at me, but played along. "Sunset over Marine Drive?"

"Yes, that. Perfect." Em flashed a grin at me. "So, are you and Leia up to with helping us brainstorm, Grace?"

"Sure," I said, laughing with Phoebe as she pretended to facepalm. "Count us in."

"Good. Now, find some space on that super busy schedule of yours to go shopping with her. Phoebe needs some 'hottest girl at the convent' clothes."

"You're not letting go of that ever, are you?" Phoebe asked, but the corners of her lips twitched up the littlest bit despite her best efforts to look stern.

Em tilted her head, her grin impossibly wide as a counter to Phoebe's expression. "What do you think?"

Phoebe made a half groan/half ugh sound and stormed down the hallway.

"Love ya," Em called after her before turning to me. "She'll thank us afterwards."

I shook my head at her. "'Hottest girl at the convent,' Em?"

Em shrugged, trying to look nonchalant, but her expression grew more serious. "She'll never complain out loud, and don't tell her I told you this, but she's really not happy about the boarding school nun chaperone thing. She was already super stressed about her sister's wedding and all the stuff everyone expects her to do as maid of honor considering that Trixie just *had* to time it so all the work falls on Feebs right now, right before graduation—"

"I know," I said, cutting her off. "Remember? Me and Leia are trying to help her out as much as you are. And my mom volunteered to help her mom with planning Trixie's wedding." I could practically picture the layout in my planner—I'd used a teal pen for all of Phoebe's things, and they had been neatly slotted between all the other things I needed to do for the rest of the school year. It was easy enough to add a shopping trip to the list.

"Yeah, but she's been trying to put a really good face on things. Think about it, the only two things that were actually all about her were graduation and this trip, and now this convent thing is happening. She was really looking forward to late night movie watching and hanging out on the apartment balcony to see the sunrise and stuff, and instead she's getting twenty-four-hour surveillance. Feebs was crushed last night."

My eyes grew wide at the details. Phoebe's easy smiles and banter hadn't even hinted a problem. "And, so, you remedy this by reminding her of the thing that upset her? That's a great way to upset her more."

Em shook her head so hard, her curls bounced against her cheek. "Nope, nope, nope. I'm just trying to cheer her up."

That last sentence didn't compute. "By teasing her?"

"Ah, but," she held one finger up in the air to make a point, "she was about to start laughing just now, wasn't she?"

"Because you were being ridiculous."

"That was the point," Em said with a nod. "I know what makes her laugh and I have no problem being ridiculous if it helps cheer up the people I love. Ignoring the problem isn't going to make it go away, but making it something she can laugh over might help a little. You do the same thing, in your own super logical life guru way." She checked her phone and grimaced at the time. "I've got to go, but schedule that shopping trip with her. I know you're busy, but she could probably use a little one-on-one Grace time." Without waiting for my answer, she started down the hallway with a wave. "Thanks!"

I blinked at her retreating form, absorbing the whirlwind of the last few minutes. Em always seemed to find new ways to surprise me.

My phone messenger dinging broke me out of my thoughts, a message from Leia popping up over my lock screen. *After school studying still on the schedule?*

I smiled down at my screen as I headed for my own locker, typing: *Definitely. Library?* Maybe she'd have some ideas about things we could do to help Phoebe a little more, too. Leia was good at things like that.

Leia's response came quickly. *Perfect. See you in a few. <3*

□Chapter 4

The park outside Lambertfield's library looked like the encyclopedia entry for a perfect spring afternoon, complete with singing birds and kids floating little boats in the fountain, but all that had quickly faded into the background after I'd opened my latest email. I shifted uncomfortably on the wooden bench, staring at the screen of my phone for a solid minute before hitting refresh again, nausea washing over me. The list of names didn't change, no matter how many times I re-read the announcement.

Leia's familiar short hair brushed my jaw as she came up from behind to softly kiss my cheek.

"Hey, sorry I'm late, Ms. Murray and Miss Royal stopped

me to talk about graduation and class day exercises and I—"
She stopped the second she saw my expression. "Grace,
what's wrong?" Leia asked, coming around the bench to
sit next to me.

"Next year's cheerleading team was announced," I said,
trying to keep the disappointment and disbelief out of my
voice.

"You're not on the list," she guessed, her voice growing
softer with sympathy as she reached out to tug my phone
from my hands to check for herself. After a moment, she
shut off the screen and dropped the phone into her lap, covering it with one hand to keep me from getting at it, then
wrapping her free arm around my shoulders and squeezing
lightly. "Well, it's their loss."

I ignored the urge to take back my phone and check again,
instead leaning into her squeeze and taking comfort in her
just being there. Leia gave the best hugs. Maybe even good
enough to help squeeze away the sting of rejection. "Thanks."

Leia didn't say anything for a minute, just dropped her
head to my shoulder and tightened her side-hug. I dropped
my head on top of hers, breathing in the familiar, spicy san-
dalwood scent of her perfume and soaking in her calm aura.
As soon as the tension in my shoulders dropped a notch, she
handed me back my phone. "We knew it was a long shot,
anyway, especially since you're an incoming freshman."

"Yeah." It still stung, though. Part of me expected to
get on the team, anyway, especially since I'd driven up to
State College for the audition and had given a textbook

audition and interview. I'd out-handspring-ed and out-heel-stretched half the girls there and danced better than at least three-quarters of them, so I couldn't wrap my brain around why I wasn't at the top of the list. "I should call them to make sure this list is complete." There simply *had* to have been some sort of mistake. Maybe they'd confused me with another girl or—

"You're not used to not getting rejected, so I'm sure it hurts even more," Leia said, ignoring my last sentence and breaking my train of thought. "It definitely must be a blow to your ego."

"Excuse me?" I tried to lift my head to narrow my eyes at her, but she reached up and held me in place, her shoulders shaking slightly as she held back a laugh.

"Even Princess Grace needs to hear 'no' once in a while," she said, softly. "But you can't blame them. They didn't know they turned down royalty. And, like *you* even said, it was a long shot to begin with."

"Hmph."

"Anyway, this will make you stronger," she said in direct imitation of my cheerleading coach.

I felt the pout growing on my lip. "I think I'd prefer staying weak and getting on the team."

"You will, next year. You can build up your skills and show them why they'd be crazy not to have you on their team. Until then, how about the club teams?"

I tried not to make a face at her suggestion. In my opinion, club teams were either for people who couldn't make the cut or weren't totally serious about the sport. Leia had called me a snob the last time I'd told her that, so, instead, I said, "I don't know. Maybe I need to focus on my classes next year."

"Ten dollars and a plate of disco fries says you'll miss cheer and you'll be on one of the club teams by October."

I shook my head hard enough to mess up her hair, knowing that doing so would annoy her later when she tried to smooth it back down. "You know I only did cheer to bulk up my transcript and up my social quotient. Otherwise, I'd have stayed in dance. It was a means to an end."

Leia made a humming sound that was the non-verbal-equivalent of a disbelieving "sure."

"Really, I won't miss cheer. In fact, it might be nice to get some free time back." I said, and she made the same humming sound as before. "It's true. It's not like I love the sport or anything. It was just a logical filler." The words flowed out easily, but the moment she laced her hand with mine, it was hard to keep up my façade. "Fine. It sucks," I said, my voice breaking slightly.

"It totally does."

"But right now I want to wallow and quit cheer forever." The thought of not cheering or competing next year was hard to process, and I squeezed her hand.

"I know," she said, squeezing back.

"And I want my girlfriend to be supportive and not to call me out while I'm trying to talk myself out of being disappointed."

Leia let out a small, almost exasperated sigh. "I am totally being supportive. I just want you to remember that you're allowed to love things just for the sake of loving them, and that it's not the end of the world that you didn't get picked for this one team at this one school."

"I—" I couldn't quite argue with her on that. We sat in silence for another minute. "The textbook scholarship would have been nice." I said while playing with her fingers.

"Not like you need one, Miss My-Piggy-Bank-Practically-Has-Its-Own-Financial-Advisor. And don't give me one of those 'a penny saved is super practical' lectures when you just bought a three-hundred-dollar scarf to tie onto your back-pack." She laughed at my *hmph* and snuggled further into my side, giving me a tiny jab with her elbow. "Save the scholar-ships for those of us who need them, 'kay? I would definitely have taken up cheerleading if my school had one of them."

I lifted my head off hers and turned to give her my best scrunch-nosed grin. "I can't picture you as a cheerleader." Leia, for all her grace in everything else in life, had the coor-dination of a television nerd trope when it came to things like hip-hop and acrobatics. I had to hold back a giggle at the memory of the one time I tried to teach her a basic cartwheel and she'd ended up splayed out on her back on my lawn, declaring that she'd never try tumbling ever again and that I'd been the devil for suggesting it in the first place.

"Your imagination just needs work. I'm sure I can do a roundhouse with tons of school spirit."

I knew she had gotten the name wrong on purpose just

to cheer me up, but I played along. Leia was the queen of listening and remembering details. "Roundoff."

"Potato, pesticide, whatever." She waved the hand that was hugging me dismissively.

"That's Round-up. And Round-up is an herbicide, not a pesticide."

"Know-it-all." She pulled back from the hug to poke me in the nose lightly with her finger and said, "Whatever it is, I could pull it off. I'd be in the hospital for a week afterwards, but textbooks for an entire year probably cost more than a hospital stay."

"The truth in that really hurts."

"Tell me about it. The way my student loans look, I'm going to be in debt until my great grandkids go to college." She reached up to fix my ponytail. "Feeling up to our study date, or do you want to, I don't know, mope some more?"

"Study." I tried to return the favor and smooth the mess I'd made of her hair, but some of the shorter layers in the back refused to stay down. "At least that's something I know I can control."

"Fine, then let's get to the library before all the good study carrels are taken." She stood and leaned down to plant a small kiss on my lips. "You are amazing and talented and I know how hard you worked to prepare for those tryouts. I'm still super proud of you, whether you made the team or not."

"Thanks," I whispered, turning my head while I stood so she wouldn't see the tiny bit of wetness that started tickling at my eyeballs. Leia knew me all too well.

☐ Chapter 5

The house was so quiet at 4:30 a.m. that, like every morning for the past month, I'd tiptoed downstairs to do my homework in the study so I wouldn't wake up my parents. The quiet was perfect for studying, but, combined with the squish of the overstuffed armchair I'd dropped into that morning, it was way too easy to imagine taking a nap, instead. My food sensitivities wouldn't let me eat fistfuls of chocolate covered espresso beans to stay awake like Em and Phoebe always did, so, instead, I dug up Mom's little essential oil diffuser and her "wake up" mix of oils filled the air in the study with the smell of grapefruit, peppermint, and pine.

I yawned and took another sip of water before diving into

the final paragraph of my essay on math in Lewis Carroll's books. Phoebe had teased me about my chosen topic, but it had been so much more fun to work on *this* for my senior honors English essay rather than trying to figure out the symbolism of a blue door some dead author had written into his book a century ago. At least by talking about how *Alice in Wonderland* was a lesson on why, according to Carroll, geometry and classic math was better than the new, "modern" mathematics of his time, I'd gotten the chance to learn more about Euclidean geometry and the adoption of symbolic algebra. Like Dad always taught me, I'd looked for the thing I might love in a task I might not like, and ran with it.

Just as I dropped that essay into my teacher's digital homework folder, I heard the shower turn on upstairs and Mom's pre-coffee heavy-footed steps coming down the stairs. 5:15. I still had plenty of time to finish the rest of my homework. I switched my focus to Calc, filling the little boxes of my green engineering pad with arcing integration swirls, numbers, and letters. There was something comforting in the way the neat grid made everything I wrote line up so cleanly, from calculations to doodled ideas. No theories or guesses necessary because there was always one right, logical answer in those crisp little rows of calculations. I dove in and got lost in switching between pencil, paper, and my TI-84, knocking out the homework at a speed I could never manage in the afternoons, what with all the texts and DMs and other things that always broke my train of thought.

But, just as I got to the end of a calculation, Dad's and

Mom's muffled voices came through the study's open door and pulled me out of my homework bubble. I debated going up to my room, but one look at all my things laid out on the side table and floor and I decided to just slide the door shut and keep working for the half hour I had left. I tiptoed to the door and my hand paused on the handle as their voices drifted down the hallway, growing louder and unhappier with every new sentence.

Mom's voice was tight, far from her usual cheery tones. "Honestly, David, can't we just have one family dinner together for once? You can't make it tonight and now tomorrow night, too? You know I asked you to keep them both free."

"It's Taiwan." Dad said, clipping his words in the way he did every time he was annoyed with someone. "That's the only time I can hold these conference calls. If you can't understand how time zones work, I don't know what to say to you."

"We had a deal. I've already invited Drina. Besides, very soon, Grace is going to be living hours away from us and you're going to regret missing out on dinner with your daughter." At the sound of my name, my stomach twisted as if I'd had eaten a bowlful of all of the foods I was sensitive to in one shot. Mom continued, the sound of water running making her words hard to hear. "Heavens know between your schedule and hers, we never eat together now, anyway."

A series of metallic thuds followed, as if someone put down the breakfast silverware with a little more force than usual. "There you go, exaggerating again. We have dinner together every other night. I can't afford to lose my job or miss out on promotions because of a meal."

Another thud, this time as if someone had dropped a bowl down onto the table, followed by Mom saying, "So, you'd rather miss out on your family?"

I could make out the refrigerator door slamming and the rattle of Mom's glass butter dish being manhandled. I shouldn't have kept listening, but, churning stomach or not, I couldn't pull myself away from the door.

"You're blowing this out of proportion," Dad said.

"And you're killing yourself and missing important family stuff, for what, a new corner office? Companies don't put up tombstones or come to funerals for their employees, families do. Are you going to tell Grace that your work is more important than her?"

"Inez—" Dad was using the same tone he used whenever I'd done something he didn't approve of, and I quickly slid the door shut the rest of the way, muffling whatever he was about to say. I leaned against the door, trying to push away the nauseating feeling of guilt for eavesdropping on them.

After a moment, I took a deep, resolute breath, straightened up my spine, and made a beeline back to the desk, turning to my planner and tomorrow's carefully planned hourly layout. I couldn't fix everything, but I could make *something* work. Mom had mentioned my missing family dinners, too, and maybe there was something I could change to help the situation.

I had my meeting with Oliver until 4 and was supposed to help Leia and her best friend, Emily, with their volunteer program in the library garden from 4 to 6:30, but… I set my jaw against the extra wave of guilt that ran over me as I pulled out my corrector pen and cleared that slot. I'd help out next time. As long as nothing else came up, that meant I would be home in time for an early dinner, early enough for Dad to have his call right afterwards, and I could still make it to the National Honor Society's induction ceremony for next year's seniors at 8. If I ignored the glaringly bright edges of the correction tape all over my schedule, it looked like I'd planned everything out that way to begin with. Not only did everything fit perfectly together, but I'd gotten back almost an hour of study time in the process. I could feel the tension draining from my shoulders as I checked my planner one more time. There was something comforting about fitting everything into timeslots, like I was moving around time with just my pen and my planner.

The study doors slid open and Mom popped her head inside, a cheery smile pasted on her face. "Hey, I thought I heard you in here. Are you planning on eating breakfast? I made a triple dose of quinoa porridge."

"Thanks. You know I can make my own stuff, right?" I started shoving all my things into my backpack and tugged at my pajama pants—I still needed to change before school, but at least all my stuff would be packed.

"I was already making it for me and Dad, it really isn't too much trouble."

"Oh, is Dad still here?" I asked, trying to sound as casual as I could.

Mom shook her head, her expression not changing. "No, he had an early morning meeting." Her voice was as carefully casual as mine, but I could hear the slight annoyance in her tone. "You know how it is. Time zones."

I nodded and turned off her diffuser before following Mom back to the kitchen. "Speaking of time, I was wondering if we could eat an early dinner tomorrow? Like, 5? Something got cancelled and I was able to move my schedule around."

Mom turned around halfway through spooning porridge into a bowl for me and scanned my face, which I tried to keep as neutral as possible. After another second, she turned back to the bowl. "That works perfectly. You don't need to move things around for us if—"

I cut her off as I took the bowl and spoon from her. "I didn't. If we can eat then, it would be a huge help for me so I don't feel like I'm running from one thing to another."

"5 it is." She turned to the whiteboard schedule near the sink and scanned it for a minute. "That'll give your Dad time to eat before his meeting, too. I'm meeting with Ana Martins at 4 to go over some of Trixie's ideas for centerpiece options for the wedding but it should be done by then. And Drina doesn't have classes tomorrow night because her school is competing Saturday—" She nodded again as she stared at the board, and said, a little under her breath, "Yes. I can definitely make it work."

For the first time that morning, I felt the weight lift off my chest enough to let me breathe. "Awesome, thanks."

☑Chapter 6

I flipped between my notebook and tablet, rotating the paper or screen as needed to get my idea across to my one-person audience. The library was fairly empty at this hour, but I kept my voice low, anyway.

"So, thoughts?" Through the window behind Oliver, I could just barely see Leia outside working with the kids and I had push down the guilt that bubbled up in my throat. I hadn't even said hi before heading inside because I didn't want to distract her while she was working—it was bad enough I had bailed on her last minute. I forced my attention back to my screen and said, "Does it make sense?"

Oliver had been nodding throughout my whole

explanation, but now he looked up and his dark brown eyes met mine, his broad face scrunched into a grin. "You know, I'm majoring in mechanical engineering with a focus on biomedical and biomechanical, so you've definitely been assigned to the right mentor." His words were tinged with a faint Irish accent Phoebe would have loved. Knowing her, she would have spent the whole time asking him to say lines from her favorite book series, but for me and Alec, his home country was just a cool discussion point with him whenever we needed a break from project work.

Well, at least for me. Alec seemed way more interested in the video game work Oliver had done before switching over to biomedical engineering.

"Considering Grace's last two projects in class had to do with fixing body parts, it's not a huge surprise Dr. Aubrey and Mr. Newton put her with you," Alec said without looking up from the glove he had slipped on his hand.

I hadn't even realized that, but he was right. Each of the other projects I'd done, though, just seemed to be fun ideas at the time, a way to improve everyday things because I could see how I could make them better. I still needed to see if I could commission Trixie to work some sewing magic on the knee brace I'd designed for my first semester project. Dr. Aubrey had even called my design "innovative" the first time she'd seen it.

Oliver grinned at me. "You're thinking of doing something in medical?"

I shook my head and flipped to the next page, where I'd

detailed out some thoughts on materials I could use in the design. "No, I'm going for Petroleum Engineering."

"Highest median salary," Alec said behind a fake cough.

I side-eyed him and Alec threw me an innocent look. He was right, of course, but I didn't need to give him the pleasure of knowing it. "No, I just like the challenge."

Oliver looked up at the ceiling and spread his hands in a 'Lord grant me patience' way, but a little smile snuck through, anyway. He flipped open his laptop and logged into his CAD program, a familiar modeling environment filling the screen. "Do you guys do any 3-D solid modeling?" He clicked away as we spoke, sliding shapes across the screen and assembling components into what looked like linkages.

"Yeah," I said, and cringed a little at the *duh* in my tone. Widening my eyes and trying to sound less snotty, I added, "That's part of this class, and I've been taking engineering drawing and design classes since freshman year. And Alec is a modeling and graphics genius."

"Okay, good. So, what I'm doing right now is making an assembly of some components I modeled earlier today."

Oliver made one of the parts on the screen move and suddenly, it looked familiar. "That looks a little like a finger," I said.

"Good catch. I'm working on the exoskeleton glove I showed your class during the tour. The glove offers support and acts like extra muscles for paralyzed or weaker patients so they can do things like pick up a mouse." He waved his mouse around as an example.

"You explained that last time," Alec pointed out.

"What do you think are the challenges with lots of current robotic gloves, then?" He asked casually. He still didn't look at us, just kept assembling components together on the screen.

Alec looked over at me and shrugged, but I flexed my hand open and closed, focusing on the feel of each individual finger bending.

"They're still pretty big and don't really talk to the patient's brain like most people's hands and muscles do? And..." I thought about how my cell phone ran out of battery if I just looked at it the wrong way, "battery power?"

Oliver stopped clicking, leaving his thin metal version of what looked like a hand skeleton sit on the screen while he reached into his backpack. Pulling his exoskeleton glove out of the bag, he gestured for my hand and slipped it on. A little pack with a joystick was attached to it by a few thin wires. "Yes. Now, this is just a rough prototype and not as good as the one you saw the other day, but it should give you a pretty good idea of what they're like."

"Cool." I rotated my hand and stared at all the little servos and motors built into the "joints."

Oliver flipped a switch on the side of the joystick box and placed it near my other hand, gesturing for me to play around with it. "You were right about the bulk and the battery. First, we need to make sure the device has enough power. Second, we need to think about the patient's limitations and how they'd be able to control it. There are a few out there that work with sensors and even fewer with really rough neural interfaces, but many of them assume you have some use of your hand or another hand." He watched me poke at the glove and play with it for a little bit before asking, "What's one thing I need to think about if I want to slim this down?"

My brain ran through all the different possibilities. Getting really tiny gears and servos were probably two problems, but as I flexed my finger and felt the plastic of the frame flex a little too much so it made a not-so-good creaky sound, I said, "Making it strong enough to do everything it needs to do even after it's been thinned down? If it's too thin, it might not handle the stress."

"Good answer," Oliver said. "That applies to any of the gears or mechanisms for the joints, too. Any ideas on what you'd do for that?"

"It sounds like you're trying to con us into doing your work for you," Alec said, but flashed us both a wide grin to show he was just joking.

I was too deep in thought to really pay attention to Alec. I studied the glove and the screen, squinting as if it would help me focus. "I'm going to have to guess you've got some good materials to make that," I gestured at the super-thin image on the screen, "possible."

"We do," Oliver shrugged sheepishly, "or, at least, I hope we do. I need to run a finite element analysis on this to see if it's even worth building another prototype, which can get expensive even if school is paying for it." He took back the glove and I cringed as he tossed the delicate prototype back in his bag. "Good answers. Engineering is all about problem solving, no matter what you're designing or improving. We'll make an engineer out of you, after all."

My whole body was vibrating with excitement and ideas both for his glove and for my own project. It took everything in me to keep from asking every question on the planet. What came out of my mouth wasn't the smart question about motors I'd planned, though. "Why medical stuff? I mean, with a mechanical engineering major, you could do power or automotive or anything like that."

Oliver cast a grin my way before turning back to his computer. "I don't know. I mean, part of it is just because it's an awesome challenge. The human body is this incredible machine and I really want to help figure out how it works and how we can fix it."

I'd never thought of it that way. I curled and flexed my fingers, looking at them in a new light. Thoughts of everything that had to happen to make my hands move the way they did swirled around my brain, waking up more questions and ideas, like a biological rabbit hole.

"Plus, it's not just about the mechanics." Oliver continued, rotating the assembly on his screen. "There's real art to product design that you don't find in things like thermodynamics or pure math."

I thought about the satisfying feeling of knowing I'd nailed a calculation with neat, precise rows of symbols, letters, and numbers filling a page. "A good calculation is really beautiful," I shot back, feeling my cheeks warm as I realized how nerdy that had to sound.

"Yeesh, you really are cut out to be an engineer, aren't you?" Alec said, reaching out, hesitating over the mouse until Oliver nodded an okay, to check out the model tree of the assembly on his laptop and rotate the model. "I'm surrounded by nerds."

I poked him lightly in the arm. "Oh, hush. You know you love this stuff, too."

Alec didn't even bother to take his eyes off the screen. "If I ever call a calculation 'beautiful,' take me straight to the ER."

I made a pfft sound. "You're a sciencelete. You can't talk."

"Yeah, but you're the one who wants to make a career out of it," Alec shot back.

Oliver snorted and pulled back control of his laptop, opening it to a document that looked like some sort of questionnaire. "So, you're both at the beginning of your final projects. Have you done any voice of customer work for them?"

Alec shook his head. "Not really. I mean, I guess since I'm the customer, I kind of *am* the voice of the customer."

I blinked at Oliver and pointed at my notebook. "And like I told you, I did some research and I know something about this because my grandmom used a glove like this."

"Voice of customer is more than that, though. If you don't really get a broad idea of what the problem is and don't understand what the user population really needs, you can't figure out the solution." Oliver scrolled through his questionnaire as he spoke. "I'll give you examples of what I did for my project and, if you want, we can figure out a good way for you both to talk with end users and understand their problems so that you can design the best product you can for them. Grace, if you want, Dr. Aubrey knows some doctors and physical therapists who might be able to help you get some input."

I nodded, even though I was sure I was already on the right track with my design. It wouldn't hurt to get a little bit of extra information for my report and presentation slides and I didn't want to sound ungrateful. "Thanks."

"Great. Now," Oliver said, pulling my sketches back in front of him, "let's talk about hand anatomy and design for human factors."

☐Chapter 7

"Your mom showed me your prom dress," a familiar voice said from the table as I tossed my backpack into the study and made my way into the kitchen for dinner. Aunt Drina turned in her chair and smiled at me. "It's beautiful."

I threw my arms around my aunt, her hug and her jasmine perfume engulfing me. Even though she lived only a half hour away, I never saw her enough anymore.

"You should come over and join the mom-arazzi next Thursday. I'm sure they'll appreciate a fourth photographer." Aunt Drina looked like a younger version of my mom, from the dark brown eyes and freckled skin to the reddish light brown hair she always had up in some sort of bun or twist.

Just like my natural color, except I always had my hair highlighted down to strawberry blonde like it used to be before I hit puberty.

"Recital stuff. You know how it is." Aunt Drina pulled back and tugged at my high ponytail. "Is cheerleading season winding down?"

"Pretty much." I slid into my seat at the dinner table and spooned a massive slice of shepherd's pie onto my plate. "Just one more game to go and we start prepping next year's squad."

"Good," Dad said, waving his fork at me and Drina. "Because your aunt needs your help."

Mom shook her head and just spooned more shepherd's pie onto his plate. "Blunt as always, David."

"It's a skill. That's how I get consensus in meetings. no beating around the bush." Dad tried to look serious, but he wiggled both of his greying eyebrows at me and his lips curled up very slightly at the corners. "Grace needs to learn the family secret to being successful."

I copied his expression. While I might look more like my mom, my personality was all Dad's. "Didn't they say on *I Love Lucy*, '*Nunca se haga necocios con familia ni parientes?*'" I quoted the line about not doing business with family in my best Desi Arnaz voice and was rewarded with his almost-smile growing into a full one. He and I had watched so many episodes of that show together that quoting lines at each other had become our thing. "So," I looked from my dad to my aunt. "What's up?"

"I was wondering if you could help out at the school,"

Aunt Drina said, laying down her fork and folding her hands together on top of the table. "My contemporary teacher got a great offer in New York she couldn't turn down, so now I don't have anyone to teach her classes. She told me the other day and when your mom called to invite me over, I figured it was a sign I should ask you."

I nodded slowly, understanding flooding me as I put the time of year and her situation together. "And it's less than two months before the recital."

She nodded. "So, I'm hoping you can do me a favor and fill in until the recital? I'll pay you, of course."

"Contemporary?" Contemporary had been my favorite style before I'd given up dance, but the thought of actually teaching it… "I'm not a trained dance teacher." The thought of teaching some of my former classmates also sent a cold shiver over my skin. How could I possibly teach anyone?

"You were my best student and you were a class assistant for years. It's only two months. You'll be fine." Before I could protest, she added, "I'm taking the rosebud and starshine classes and Natalie can take the seniors. You just have to teach the juniors and junior preps."

My brain translated her school's naming system into age and skill levels. Nine- to fourteen-year-olds, maybe some fifteen- and sixteen-year-olds who started late. At least everyone would be younger than me.

"Juniors and junior preps?" I repeated, slowly.

"Oh, and the adults. But don't worry, they're easy to

teach, just don't work in any tumbling." She didn't look away, just kept her eyes trained on mine with the tiniest concerned expression. "I'd really appreciate it. Natalie can't take on any more classes. I've already over-stressed her and these groups need someone who can demonstrate everything full out for them. And every other dance teacher I know is overbooked because of recital season, too."

I ran through my schedule—if things hadn't changed, all her contemporary classes met later in the afternoon or at night, which were probably the lightest times of my day, but with everything else I needed to do in the next two months, I couldn't imagine taking on one more responsibility. "I... I'm pretty busy."

"If you're worried about being out of practice, don't. It really shouldn't be too bad, just the usual warmups and a few easy combinations to keep them from getting bored. It will be a piece of cake for you."

"That doesn't sound hard," Mom said, in a 'trying to be helpful tone.' "I definitely think this is something you can squeeze in, Grace."

I held back the urge to remind Mom that she wasn't the one being asked to add another thing to her overflowing schedule. After all I'd done for Mom to make family dinner work, I didn't expect her tag-team me about something like this.

"Think about it." Aunt Drina went back to her dinner, then waved her fork around in the air and swallowed to add, "And start thinking about recital pieces for them. April didn't get a chance to choreograph anything before she left."

I quickly ducked my head down and tried to look like I was focused on eating so no one would see my horrified expression.

Perfect. Just perfect.

□

"You need to help your aunt," Dad said, as he followed me into the kitchen with the dirty salad plates. "It's the right thing to do."

I focused on carefully lining up the dinnerplates in the dishwasher rack, my brain spinning with everything I needed to do over the next two months. "I really don't have the time. Between studying and my final projects and cheer—"

"Grace," Mom broke in as she slid past me to drop some dishes in the sink, "Drina's done so much for you, this isn't asking much in comparison."

"Correas don't leave family hanging, ever," Dad added. "She's your only aunt and she needs your help. Plus, with the amount of money we spent on dance lessons and dance shoes, you could at least—"

"David," Mom said abruptly, raising her eyebrow, "It's not about the money, it's about helping someone out of a tough situation."

I didn't need them to start fighting again, this time over me. I blew air through my lips and did a quick mental reshuffling of my schedule that made my heartburn even worse. "Fine, I'll tell her I'll help."

"Wonderful," Mom said, giving me a one-armed hug. "Now, for dessert, I made a coconut milk panna cotta from a recipe I found online the other day, It's a shame Drina had to leave before trying it, but I think you'll both love it." She headed back to the table and placed the jiggly white thing on it with a flourish. "You both still have a few minutes before you need to run off and do your other things, right?"

Dad and I shared a grimace while her back was turned and, before I could bow out gracefully, Dad quickly pulled his phone out of his pocket and said, "Sorry, can't keep Taiwan waiting," and then hurried out of the room.

"Your dad has always been picky," Mom said absently as she scooped a big bowlful of the panna cotta for me. "Aren't you glad you inherited my tastes?"

I stared at the panna cotta and tried to force my brain to believe it looked good. Between my current heartburn and the bowlful of coconut in front of me, I was definitely going to be a nauseated mess through the whole Honor Society ceremony. "Definitely."

☑Chapter 8

"You're ridiculously pretty, you know that? It was really hard to pay attention to Oliver yesterday with you out there being all gardener-y and stuff." I said casually, twirling my spoon in the water ice Leia had picked up from Marranos on her way home from the library. We were perched on the front steps of my house, doing our best to ignore the damp chill starting to settle over the neighborhood.

Or, at least, Leia was ignoring the chill. Considering she was one of those people who believed you should only eat frozen desserts in the winter because then you didn't have to worry about it melting, I wasn't totally surprised. "Really? Mud and all?"

I laughed and reached over to wipe at a blotch of dirt on her cheek. "Mud and all."

"I'm trying to start a new trend. Mud masks on the go. Watch out, Photogram influencers." She struck a silly pose, lips pushed out into a duckface expression, bright red from the cherry water ice she'd gotten. "But you forgot to also tell me I'm incredibly smart. Us pretty girls like to hear that sort of thing, you know," she added, scrunching her nose to let me know she was joking. She waved her spoon at me. "Pretty can go away but smart lasts forever."

"Truth," I said with a laugh, but then added, "But that doesn't negate the fact that you're ridiculously pretty."

She scrunched her nose and used her free hand to push her hair out of her face. "Okay, now you're exaggerating. I know I look like I was attacked by the swamp thing."

"Dirt looks cute on you."

"Thanks." She leaned closer, bumping her nose with mine. "Well, you're ridiculously pretty and ridiculously smart, too."

It didn't matter how many times I heard something like that from Leia, it always made me feel like there was a chemical reaction fizzing through my body, bubbly and energizing. "We're obviously a good match," I said, dropping my chin so my forehead touched hers, then took that moment to close the distance between us with a kiss.

When we broke apart, she pursed her lips at me and said, "Remind me never to mix cherry with key lime." She made a big show of scooping up a big scoop of her water ice and popping it in her mouth.

"Noted."

"So, tell me something interesting. We've already established we're the world's prettiest couple at the moment, and I told you about my and Emily's plans for the children's garden, but you've been so busy lately, I feel like I never really know what's going on with you." Leia leaned into my side and dropped her head on my shoulder.

I popped some water ice in my mouth and let it melt on my tongue while I thought through to the last time we'd talked. "Fair enough. Here's something you haven't heard yet—my parents want me to help teach some classes at Aunt Drina's school until the recital."

"And you?"

"I'm doing it against my best judgment. Mom and Dad pretty much guilted me into it even though they know my time is already overallocated." I loved that last word, "overallocated." Not because I loved having more tasks than time, but it was so efficient.

"I hate to say this, but I agree with your parents. Your aunt has always been there for you."

Side-eyeing her was hard when she had her head on my shoulder, but I tried, anyway. "*Et tu,* Leia?"

I could feel her shoulder shift up in a shrug. "She helped you when it came to figuring out things with me."

That was true. Not only had Drina helped me draw up a plan of attack for telling my parents about Leia, but she had comforted me and was my confidante through my overanalysis ("Does she like me? How can I tell? Should I invite her to my party? Does kissing mean she wants to be my girlfriend? What about handholding?")

Leia continued without waiting for a response. "Besides, you loved dancing. Maybe it will help you relax a little."

I scrunched my nose at her, even though I knew she couldn't see my face. "I don't have time to relax."

I didn't have to see it, but I could practically *feel* her eye roll. "You're a senior with an awesome GPA. Unless you totally fail everything, you're going to be fine."

"Tell that to the AP test graders. And what if I wanted to be valedictorian?" I flung that last bit out knowing it would get a laugh out of her.

As if on cue, she let out a little "Ha." "You can't pull that with me. I know that ship sailed freshman year when you decided you wanted to have a life."

"I could still do it if I could get Christian Washington and the brain squad to drop out…" I said in my best super-villain voice.

"No sabotaging your classmates, Grace," she said in her Mom voice.

"Not even for the chance to give a really boring speech at graduation about how we're embarking on the next, exciting phase in our wonderful life journey and how we'll always have Pine Central muskrat pride to carry us through the tough times?"

She tried to stifle a giggle, but I could feel her shaking next to me. "That muskrat pride is a powerful thing."

"Don't mess with us, we're like the seals of the rodent family. Noble and web-footed."

She set aside her cup of water ice and reached out to cover my hand with hers. "Well, noble seal-rodent-person, I think helping your aunt is the right thing to do and that it will be good for you."

I felt the air deflate out of me and resisted the urge to let my voice grow whiny as I said, "She wants me to do a teacher dance. It's going to take so much of my time to prepare for it."

Leia grinned at me. "Even better. I loved watching you dance."

"You did?" Maybe I was fishing for flattery, but a part of me still wanted to hear her say what I knew she was about to say.

"Yes. You're so talented and I loved your costumes... I mean, spandex looks really hot on you," she said, with a small giggle, "*much* hotter than a cheer uniform. And..." her voice dropped into a more serious tone, "it's probably one of the few times when I see you actually let go and enjoy yourself. It's a part of you that you don't let people see a lot and I love it."

I had no idea what she was talking about. "I let go all the time."

"Sure," she said, drawing out the word.

"No, seriously, I do."

Leia had the temerity to actually roll her eyes at me. "Grace, I love you, but you're the definition of 'wound up.'

Your entire life revolves around your plans." Her phone alarm went off and she sat up, frowning at the screen. "Well, time to turn into a pumpkin." She stood, but not before dropping another soft kiss on my lips. "I've gotta go, but I'm glad you're doing this. It's good for you."

"Yes, Mom."

She leaned down to drop a tiny kiss on my lips. "Love you."

"Love you, too." I watched as she picked up her bag and headed for her car. She started the car with a painful-sounding grinding sound that turned to a rattle, stuck her hand out the window to wave goodbye, and drove off.

May

☐ Chapter 9

I was used to walking past our dining room and seeing one of Mom's friends or Dad's coworkers at the table, either flipping through party plans or shuffling spreadsheets. This time, though, familiar shoulder-length hair tipped in bright red and orange made me freeze and back up the second I passed the entryway. Two women were standing with Mom around the dining room table, studying a big piece of white paper. The younger woman with the fiery hair looked up and her grin, which was just like Phoebe's, confirmed my guess. Phoebe's older sister was shorter and thinner than her and had way more daring hair and fashion sense, but even though they didn't look too much alike, they shared the same smile and big eyes, although Trixie's were brown to Phoebe's grey.

"Oh, hi, Trixie and Mrs. Martins," I said, poking my head into the entryway. Mom had offered to plan Trixie's wedding as a wedding present, but it was still a surprise to see them both actually at the house.

"Hey, Grace," Trixie said in return, walking over to give me a hug. "Long time no see."

"You know Feebs has been trying to keep us apart since the Chloe Marks incident." It had become an in-joke in our group that Trixie and I had a running war over my favorite new designer and her most detested ex-classmate and that Phoebe had to separate us to avoid bloodshed. In reality, it was fun having someone, other than Mom, with whom I could debate the latest fashion trends. I reached up to flick at her hair. "Your hair has definitely gotten longer since New Year's."

"Yup, I'm growing it out for the wedding. I like it short but I kinda want to do this epic up-do I saw during fashion week on the Vivienne Chen runway."

I'd been glued to coverage of that runway show and remembered loving one updo on the next-to-last model. "Oh, I think I know the one you're talking about. The looped buns? That was gorgeous. Really modern."

"Exactly. Mom thinks I'm going to regret it when I'm forty and looking over my wedding album."

"You will," her mom said with a laugh. "May I remind you that you and Phoebe laugh over my wedding album every chance you get?" She looked at me and my mom with a grin. "I wanted to look so much like Cameron Diaz in *My Best Friend's Wedding* and the girls always ask if I were able to lift my arms in my dress. I really couldn't, but I looked fabulous."

Mom stopped midway in her drawing and laughed. "Oh, you have to see how much smoky eye makeup I piled on for mine. It's hilarious looking back at those pictures now." She picked up her marker again and grinned at me. "Grace, you have fantastic timing. We could use your opinion."

"But I was heading out," I gestured at my dance bag. "I'm supposed to teach the adult class tonight. You know, the class you and Aunt Drina guilted me into teaching?"

Mom ignored my pointed comment. "Just one second, okay?"

I glanced at the grandfather clock, made some calculations, closed my eyes, and took a deep breath before dropping my bag in the hall and heading inside. "What's up?"

Mom smoothed out the paper she had been drawing on before stepping back to make room for me to see. At first, it looked like one of the seating charts she usually drew up for events—all circles in perfect formation and spaces for names, but then I noticed a squiggly line had been drawn down the center with a completely different layout on the other side. "Okay, so we're trying to figure out seating for the reception…"

"Even though it's not a sit-down," Trixie chimed in forcefully with a look over at her mom, who frowned in response.

"Yes, not a sit-down, but people will need places to drop their things and I think they'll want to be able to sit and eat or rest," Mom continued smoothly, not even batting an eye at the unspoken tension between Trixie and her mom.

"Especially for people who want a sit-down," Mrs. Martins said, "like anyone over the age of forty. And it will need to look elegant."

"I want people to be comfortable. And I want them to be able to mingle." Trixie looked over at me and said, "Amani is my only high school friend coming to this. Could you imagine if I just forced her to sit at a table with my college friends or you guys or Petur's friends? This way, she can, like, eat an appetizer while listening to Aunt Sophia talk about her last trip to the gastroenterologist, then escape to hang out with Petur's really cute cousin from Keflavik without feeling like we're trying to set them up."

"Honestly, you and Phoebe make it sound like the only things Sophia talks about are her health problems," Mrs. Martins said.

"She does," Trixie said, adding, "And she'll be especially worse since she knows Amani is in med school."

Mom looked over at me and shrugged her shoulders ever-so-slightly as if to say, *See what I'm dealing with?* "So, I drew up a more traditional cocktail hour table layout, but what if we mix standing tables with a few sitting tables and have a few *elegant*," she said, looking over at Mrs. Martins as she said it, "—lounges set up on the sides and back, away from the DJ, with comfortable sofas, chairs, and low tables, so people could sit and chat *casually.*" The last word was aimed at Trixie. Mom then looked over at me. "Grace?"

I stared at the second seating plan for a minute, impressed by Mom's neat lines and the whole flow of the room. She'd even thought to put what she'd marked as a "hot chocolate and coffee bar" between two of her sofa-lounge seating layouts, and left space by the walls for people to check out the artwork in the gallery. For someone who wasn't into technical things, she would have blown everyone else away in my engineering design class. "I like the idea of the lounges. They'll probably be more comfortable for some of your older guests rather than forcing them to sit at a table all night. You can still see the dance floor really well from them."

"Great-Uncle Antonio is going to fall asleep on those," Mrs. Martin pointed out.

"And he'll say it was the best wedding ever," Trixie countered.

"Why did you do standing tables?" I asked Mom, already knowing her answer.

"It's good for mingling, but people like Amani won't feel like they're stuck talking to the people at those tables forever," Mom said, looking at me but directing her words at the two Martins.

For two people with very different tastes, Trixie and her mom had identical appreciative hums.

"Got it," I said, making sure to look over at Trixie and Mrs, Martins, too. "I honestly like it. It has a really nice flow from food to different seating options, and it looks like a layout that might get more people out on the dance floor or checking out the gallery."

Mom nodded, a tiny smile on her lips, then turned to the other two women, who were also nodding with her. "So, what do you think?"

"It's an elegant compromise," Mrs. Martins said, slowly.

"It looks comfortable," Trixie added, with a glance over at her mom. "I'm positive Petur will love it, too."

"Then, done." Mom put a checkmark on the side of her paper with the sofas and standing tables. "I'll start looking into rental costs for the tables and lounge furniture and I'll get back to you."

I looked at the three of them, then over at my backpack. "Can I go now?"

Mom didn't look up from her notebook, but she had a wide grin as she waved me away. "Yes, thank you, Grace."

Trixie pulled away from the table to come to my side. "I'll walk out with you. I'm meeting up with Amani to hit up some of the vintage stores in Mt. Holly. Thanks, Mrs. Correa," she called out as she shouldered her purse. "I'm doing a brooch bouquet and I'm kind of hoping to find some fun pins for it."

"No flowers?" I'd seen those kinds of bouquets made up only of pins and brooches in pictures from one of the fashion weeks a few years ago and wasn't surprised Trixie would pick something like that for her own wedding.

"Flowers die, but tacky rhinestone pins from the seventies

are forever." With a glance over my shoulder, I could see both my mom and hers shaking their heads at Trixie's comment, but she didn't seem to care. "I have a bunch I picked up in the city, but I need a few more to fill it out. And Amani has this magical ability to find the best pins in the bins in seconds."

Amani was the name she had mentioned earlier. I tilted my head at her, asking the question that had popped into my head during the whole seating discussion. "You said you only had one high school friend coming to your wedding? What happened to that whole art class group Phoebe said you used to hang out with?"

"Oh, you know how it is," she said, waving her hand airily. "We all went on to our own schools and kind of grew apart. It happens to everyone. Amani's the only one I really kept in touch with after freshman year."

"Wow."

At that, she glanced over at me with super wide eyes. "Oh, I'm sure you and Phoebe and the others will stay close. It's just me and you know, fashion design takes up all my free time and the city's just a pain to get to if you don't have a huge budget…" Even I could tell her excuses were weak and, with a sheepish smile, she quickly changed the subject. "Anyway, did you and your mom just tag-team me and my mom back there?"

I pushed open the front door and waved for her to go ahead of me. "I wouldn't say 'tag-team'… I just agreed that she came up with a nice compromise."

"Oh, she totally did, but it's hilarious how you two basically steamrolled us into compromising."

I stopped mid-step and cringed, realizing that we really *had* somewhat bullied them into Mom's plan. "Sorry. I can go back and argue something different if you want."

"No," she said with a laugh as she headed down the driveway. "Seriously, I love it. But you two are dangerous. Remind me to come to you when I need to convince store buyers to carry my stuff."

I grinned. "If you think we're bad, you should spend more time around my dad. It runs in the family."

"I'm not sure whether I should be scared or impressed," she said, then grew a little more serious. "Thanks again for your help back there."

"No problem. Good luck finding tacky stuff."

"Thanks, crossing my fingers for something neon this trip." With a wave, she turned in the direction of the exit to our development, probably to catch the bus off Main Street. "I'll see you at your graduation," she called out over her shoulder.

"Later," I said absently, pulling out my phone to check the time before getting into my car, and held back a groan as I tossed my dance bag onto the passenger seat. Hopefully, the green light gods were going to be kind to me today.

☑Chapter 10

"It's good for you," Leia's voice repeated in my head as I took a deep breath and opened the door to Aunt Drina's studio. The glass door, scribed with *Adamo School of Dance* in blue cursive, was all marked up with fingerprints.

Inside, it was like walking right into the past. The waiting room windows were still packed with rows and rows of trophies, and the same worn benches were filled with gossiping dance moms and the lone dad waiting for a class to let out. Except for the waiting room walls changing from a bright violet to an even brighter green, nothing had really changed from my time there as an uncertain sixteen-year-old constantly reminding herself that dance was taking up too big a chunk of her life, always on the verge of quitting in favor of things with bigger payback. If it weren't for today's date tacked onto the top of the corkboard with the class schedules and competition information, I would have sworn the dance studio had simply frozen in time the moment I walked out two years ago.

Aunt Drina waved me over from the office door, wrapping me up in a big hug the second I was in arm's reach. "Thank you so much for agreeing to help. You're an angel. I would have been so stuck without you."

I squeezed back, the hug dragging up so many memories of dropping into Aunt Drina's office for a chat or a hug whenever I felt sad or overwhelmed or needed advice. It wasn't like I'd stopped talking to her after I'd stopped classes, but now, instead of seeing her practically every day, sometimes for hours, I maybe saw her once a week. I'd forgotten how much I missed this part of my dance life.

"I didn't really have a choice. Leia guilted me into it," I said into her shoulder.

My aunt laughed and let go, stepping back to regard me with an amused look. "Of course she did. Remind me to thank her the next time I see her." She glanced up at the clock and then back at me, still grinning but trying to look all business. "Okay, so the adult contemporary starts in ten minutes. That class is in the rose studio. Usually about twelve or so show up. Keep it at an advanced beginner level, max."

Nerves bubbled up in my stomach and I leveled my gaze at her. "Are you still sure about this?"

"Definitely. Mila will probably tear another ligament if you even hint at doing something close to intermediate or advanced," she said, "and Sandy will complain that you're making it too hard for her to keep up if you go too fast. Stick to beginner."

"I mean, me teaching adults," I said, wondering if she even saw the problem. It was one thing teaching people younger than me who didn't really know better, but these people probably expected their dance teachers to have degrees and actual experience. "Won't they get upset that I'm not, you know, a real dance teacher?"

"You'll do great," she said with a dismissive wave of her hand. "Amy was only a few years older than you and they had no problem with her teaching them." Her eyes drifted to the clock again. "Go on, I'll catch up with you after."

I shouldered my dance bag and nodded.

"I'll be in the little studio if you need anything," she added, before practically pushing me back out into the waiting room.

The rose studio was just as obnoxiously pink as it always had been, the walls above the barre cluttered with pictures of kittens inside pointe shoes and close-ups of tutus and roses. The gray marley floor had lost its sheen from when it had been replaced when I was fifteen, and the old sound system in the corner was perched on neon pink shelves and packed with layers upon layers of CDs. I dropped my bag in front of the shelves and, after a glance at Aunt Drina's museum-worthy collection of music, hooked my phone up to the system and pulled up one off the playlists I used when I needed to warm up for cheer.

"Oh my goodness, is that you, Grace?" A voice came from the doorway and I turned, seeing a woman with dark curls pulled into a messy bun on the top of her head step inside the studio with a wide grin. "It *is* you. Wow, what a blast from the past. Are you taking over for Amy?" Little wrinkles had cropped up around her eyes, but I recognized her as one of the adults who had been taking classes with Drina as far back as I could remember.

I nodded, wracking my brain for her name. "Yup. It's good to see you again…Mila?" I hoped she didn't hear the uncertainty in my tone when I said her name.

"It's good to see you back. This school just hasn't felt the same without you hanging around all the time. I remember you sitting over there—" she nodded at the far corner of the studio, "—doing your homework between classes. How are you? Did you graduate yet?"

"June 21st," I said, looking past her to wave in a few uncertain students standing in the door. "Come on in, I'm Grace, I'm taking over for Amy." The room was starting to fill, a few other familiar faces joining the group of about ten adults that ranged from their twenties to a small woman with completely white hair. I was the youngest person in the room by at least five years.

"Congratulations." Mila continued. "Are you going to college after?"

I felt like I was being cross-examined by a PTA mom,

but tried not to show my annoyance. "Penn State."

She lit up. "That's great. I remember you mentioning you wanted to go there. Are you going for dance? I hear they have a great program."

"Um, no, for engineering." Before she could drill me anymore, I hit play on my playlist. "Um, let's get started. Is everyone here?" I looked past her to the rest of the group. At the nods around the room, I slipped my phone on top of one of the speakers and reached up to tighten my ponytail.

"Grace is Drina's niece. She used to dance here," Mila explained to the general room, finally taking what I assumed was her usual spot on the floor, center front. "It was such a shame when she stopped. She's such an amazing dancer. You'll see when we get to the combination. I think she held the school record for individual awards in competition."

"No pressure," I said under my breath, then pulled up my spine and chin to try and look a little more teacher-like. "Okay, let's start with a nice and easy warmup and stretch. Follow me, and if you can't do something, adapt or let me know so I can show you how to adapt." I waited for the right spot in the music and started my usual set of warmups, the same ones Drina had been teaching at her school for decades.

"See, I told you. They all go through that stage where they rebel, go off to become cheerleaders, and then they always come back because they realize dance is so much better than cheer," Mila whispered to the man stretching next to her. I shut my eyes and didn't bother to correct her, only pretended I didn't hear as I melted into a deep plié and arched my arm over my head to stretch to the other side.

This was going to be a long class.

☑

Warm up and technique had gone smoothly, with only one of the adults rubbing her ankle after we'd worked through a few basic pencil turns. My worries about having to actually teach different turns and jumps from scratch had faded as soon as I realized the class had enough experience to keep up and that I wasn't going to break them if I asked them to try something new.

I hadn't had time to prepare a center combination for the class, so I racked my brain to remember a simple one from one of my early competition dances.

"Okay, I'm going to do this straight through at first, but try to follow along. I promise it's not too complicated." I cycled through my playlist to find a good song to match the choreography, then put it on repeat and hurried back to the center front of the room. I counted down the beat for the class before stepping straight out into a deep second position plié. The familiar combination poured out of me into simple steps I'd done a million times before. It was only a few bars of music, but an unexplainable feeling of loss and missing tightened in my chest and I forced out the last few steps. I glanced in the mirror, hoping no one else had noticed the emotions that were running across my face and pouring into my movements. I wanted to run out of the room.

Trying to hide the tightness in my throat, I said, "Mila,

you seem to have picked up the pattern, can you go over it with everyone while I step out for a second?" I was betting she'd done this combination before in one of her classes. I couldn't be the only former student who had recycled this choreography.

She nodded, rolling her shoulders confidently as she tried to hide how out of breath she was. "Sure."

"Thanks," I said, and tried to look unconcerned as I headed for the door. "I'll be right back."

As soon as I was out of the room, I leaned my head against the wall and took a deep breath, letting the much cooler hallway air wash over me. Aunt Drina was letting me "ease back in" to dance the first week by only taking on the adult group, but if I couldn't even hold myself together for them, I had no idea how I was going to make it to the recital.

"You agreed to do this. People are counting on you," I muttered to myself under my breath. "So suck it up."

One of the other teachers I didn't recognize passed me, paused to take in my sweaty pose, and asked, "Um, is everything okay?"

"Just taking a minute," I said, then added, more as if I were talking to myself than to anyone else, "Don't mind me. I'm weirdly emotional today. Probably my period messing with my hormones. I'll be back to practical soon."

"Okay?" she said, furrowing her brow at me for a minute before quickly adding, "Let me know if you need me to call Drina," and hurried off without waiting for me to answer.

Great, I'd just scared one of the other teachers. With my

luck, she was going to quit, too, rather than deal with the owner's "hormonal" niece and then I'd be stuck teaching yet another bunch of classes. I let out a little laugh, and, before I could potentially cause any more damage, took another deep breath and rolled against the wall to face the door again. "Back to work," I said to myself, before opening the door and stepping back into the combination as if I'd never left.

☐ Chapter 11

"The idea is ridiculously over-the-top, but your sister actually pulled it off," I said, grabbing Phoebe by the shoulders and turning her around so I could see the back of her incredibly elaborate medieval-ish prom gown. The fabric shimmered in my room's light, shifting from gold to purple and back again as it moved, and it fit her perfectly. I'd already done her hair in a loose curly bun and the whole effect made her look like she'd stepped out of a fairy tale.

"Yes, and she made me promise to take a lot of pictures or she'd strangle me with the corset laces." Phoebe looked up from trying to tug up the dress' neckline, saw herself in the full-length mirror on the back of my closet door, and froze. "It's perfect. Just like Maeve's gown in *Gilded*," she said in an awed whisper, like this was the first time she'd ever seen the dress. She caught my confused look in the mirror and added, still whispering, "Trixie didn't let me see the finished dress on. She covered all our mirrors while she checked the fit so it would be a surprise." She swayed back and forth, making happy Phoebe noises and I dove into my closet to keep from laughing.

Em came over, blindingly bright in her short yellow dress, and held out one of Phoebe's long, chiffon sleeves like it was a banner.

"This gives me an idea. What do you think of me and Kris getting jobs at the Renaissance Faire next summer?" Before I could even say anything, she added, "I'm an actress, he's a fencer. It would be so perfectly romantic."

"May I remind you," I said, pointing the heel of one of my Lebuttons at her, "that even if you could convince Kris to do it—and I seriously doubt you can—the faire means spending all day outside in the woods? And that you're not the one-with-nature type?"

"Please. I'll be wearing a corset-bodice-thing. There's no way they'd hide this behind any trees." She gestured dramatically at herself and ended the gesture in a pose that showed off the rhinestones running down her one shoulder strap to a rhinestone sun at her waist.

"Bring plenty of sunscreen and bug spray, then," I said, as dryly as I could.

Em pursed her lips, held up a finger and turned,

shuffling through her backpack before coming back over with the tape measure from her latest run in Mary Poppins. "I forgot to put this back in the prop room after we cleaned up." She pulled me away from my shoes and made me straighten up. "Hold still, let me measure you." With Phoebe's silent laughter egging her on, she made a huge show out of measuring my height and then looking at the measurement. "Just as I thought. Grace Correa, perfectly practical in every way."

I turned my nose up at her and shook my head. "There's absolutely nothing wrong with being practical."

"Being impractical is more fun. Like these." She took my simple silver heels from my hands and pulled a pair of rhinestone-covered Lebuttons out of my closet. "These are a lot more fun."

I took the heels from her and held them up against my silver column gown, studying how they looked together in the mirror. Considering how simple my gown was—strapless and draping a little at the waist—the shoes could work without looking over-the-top. Especially if I switched to a plain silver clutch instead of the beaded one I'd been planning on using. "Done. Am I impractical enough for you now?"

"Getting closer," Phoebe teased, squeezing next to me so all three of us were reflected in the mirror.

"This is as wild as it gets. Take it or leave it." My smile grew so wide it almost hurt. It was too bad mom got more worked up about Alec changing in here with us than my own girlfriend, though she banned both of them. It felt incomplete with one of our quartet missing. "I can't believe this is the last time we get to dress up for something like this."

"Until the wedding," Phoebe said, fixing one of her loose curls nonchalantly while the two of us just stared at her. "Trixie? To Petur? This August? Right after I get back from my trip? The one you're *invited* to??"

I fake-held my hand to my chest. "Never just say 'the wedding,' Fee. Never. Because you nearly gave me a heart attack."

She stepped over to my dresser and started moving things from her purse to the little shot-silk clutch her sister had made to match her dress. "It's not my fault you can't remember things."

I took away the e-reader she was trying to stuff into her clutch and threw it onto my bed. "No books at the prom." Phoebe rolled her eyes at me, but I ignored it and went back to fixing the soft Rita Hayworth-like wave I'd styled into my blonde hair.

Em swiped some gloss onto her lips. "Remind me again—did your sister go to the prom with him?"

"No, that guy dumped her freshman year right at Thanksgiving. She met Petur when she was out skating on River Rink with a bunch of friends on winter break, remember?" Phoebe dropped onto the bed close to the e-reader and pretended to study her nails. "That's why she always goes skating New Year's Eve with him."

I grabbed the e-reader again and dropped it into my

nightstand drawer, giving her a "don't even think about it" look.

"Oh yeah, Turkey Dump Guy." Em waved her hand dismissively. "Trixie rebounded like a pro from him, too. The way her and Petur got together is just disgustingly cute. What's up with your family?"

"Good readers breed good love stories?"

I blinked at the two of them, trying to decipher their conversation. When Phoebe and Em talked with each other, following their high-speed conversations was like trying to chase a starship through a wormhole. "Wait. Go back. What's a turkey dump?"

"You know," Em said, giving her rhinestone headband one last adjustment so it sat perfectly in her short, dark curls, "when you come back for Thanksgiving break freshman year of college and your significant other dumps you."

"The death knell for long distance relationships that can't make it," Phoebe said dramatically. "Which is what happened to Trixie but won't happen to any of us," she added quickly. "I hope."

An icy feeling ran down my back and I had to keep myself from shivering. I hated the cloud that had descended on the room at that moment.

"C'mon. If we don't head down now, we won't have enough time for pictures before our dates get here. And I don't want to be the reason for your death by corset," I said pointedly to Phoebe.

"Good point." Phoebe slipped on a pair of flat sandals

and grabbed my hand, pulling me along with her out the door. She must have sensed or seen something in my face because she squeezed my hand and said, "You look so pretty. Leia's going to love it."

I didn't say anything, just squeezed back.

□

"Just one more picture." Em's mom reached out to fluff Phoebe's skirt before stepping back to stand by my mom and Phoebe's mom. Practically in unison, they all held up their phones.

Alec stopped trying to balance on the arm of the living room settee and started sliding into my lap. "Hey," I pushed at his leg, "you're cutting off my circulation."

He slid even further down until he was half-sitting on my lap. "And you just touched my butt, which could be considered sexual harassment." He swatted at my hands with a fake offended look.

"Grace and Alec, can you two sit still for half a minute so we have at least one nice picture?" My mom asked, lowering her phone just enough to frown at both of us. My house had been picked to be the prom prep and picture house because I had my own bathroom and every hairstyling implement known to man, but it also came with this chair, which had to chronicle every milestone in my life.

"I'm sorry Mrs. Correa, but my tux is too slippery for this chair." He tried to get up and, when that didn't work, threw an arm around my shoulders and tried to look casual.

I inched closer to Em and he fell a little more, squishing us all into the small seat. "Ow. Okay, Mom, this isn't going to work. Can we have a second to reset?"

Mom waved impatiently at us and the moms got into a huddle—probably trying to come up with other ridiculous poses—and we untangled ourselves from the seat. "Aren't you glad you came early for pictures, Alec?" Em asked with an evil grin as she helped pull him off me and up to standing.

"So happy. You're going to make me regret going alone. I could have been doing the awkward five or six pictures with one of the girls from the science club right now."

Em bumped him with her shoulder. "Yeah, but then you'd have to dance."

Alec looked a little nauseated at the thought. "Good point."

"Ohmygosh, do you remember Poppy and that waltz thing you two did?" Em's expression lit up and she added, "I would pay to find a video of the two of you at fifth grade graduation."

Alec cringed. "Don't remind me." He looked over at us and added, "Poppy is why I don't dance."

I traded a grin with Phoebe. Em and Alec were like siblings and their banter was always fun to watch, especially if they started bringing up stuff from their shared childhood.

"It's not so bad when it's with someone you like. If you want, I can work some magic—" Em wiggled her fingers in what I guessed was supposed to be an imitation of a fairy godmother.

Alec held up a hand to stop her. "No, I'm not going to let you set me up with anyone. Ever."

"Fine. Just don't drool all over our table whenever Laura passes, okay? It's embarrassing."

"Shut up."

There was a long honk in our driveway and we all jumped up to run to the windows. Even though Mom had wanted us to rent a limo, I talked everyone into just sharing two cars. Some of my friends had tighter budgets than me, and I wanted them to have fun, not stress. Em peeked through my curtains and jumped back when I opened them all the way, poking nervously at her short curls. For someone who acted so confident, it was fun to see her get flustered.

While we watched Leia and the boys make their way up our walkway, I glanced over at Mom, who was clicking away on her phone. "I still don't understand why you didn't let Leia get changed here."

"While I've been rather accepting of your choice to be… nontraditional, at least let me have something traditional. I didn't pay that much for a prom gown not to see your date walk up to the door and see you in it for the first time."

I was lucky. When I first came out, my parents were almost unsettlingly okay about it—Dad just ignored the whole situation, murmuring something about how I was too young to date and that school was my job. Mom, on the other hand, was probably still convinced it was 'just a phase,' I'd get over it all, marry some trust fund manager, and have a 'normal' life with two-point-five kids and a dog. That was always a possibility, if the trust fund manager had two X chromosomes, but that was not the way Mom wanted it. Still, hearing something like that made my heart swell a million sizes and I threw my arms around Mom, giving her an impromptu hug.

"Thanks for thinking of everything."

Mom's dark eyes looked a little watery, but she tried to hide it with a smile. "You girls, and Alec, of course, grew up so fast. Now, go upstairs so we get a real entrance picture."

"You're kidding, right?"

"I did not pay that much for a prom gown…" she purposely trailed off, her smile widening.

"How about a compromise? We only go halfway up the stairs so we can pretend we were on our way down when the door opens?" Phoebe asked, and even from where I was standing, I could see how she was giving her mom a pleading look.

"Fine, go!" Phoebe's mom shooed us towards the stairs and Em's mom tried to artfully arrange us while Alec dropped onto the little bench in the foyer to play a game on his phone. Phoebe couldn't stop laughing at the faces Em was making behind her mother's back.

And then Mom opened the front door.

I couldn't even register what she was saying when Leia walked in, dressed in a mock-turtleneck, sleeveless white gown that looked like a sleek take on Princess Leia's *A New Hope* dress, down to the belt and the white over-the-knee boots that showed through a thigh-high slit in her long skirt. I had to focus on the stairs to keep from tripping in my heels. It was like the first time I saw her, except she was a million times prettier.

"Grace, your girlfriend wins the hotness award from the geek judge," Alec said, looking up for only a second before going back to his phone. I pretended to ignore him as I walked the mom-paparazzi gauntlet to stand by her.

Leia's gaze moved slowly up my body, from the toes of my bling-y heels and up my curves, and I had to work so hard not to blush. "Wow," she mouthed at me when she finally met my eyes.

While the others were hamming it up for the cameras, Dev picking Phoebe off of the last step and twirling her around before putting her down, Kris and Em arguing whether she should pin the corsage to her dress or wear it on her wrist, we just stood there, goofy half-smiles on our faces.

"Good reaction," Mom said, peeking from behind her phone again and giving us a thumbs up. "I videoed everything for Dad."

"Thanks," I said, awkwardly leaning on Leia for support as soon as I was shaken back into the moment and realized we had an audience. "So, we should go now before we're late."

"We need some outside pictures by the hydrangea bushes before you leave," Em's mom suggested. "You kids have plenty of time to get there."

I looked up at the grandfather clock and bit the inside

of my cheek to keep from saying anything. There went our pre-prom stop at Marranos. I forced a nod and a bright smile, wrapping my arm around Leia's shoulders. "Sure. Hydrangeas it is."

☐Chapter 12

Cassie looked like she was floating as she slow danced with Christian Washington, trying her best to lay her head on his shoulder without dislodging her massive silver foil tiara. They passed our table in their spiral around the dance floor and she gave us a little wave before going back into her prom dreamworld. On the other side of the dance floor, Jake and his date were doing crazy twirls and lifts that fit with the attention-seeking backflip he'd made when they crowned him prom king.

"I seriously would never have predicted that," Dev said, taking a sip of punch and gesturing to Cassie and Christian. "It's like something straight out of one of Phoebe's books."

Phoebe looked up from her phone, where I could bet she was reading a book, and said, "The nerdier-than-all-of-us-combined nerd and the cheerleader who broke up with her football star boyfriend? I like that trope." She put her phone down and pointed at it with a tortured look on her face. "Now, you know what I can't stand? Insta-love."

Dev and I shared a knowing glance and kept our mouths shut, but Leia bit. "Insta-what?"

"Insta-love. You know, when two characters meet and fall into 'we're meant to be together forever and oh my gosh I can't live without you' love," Phoebe said, hamming it up by putting the back of her hand against her forehead in a faux swoon. "And usually it's the bad boy and the quiet, mousy, bookish girl."

"What, you didn't instantly love me?" Dev asked, nudging her in the side.

Phoebe laughed and nudged him back. "Right. The second you walked into middle school orientation, talking about how you'd gotten a chance to see *Spring Awakening* and almost giving Ms. Lintz a heart attack because you started singing that one song, I knew we were meant to be. And if you'd started dancing, I definitely would have thrown myself at you on the spot." He'd organized yet another flash mob right before the crowning, this time to a nineties music compilation, and looked like he was still recovering. Phoebe, who had refused to get involved until he dragged her in for the last half-song, kept reaching over to fix his sweaty hair. "I mean, *really*. I get love at first sight and all of that, but I think you still need to work together for it to become real. Real love, the kind that lasts, takes work. Movies and books with relationships that go from zero to eighty just aren't realistic."

Alec picked up her phone and pursed his lips as he checked out her screen. "Wild guess here, but I bet this vampire/elf thing you're reading has this insta-love."

She snatched back her phone, slipping it into her clutch. "Maybe."

I really couldn't help myself. Some of the stuff she read was ridiculous, but this took the cake. "Vampire/elf? Really?"

"Elves are immune to vampires and they're natural enemies, so… yeah." Phoebe mumbled, suddenly more interested in the trim on her sleeve than the rest of us.

"In what fantasy canon?" Alec challenged, but was interrupted by Kris and Em sliding into their seats, back from their shift hanging out with some of the other student council guys.

"You know, I could have helped any of you with a campaign to get prom queen," Kris said. He looked down at Em, who pressed her lips together and shook her head. "For someone who really likes being the center of attention, I don't get why you wouldn't want to be prom queen."

He really *didn't* get it. Em wasn't the type to get involved in what amounted to popularity contests, no matter how much she loved the stage. I answered for her. "Yeah… none of us are into that. But it was nice cheering for Cassie." Leia squeezed my hand under the table. Two points for my skill in saying just the right thing to make everyone happy and for being nice to Kris.

We didn't have to like our friends' significant others, we just had to tolerate them. For the longest time, Phoebe didn't like Leia much for some reason I never figured out. But since we were package deals, we made it work.

"As long as you're into the post-prom party, I'm okay with that," Kris said, flashing us a brilliant smile. "I'm counting on you guys to keep things fun."

I looked over at Leia and said, "Maybe, but we'll be bowing out early. Leia has something at her school tomorrow morning."

Kris nodded and quickly turned his attention to Dev and Phoebe. "Jacobs?"

"You know Phoebe goes pretty much anywhere Em goes and I go wherever Phoebe goes."

Em grinned. "Smart boyfriend. As first lady of the senior class, of course I need to be there but, you know," she reached over and played with Kris' tie, "we could have much more fun doing other things."

The tips of his ears turned red and he yanked his tie out of her hands. "You have way too much fun with that 'first lady' thing for someone who hates politics."

"Please. Who came up with this year's post-prom idea?"

"The post-prom committee?" I volunteered. This was the millionth time we'd heard this argument.

Em narrowed her eyes at me, then turned her full attention back on Kris. "*I* was the first to say glow in the dark mini golf. Totally beats the same bowling alley they've gone to in the past gajillion years."

A cloud of sparkly material wafted by our table and Alec seemed to perk up a little bit. "Hey, do you know if Laura is going to the post-prom thing?" He watched the girl as she passed our table, eyes wide.

I could see what Alec saw in her—Laura was pretty in a Lord of the Rings elven extra sort of way, with big blue eyes, long, straight hair she bleached to a white blonde, a waifish figure, and she always wore flowy clothes and sparkly things to emphasize her elvishness. I liked more curves but had to admit that she was ethereally pretty. She twirled by in her layered chiffon dress, sparkling in the low ballroom lights, completely unaware of her one-person fan club.

It was hard seeing one of my favorite people constantly trailing after someone like a lost puppy. "You know she's a lost cause, right? She's dating some guy at U of Delaware. That's probably him." I pointed at the longish-haired guy who looked like a Strider currently dancing with her.

"Yeah, but she's also going to Rutgers Newark and when she realizes she's so much better than him and turkey dumps him, I'll be there to sweep her off her feet. NJIT's right across the street."

"What's with you guys and turkey dumping?" The words twisted my stomach and suddenly the chocolate mousse I was eating tasted like sawdust. "It's the worst time to break up. That's right before first semester finals."

"It kind of makes sense. Think about it. Other than

being the first break once you get to college, it's before the winter holidays so you don't have to get presents, but it's far enough away from the holidays that you don't come off looking like a jerk," Leia said, then at Alec's cleared throat, added, "except for the times that Hanukkah happens practically on top of Thanksgiving. Then you really do look like a jerk and need to wait for the next non-gift holiday break."

The whole conversation still made me feel a little ill, so I stood and practically lifted Leia out of her seat. "Okay, enough turkey talk. Dance?"

Leia nodded and waved at the others, this time anchoring me as the pivot point, spinning us into the crowd. "This is fun," she yelled into my ear over the loud music. "Better than anything the Academy would have come up with, anyway."

I squeezed her tighter, afraid she and everything around us would just disappear, but it didn't.

It was a fast song, but we curled into each other like we were slow dancing. We were perfect together.

☐ Chapter 13

I tried to stay quiet as I made my way into the house so I wouldn't wake anyone, but, apparently, judging by the light coming from the kitchen, I really didn't need to bother. When I walked into the kitchen, Mom was still in her day clothes and was sitting at the island, her hands cupped around a mug of tea as she stared at four lists at the same time.

"Hey," I said, trying to keep my voice down. I dropped my clutch and keys on the kitchen counter and slid onto the stool kitty-corner to her. My dress made it a little hard to balance on the stool, but I managed with a little extra wiggling. "I hope you didn't stay up late for me."

She looked up at me, a small, tired frown on her lips. "Oh, no, no. Just planning a few things for Trixie's wedding and your graduation party." Her usually neat bob was mussed and her concealer had worn away to reveal deep undereye circles. She and I both had constant, awful dark circles, but I'd never seen her outside of her bedroom without concealer.

I reached out tentatively to touch her arm. "Is everything okay?"

"I just don't know," she said with an exasperated note in her voice, just before she seemed to catch herself and pasted on her 'everything is perfect' smile. "Ignore that. I'm sorry, I'm just very tired. Everything's fine."

That's when I noticed an empty spot on the key rack. "Dad's not home yet?" Visions of a big fight, and Dad storming off to sleep in a hotel or his office popped into my head and I couldn't push them away. I suppressed the urge to play with the napkin holder, pressing my fingers flat against the cold marble of the island top, instead.

Mom shook her head. "Last-minute emergency in God knows what country it is this time. He wasn't even sure if he had to fly out there or not when I spoke to him earlier." She pushed the lists together into a neat pile and focused on getting the edges perfectly lined up with the lines of the island. "Honestly, I still have no idea why everything is an emergency in that company. A few days' delay won't kill their product lines, but it will keep their executives from killing themselves working."

"A few days' delay could cost them millions of dollars," I said, repeating what Dad said every time we'd asked.

"Whatever. I just wish your father wasn't the one who had to fix things all the time."

I tapped her pile of lists with a smile. "Correas are just too good at fixing and organizing things for our own good."

She pursed her lips and shook her head. "Correas are also good at forgetting there's more to life than work and to-do lists."

That sounded way too much like what Leia had said about me earlier, so I quickly changed the subject. "So, were you waiting up for me or for Dad?" I got up and checked the tea kettle and added more water—I didn't feel like having tea, but I could tell by the lack of steam coming off the top of Mom's mug that she could probably use a fresh cup.

"Both? Either? The house was too quiet. Honestly, it doesn't matter how long I live here, I don't think I'll ever get used to how weirdly quiet these woods are. I should have tried harder to convince your dad to get something in Philly, but when your dad is stubborn about something..." She trailed off with a shrug. "I think we need to get a cat, a really noisy one."

"Once a city girl, always a city girl?" It wasn't like we lived deep in the middle of Wharton State Forest or anything—our house was just on one of the bigger lots in our development, and since we were an end lot that butted up against state owned and protected forest on one side and that had a lake in the back, it was quieter than my friends' houses, but not by much. "Besides, it's not that quiet. We have neighbors and civilization and stuff."

"Let me remind you I grew up a few apartment buildings down from a firehouse. This kind of quiet, Miss Grace, is horror movie silence compared to that." She put down her mug and slid her lists into a folder. "Anyway, enough about me, how was prom?"

"Prom-like? You know, dancing, food, the usual," I said, then smiled as she made a 'go on' gesture. It was late and I was exhausted, but I didn't just want to leave her alone in the kitchen again.

"I did not pay that much money for your dress for such a lame recap," she said, arching her brows at me as she took another sip of tea.

I tried to look nonchalant but tried to hide the relieved feeling that came over me at her lighter tone. "Fine. The food was sub-par as expected, the music was too loud but okay, Leia and I danced a lot, and Dev and some of the other theater people organized another surprise choreographed dance thing at the beginning. It was a lot like a cheesy movie, so I guess it was good?"

"Better," she said with a nod. "I hope you filmed the choreographed dance. I'd love to see it and would have loved it at my prom. Junior year, one of my friends wanted to organize something like that but she couldn't find enough boys willing to risk their reputations to dance in front of the whole class." A distant look came into her eyes and the corners of her lips turned up a tiny bit more. "But she did rig the prom queen elections senior year and that's how yours truly managed to get prom queen." She made a hmm sound as she dropped her chin into her hands. "I think Alya is in real estate now, convincing people to buy incredibly overpriced apartments in Manhattan."

"Alya?" That name sounded sort-of familiar, but in a way that was more random, distant family member than parental friend.

"We were inseparable from freshman year to graduation. She was the one who convinced me to do all the things that gave your grandparents grey hair." Mom ran a hand through her hair and laughed. "And that gave me pink hair. I know you've seen the pictures."

I had, but I didn't remember her saying anything about why she'd had bubblegum colored hair for most of her junior year beyond her usually dismissive 'rebellious phase' comments. "You know, you never mention anyone from high school. Did you stay in touch with *any* of them?"

"It's hard. Everyone changed so much in college, and then, once I got married and had you and moved down here, it just became harder. Honestly, I'm closer to my friends from Vassar now." She put down her mug and a grin stretched across her cheeks. "Anyway, Alya also managed to work her magic and I ended up going with Ivan, the most popular boy in our school, to my senior prom. Oh, I was head over heels for that boy." She put her hand dramatically over her heart.

That name, at least, was a little more familiar. "He was the other guy, wasn't he? Dad's competition?"

"No, I think we only lasted until the day after graduation. High school relationships have such a short shelf life. . . It's just a part of growing up, you know?" Mom didn't wait for my answer, just put down her mug and looked squarely at me. "Anyway, enough about my past. It's really late. Either the two of us get to bed, or you need to pull up a video of that thing Dev and his friends did."

My brain was swirling too much from what she'd said to even think of going to sleep, so I got the kettle from the stove and refilled her mug before pulling my phone out of my clutch. "Leia sent me hers. I didn't think to film it."

"Thank goodness for Leia," Mom said as she dropped a fresh teabag into her mug.

"Yup. She's amazing."

May

☐ Chapter 14

Sorry, got held up with Mom and then I got an email from Mr. Hayashi asking why I hadn't turned in my paper, I texted Leia, then put away my phone and tried not to think about the five messages she'd sent while waiting for me at Marranos. By herself. For over an hour. While I'd rushed to figure out what had happened with the file I'd uploaded two days ago. It was as if the universe was actually working to get me the title of Worst Girlfriend Ever.

Instead of turning the car around and driving straight to Marranos, I closed my eyes, dropped my head to my steering wheel, and took a bunch of deep breaths to straighten up my spinning world and push away the guilt. I had driven practically on autopilot, but I'd come to this parking lot outside the dance school every day for years and the route was burned into my brain. I didn't have the time to fix anything at the moment, and digging myself deeper into the vortex of a messed-up schedule would just bite me in the butt later. I desperately needed to prep for the junior classes and Aunt Drina had texted that there would be an empty studio for the next hour.

I took another deep breath and then I was off running through the raindrops to the school's storefront. Inside, I ignored the stares of the parents and peeked at the schedule posted on the corkboard, doing a tiny mental cheer when I saw that the little studio was still free. It would have been just my luck if one of her competition dancers had booked it for practice right before I'd gotten there. Aunt Drina nodded at my wave when I passed the window to the studio where she was teaching the advanced ballet class, all buns and pointe shoes and attitude.

The little studio was sandwiched between the two bigger studios and I could hear strains of Stravinsky coming from Drina's class and soft music and thumping bodies coming through the other wall—probably one of the lyrical classes. It smelled like dance shoe leather and sweat and the occasional rosin the ballet dancers snuck in, even though Aunt Drina had marley floors and rosin was against the rules. I closed my eyes and took it all in—the sound, the smell, the vibration of the floor from the music. *Home.* Kicking off my shoes and dropping my car keys into them, I hooked up my phone to the sound system and pulled up the dance playlist I'd put together the other night. I was already wearing my sports bra and jazz leggings, so I just stepped into the middle of the floor and started warming up, my muscles and joints stiff and protesting before turning to butter with each plié and roll of my hips.

As soon as I felt warm enough, I threw myself into the next song that came on my playlist, feeling my body disappear until there wasn't anything but the beat and the music. It had been so long since I'd felt my body become the music, like how Em always transformed on stage into whatever character she was playing. Competition songs were always cut shorter, but, this time, I danced the full five minutes, collapsing at the end in a pile of sweat.

Only when I stopped did I notice that the balls of my feet were raw from turning on the floor without my old calluses. I cringed and pulled my planner out of my dance bag to add a note to dig up my old foot undeez until my skin toughened up again.

Clapping from the doorway made me look up to see a pretty girl, with shoulder length brown hair, poking her head around the doorway. "That was really nice." I was too out of breath to answer, so she continued on. "You must be Drina's niece. I'm Natalie."

I finally had caught my breath enough to stand up and walk towards the door. "Yes, I'm Grace."

"Nice to meet the prodigal niece," she said, stepping into the studio. "Drina talks about you all the time." She didn't look too much older than me and, even though she wasn't wearing the school's mandated pink tights and a black leotard and didn't have her hair up in a bun, she looked like a stereotypical ballet dancer, long and lean with natural turnout. Out of habit, I looked down to check out her feet and legs. That's when I noticed the physio tape around her left ankle that even her legwarmers didn't completely hide.

I tried my best not to stare at her ankle and forced myself to look back up at her face, the obnoxiously purple wall, anything but whatever injury she could have.

"Don't believe anything she says about me, especially if it involves matches and pointe shoe ribbons," I said, forcing a wide smile on my face. "I'm definitely not the reason behind why she had to replace the floors in the rose studio."

Her light brown eyes practically sparkled at my reaction. "I already like you more than April. Amazing dancer, but no sense of humor. And she called me Nat all the time."

I latched onto the barre and started stretching out my protesting hamstring as we talked. "I'm definitely not April. I can't promise I'm an amazing dancer because I haven't taken a class in three and a half years, unless you count the choreography for our halftime routines."

"Hmm." Natalie stepped further into the studio and the contrast between her right foot and bandaged foot was too hard to ignore. Maybe a normal person wouldn't notice, but as a dancer, I couldn't help but see that something was going on. "Do you want advice?" I nodded and she walked over to the speaker system, pointing at my phone to ask for permission to touch it. While she scrolled back on my phone to the song, she said, "You don't look like you haven't danced in over three years, but there were a few rough spots. First, you need to point your toes a little more, especially on your pencil turns. It was really obvious, especially here." The music started playing again and she waited for the chorus before marking out the sequence I'd been dancing on the floor. Her injury didn't stop her, though she did all the turns in the opposite direction from the way I'd turned, and she only barely pointed her left foot, making it look like she was trying to flex, instead. "And here, it might be nice to have a jump—any jump—that curls into a roll. You know, to counter the emotional low the music hits on the word 'now.'"

What she said made total sense. I waited for the chorus to repeat and followed her as she marked ahead of me, kicking into a barrel jump right before the 'and' in the song and falling to the ground on 'now,' my arms wrapped around myself as I rose onto my knees.

"You're right." The choreography played through my brain and I did it again when the chorus repeated a final time, tweaking the barrel into a tour jeté to make even more of a contrast between the open legs of the jump and my completely curled-up body on the landing. I felt powerful and vulnerable at the same time. "That's perfect." A little more work and it might actually be useable. "Do you think the juniors can handle a song like this?"

"Working already? I definitely like you." She rewound and listened again. 'I don't know if they'll like the song, because they're all dying to dance to something by that new K-pop group, but I think they can handle it. Put single piques instead of the pique-fouette, and they might pull it off."

"Okay." I made a mental note to work on that with the class—at their age, I definitely wasn't substituting out fouettes. The next song in my playlist came on and I realized I didn't know what to say. I wasn't used to awkward silences. "So, um, sprained ankle?" I asked, pointing at her leg.

"I wish," she said, shaking her head. "It's a little swollen because I pushed too hard yesterday in PT. Sometimes I forget I can't use it like I used to."

"I know the feeling," I said with a smile. Physical therapy was amazing but I was the type who would do an exercise twenty times if someone told me to do only ten. "What's the therapy for?"

"Ruptured and repaired Achilles tendon, and a few bones in my foot and ankle are fused together with little metal plates." I felt my eyes grow wide and my shoulders go up in an involuntary cringe and Natalie added, "Want the gory details? I don't mind, unless it bothers you."

"No, it doesn't," I said quickly, maybe a little too fast. I hated to admit it, but all the time spent looking at Oliver's project and doing research on hands for mine had made me extra curious about this type of stuff. It was weirdly fascinating, not in a train wreck sort of way, but in a 'understanding a super complex system' way.

"You know how subway doors are supposed to open back up again if something gets caught in them?"

I nodded. "Yes?"

"Well, one time, they didn't. The sensors must have malfunctioned and the subway kept moving and I had been in a rush to get on the train and—" She gestured at her leg, "—voilà, career-ending injury." Before I could say anything, she tapped at her ankle. "I can't do pointe, so professional ballet is out. It's hard to find even modern or contemporary companies and choreographers willing to deal with a dancer who can't fully articulate her foot and is a little shaky on one side…" she trailed off before smiling at me, "but we haven't given up yet. Drina won't let me."

I tried hard not to stare, instead forcing my eyes back to hers, which were just as hard not to stare at because of the dark ring circling an almost cat-like amber. "I…can imagine."

"Because she's still one of my best dancers. Stubborn, but good," Drina said, making her way into the room with an armful of CDs. She was still old-school enough to use them in her classes. "If we can just get that Achilles of yours close to where it was, I bet companies will be falling all over themselves to take you. If that figure skater, Zhao, can get an Olympic gold medal after rupturing his Achilles and Alex Wong is still dancing with two repaired Achilles, I know you can get back up to full relevé."

"I'm only as stubborn as my dance teacher," Natalie shot back, walking over to take a pile of the CDs and help re-shelve. "When are you joining this century? I told you I could convert this all to digital so you don't have to drag these all over the studio."

"It's not the same." Aunt Drina said without any further explanation, running her fingers almost lovingly over the rows and rows of CD cases. "Anyway, it's nice to see you two getting along right off the bat."

In the lull between songs, I heard my phone buzzing, but I ignored it and the tiny wave of nausea that came with it. I was not looking forward to hearing Leia's hurt voice. "Natalie was helping me with my choreography." The phone stopped buzzing and I practically slumped with relief.

Drina looked at me in that really disconcerting way she had that almost felt like she was seeing through me, and, with only the littlest glance at Natalie, asked, "Is everything okay?" She was always better at reading me than my parents ever were, and I caught her eyes shifting toward my phone and back to me.

I changed my focus to stopping my phone mid-song and slipping on my shoes, not looking her in the eye. A second later, I was able to look back up again with a grimace and slipped my right foot out of the shoe and flexed it at her so she could see the red and torn skin. "Perfect. It's just that I've gotten soft."

"Epsom salts," Natalie said absently, then glanced up at the studio clock. "Oh, gotta go. It was nice meeting you, Grace."

"Remember, you're covering adult ballet for Adam tonight," my aunt called after her and Natalie waved a hand with a thumbs up at the doorway before we heard the studio front door's bells chime as it opened and closed. "Dancers,"

Drina said with a shake of her head before turning back to me. "She's right about the salts. But is everything else okay? How are things with Leia?"

"Good. Really. I just popped in to get back into all this again." Before she could dive in deeper, I shoved my phone in my pocket and picked up my keys. "I have to go, too. With Dad in Belgium this week, I don't want to leave Mom all alone for dinner."

She heaved a little sigh that meant she really didn't believe me, but that she was letting go. "Okay. I'll see you tomorrow, around 3:30? And don't worry about dinner tomorrow night, I'll pick something up for both of us between classes."

"Great. Bye." I wasn't the little fifteen-year-old who came to my oh-so-cool aunt with my problems anymore, especially since those things were partly caused by my helping her out. I was definitely too old not to handle things on my own.

I wished I weren't, though.

☑Chapter 15

"So, we're meeting at 3:30?" Phoebe asked, stopping next to my locker.

I blinked at her for a second, trying to figure out what she could possibly mean. At 3:30, I was supposed to be going over my Junior recital dance ideas with Natalie, then cramming in a half-hour study session with Leia before teaching my class at 5. "For?"

"You were going to help me shop for my trip?"

I shook my head and pulled out my planner. "That wasn't today, it's..." I scanned my weekly layout and felt my heart drop into my stomach. "Shopping with Phoebe: 3:30" was right there, in impossible-to-miss teal ink. With my dance schedule written in the box directly below it in pink ink. "Today." I resisted the urge to pound my head against the locker in response to my stupidity and instead looked up, noticing how Phoebe's smile had drooped slightly into what Em had termed her "disappointed kitten" look. "I am so sorry, I don't know how I managed to double schedule you and dance."

Phoebe forced a bright smile. "It's no problem. We can go another day."

"We can go this weekend—" I started, but trailed off when I saw my packed Saturday and Sunday, starting with a design session on Saturday morning with Alec and ending with helping Aunt Drina recut and digitally arrange all the music for the recital. "Or next weekend."

"It's not important, Grace," she said, readjusting her messenger bag.

I shook my head, tapping at my planner. I was *not* going to let her down just because I'd made a stupid mistake. "No, I can make this work. It's just going over a recital dance; class isn't until 5. I'll cancel with Leia and, if I can get Natalie to stay late and Aunt Drina lets us use the little studio, we can work on it after my class and," I added the homework my teachers had given us today—it was about three hours' worth, and if I got home at 8:30, I could still get it done before getting to bed, "I'll just let Mom know I'll be late to dinner. I can make it work."

"It's okay, really. Technically, I won't need these clothes until June. And it's not like there aren't clothes in my closet or stores in Mumbai, either."

I shook my head, remembering what Em had told me about Phoebe needing some friend time. "Yeah, but I promised, and I saw a few things the other day that I really want you to try." I pulled out my phone and started texting Natalie. "I can make this work, just give me a minute."

"But there will be other clothes—" Phoebe said, then seemed to give up. She leaned against the pillar next to my locker with a frown on her face.

"As your official stylist, I refuse to let you down." My phone buzzed and Natalie's "No problem" popped up on my screen. "See, it's okay with Natalie. And, as soon as Mom hears I'm coming home late because I was helping you, she'll be okay with it."

"Are you sure?" She asked, hesitantly.

"Definitely." At the unsure look on her face, I reached out to pat her arm and added, "I promise, this is fun for me. Like Em would say, I'm the shopping queen. Bow before my retail greatness."

Phoebe snorted. "Okay, shopping queen. We'll meet in front of Oh, Knit! then? I promised Cassandra I'd stop by to drop off a sample knit after school."

"Deal." I shoved my planner in my backpack and watched Phoebe hurry to go catch her bus. As soon as she turned the corner, I leaned back against the lockers and tapped the back of my head against them loud enough to hear the metallic thud. Tomorrow morning, I was going to go through my entire planner and make sure this wouldn't happen again.

☑

Good fashion was a mix of geometry, symmetry, physics, and knowing the rules well enough to break them all in breathtaking ways. It was really satisfying to analyze a situation and put together the perfect outfit or figure out a way to make things work on someone's body. It was like a visually appealing equation…always perfect.

When Phoebe stepped out of the dressing room and twirled, a giant smile on her face, I knew I'd gotten another equation right. The black, floaty skirt hit her perfectly mid-calf and swirled out as she turned, and the half-sleeve teal top fit her closely enough to be cute without overdoing it. She adjusted the bow at her neckline so it sat half-on her shoulder and nodded slightly. "I really like this."

"And it matches the scarf Dev's mom gave you for your birthday," I said, remembering how Phoebe had practically lived in the teal silk scarf the second half of the winter, even in lieu of some of her beloved wool. "Wear that with it. You'll need a scarf sometimes to cover your head, right?"

"Mmmhmm." She didn't seem to be listening as she turned from side to side in front of the mirror. "I really like this place, it has the cutest stuff."

"Now do you see why I didn't want to wait?" I gestured to the rack next to us. "Everything in here is upcycled or made from sustainable materials without being super expensive. Leia found this store ages ago, and when I saw that top in the window, I knew it would work for you."

"I like sustainable. And my yarn and book budget thank

you." She twirled again, then tugged at the skirt. "This won't be too hot? We're probably going to be there during the monsoons but it's still going to be summer, you know."

"It's all-natural materials, they'll breathe fine," I said. "And you can make a bunch of other outfits with these two pieces." I pulled the grey capris we'd bought at another shop out of the bag I was holding and put it in front of her skirt. "See? Just make sure you pick colors that work together and then you don't have to pack a million things."

"Yes, Style Mom."

I snorted and made a dismissive motion towards the dressing room. "Go try on the other outfit now. I want enough time to squeeze in an oh-so-exciting oatmeal bar or two before dance."

"You're back to those?" Phoebe's voice was muffled through the curtain and probably by a layer of fabric as she changed. "I thought you were finally eating kind of normally again." She paused, then added, "I mean, not to say you're not normal, but normal as in general wheat-free public food consumption normal, not that it's everyone's normal but…you know what I mean."

I snorted at her word-gymnastics. "Yeah, back to those. I've been extra sensitive lately. Probably the change in the season or something." All my friends knew that when I stopped eating even the tiny amounts of wheat or apples or dairy that my body could tolerate, I always switched to homemade oatmeal bars my dietician had taught me about when I'd first been diagnosed with all my sensitivities.

"Or it's stress. You have a really bad habit of doing too much." Phoebe stepped out again, this time in black leggings and a long pink tunic top. "Your doctor told you stress could do that to you, too, right?"

I studied her for a minute before pulling a black ribbon belt from the display next to me and looping it around her waist. Better. "We're all stressed. You also just finished up AP exams and needs to study for finals."

"Yes, but I ask for help and I'm not a perfectionist like you. You're extra stressed and you know it." Phoebe played with the bow I'd tied around her waist, keeping her eyes focused on her own reflection as she said, even more firmly, "You told me stress can shift your bacterial something-or-other and make you more sensitive to all the stuff that already makes you sick. Which means it has to be really affecting you right now."

I didn't try to correct her mangled attempt to explain the science behind food sensitivities. This was supposed to be about cheering her up, not talking about what I could or couldn't eat. "I'm fine, seriously."

This time, she looked straight up to study me, grey eyes narrowed. "You know you can say no to things like this and helping my mom, right? And do you need me to talk to Em and Alec about us helping you for once? I can't dance, but maybe I could help with the recital stuff?"

I shook my head. "Seriously, forgetting about this shopping trip was just a planner mistake. And you have your trip and your sister's wedding stuff to worry about. I wouldn't trade places with you in a million years."

"Oh, please, if Trixie was your sister, you and your mom would be planning the wedding of the century. The two of you love this kind of stuff." She twirled in front of the mirror and added, "The two of you should go into planning business together: 'Unique Weddings by Correa and Daughter.'"

"With a hot-chocolate bar, of course," I said with a laugh, then gave her a gentle nudge towards the changing room. "Okay, you're going to look adorable, and I'm sure you'll pick up a few cute things in Mumbai. Dev's mom has great style and I bet she can take you to the best places when you're there."

"Mmmhmm." She said over her shoulder before closing the dressing room curtain. "She was talking about this one designer she loves who's supposed to have a pop-up shop in Breach Candy while we're there."

Mission accomplished. Phoebe was looking forward to pop-up shops and shopping instead of convent schools and chaperones. "See? Now, hurry up, the oatmeal bars are calling me."

☐Chapter 16

My phone's ringtone shook me awake and I forced my eyes open as I slowly pulled my head off my forearms and cracked one eye open to stare groggily at the phone screen. Leia's name was unnaturally bright under the time—10:45 p.m. "Crap." I hit answer on my phone while rubbing at the divot I'd gotten on my nose from pressing against the edge of my history textbook. Apparently, based on the evidence before me, I'd fallen asleep over my homework and had lost two hours of precious study time. "Hey."

"Hey, yourself." Leia's tone was way too perky for me at that moment. "I tried calling a few times earlier, but you didn't answer."

I stifled a yawn. "Sorry, studying." I searched my desk for my mug and took a sip of cold peppermint tea, which had obviously been useless at keeping me awake earlier. "What's up?" Along with the crick in my neck, a pang rang through my abdomen as I straightened up. I pushed lightly at my stomach around where my lymph nodes were and cringed at the corresponding pain, familiar and definitely not cramps. While she talked, I opened my planner to the monthly layout and checked it just in case I was wrong—nope, I wasn't scheduled to have my period for another two weeks.

Leia had been going on for a full minute but paused mid-sentence. "Um, are you listening?"

"Yup. Emily's idea for the library garden?" I said, repeating what I'd picked up from her last sentence, something about starting a cooking class for the kids to learn how to use the vegetables they'd grown. Meanwhile, though, my brain kept cataloging what I was feeling. I'd been bloated and headache-y for a few days, and I knew the symptoms way too well to ignore them. My food sensitivities had kicked up with a vengeance, and this current pain was probably because of the apple I'd eaten after I got home from school. Or maybe the French toast stick I'd stolen from Em's lunch tray. My body already wasn't a big fan of fructose or oligosaccharides, but something I'd eaten seemed to have really triggered it in the past month.

I made a mental note to start food journaling again and then tried to focus back on what Leia was saying.

"Anyway, I wanted to know how your first non-adult

dance class went." I could hear her bed creak in the background and realized she was settling in for a long call, which I definitely didn't have the time or energy for. "How did it feel to teach kids again?"

I did *not* have time for this. I stared at the unintelligible page of notes that were supposed to be the research for my history paper. "Good. Dance-y," I said, distractedly, flipping through the library books I'd marked up with page flags and breathing a sigh of relief. At least I'd been conscious enough when marking the pages to have something remotely useful, unlike my actual notes.

Leia seemed completely oblivious to the distraction in my tone. "Awesome. How many kids are in the classes? Are they really big?"

"Twelve in Junior, eighteen in prep." I kept my words short, hoping she'd get the hint. I didn't have time to talk— the paper was due tomorrow, I'd procrastinated on it for a week because of dance and other school stuff and now I'd lost all the time I'd planned to actually write it. And the time I was going to spend writing the paper was going to bump my physics homework out, and—my brain spun, trying to weave my plans back into some semblance of organization.

Apparently she hadn't gotten the hint, because she went on to say, "Grace, is everything okay? It feels like you're not all there."

"I'm fine." I cleared some sticky notes off of my planner and stared at my schedule, trying to think. I had to go meet with the physical therapist for my project tomorrow afternoon, but maybe I could figure something out afterwards.

"No, really, something's up. You sound annoyed."

I pulled out my correction tape and planner pens and started moving things around on my schedule. "You know, maybe nothing's up and I just don't have anything to talk about."

She made a disbelieving noise on the other side of the line. "You know," she said, in what I could tell was a deliberate imitation of my tone, "if anyone should be annoyed, it's me. I'm the one you stood up, again."

"I know," I said, trying not to sound exasperated. How many times did she want me to apologize? "I would have loved to have been there, but—"

"But your friends' needs always come before mine." Her tone was flat, more of a statement than a question.

"That's not fair," I said. She had no clue how much work I had to do, scrambling to squeeze her in between all my million other priorities.

"You're always cancelling on me," she said with heavy emphasis on "always." "I don't even get it. It's the end of senior year, your AP tests are done, you got into PSU, and you're not up for valedictorian. Who cares what kind of grades you get now?"

"I care. But you apparently don't."

"I'm going to ignore that comment because you're obviously stressed."

I held back the urge to say, "No, really?" and instead

stared down at my phone incredulously and said, "Yes, I'm stressed. I have a paper due tomorrow in history class and I haven't even started writing it. Instead of figuring out how to write about post-September-11th US foreign policy practices, I'm talking on the phone."

Leia paused for a long moment before saying, her tone a bit softer, "Have you asked Em for help? She loves this stuff. You know she probably even knows more than all the history teachers in your school."

"I don't *need* Em's help. What I need is a few hours to get stuff done without people interrupting me."

I could hear her take a deep breath on the other side of the line, the same way she always did before pasting a faux smile on her face to talk to people like Brooklyn. "Fine. If you want me to leave you alone, just ask. You don't have to snap at me like that."

Her tight tone popped the bubble of frustration and I imitated her deep breath before saying, "Sorry, you're right, I'm stressed. Can I talk to you later?"

"Sure. I'm going to bed soon, though."

I dropped back into my desk chair and mentally ran through my schedule. "How about Wednesday? I was going to cram some studying in for a half hour at the patisserie by the dance school. Want to meet me there at 4:30?"

"That works. I'll head over right after I finish with the kids at the library. We're making rhubarb cobbler from some of yesterday's harvest. Emily found a really simple recipe for them."

"Exciting."

Leia's laugh was tight, but at least it was a laugh. "Very. Okay, see you tomorrow. Good night."

"'Night." I didn't wait for her to add on anything else, just hung up and stared at the clock. I could get another three hours in before going to bed and finish everything else up in the morning. "I can do this," I muttered to myself, as I slid my history book back towards myself and tried to find where I'd last left off.

☐Chapter 17

"If I were you, I'd raise tuition for next year if you want to keep operating. You can't keep afloat if you keep charging the same amount as you did a decade ago. Inflation *is* an actual thing." Dad's voice drifted out of his and Mom's bedroom and I paused on my way past their door, popping my head in the doorway. Dad waved and gestured for me to come in. "Just packing," he mouthed at me, then pointed at the phone he'd perched on the dresser. I dropped onto the floor and maneuvered my legs into a butterfly stretch. Ever since I'd been little, I'd enjoyed listening to Dad giving people advice—he always made sense and always seemed to know exactly what to say. Since I'd managed to finish my paper in record time that morning, getting ready for school could wait a few more minutes.

"Inflation might be an actual thing, but I have a lot of students who won't be able to afford to dance if I raise prices. As it is, I'm the only affordable school in the region." Aunt Drina's voice sounded stressed as it came through the speaker.

"You won't even have a dance school if you can't afford to pay your lease." Dad expertly rolled a pair of perfectly ironed trousers into a neat log and put them into his small carry on. "And how's that air conditioner working?"

Aunt Drina seemed to ignore the dig about the air conditioner. "I'm sure if I can have a successful summer session, I can avoid raising tuition next year. I was thinking of setting up a Zumba class on Saturdays all summer."

Dad didn't pause as he turned to pull a few polo shirts with his company logo out of his dresser. "Will you have any students? If they're not at the shore on Saturdays, they're avoiding shore traffic. I wouldn't count on a big break in the summer, Drina."

"I just can't raise tuition like that, David. I opened this school because I love dance and want to share that love with all kids who want to dance, not just the ones who can afford it."

Dad looked over at me and raised an eyebrow, giving me a 'see what I'm dealing with?' expression. "Love doesn't pay the bills. Speaking of, how many full scholarships are you floating this year?"

She made a huffing sound. "That's beside the point."

"Probably more than enough to pay for that air conditioner and replace all those floors you keep talking about," Dad said. "Not to mention the shoes you've bought for a few of those girls. I know how expensive those ballet toe things are. Look, I know you want to help everyone, but you have to think about your bottom line. The bank won't even think about another loan if your business plan is all about giving away free classes to everyone who says they need them."

"This is kind of a non-negotiable," Aunt Drina said, her tone light but firm. "I know turning around underperforming business units is your specialty. Can you help me with any ideas that don't involve leaving some of my students behind?"

Dad shook his head, but there was a good-natured expression on his face. We'd both expected that answer. "Fine, email me your budget and business and marketing plans. I'll see what I can do."

I could hear the sound of what sounded like excited typing on the other side of the line. "Thanks so much, I know you can make this work. You're a miracle worker."

"Miracles are easier if you're practical," Dad said, and I resisted the urge to nod like a bobblehead doll.

Aunt Drina laughed. "Practical may pay the bills but it doesn't always fill the heart."

"Paid bills keep the heart healthy. But I'll agree to disagree with you," He responded with a chuckle as he rolled up the last polo on his bed and squeezed it into his bag.

"Perfect." She made a loud "mwah" sound over the phone. "You're the best brother-in-law ever. Thanks for the early morning call. Have a good trip."

As soon as Aunt Drina hung up, I smiled up at Dad, who was rubbing at the bridge of his nose like he was trying to ward off a headache. "You know Aunt Drina won't raise tuition or cut the scholarships, right?"

"I know. She's not exactly cut out to be a businesswoman. Corporate America would have eaten her alive."

I tilted my head and studied him with a smile. "So, what are you thinking?"

"I'll take a look at her expenses and see if she can cut something there, maybe see if she can figure out if her marketing costs are impactful or if she'll have better luck doing something else. This isn't exactly consumables, but business is business. You can do good things and be practical at the same time, it just carries more risk."

"Hmm." I stretched out my legs and wiggled my toes at the ceiling. "Do you think she'll have to close the dance school?" At those words, my throat clenched up a little bit. That school had been a huge part of my life for so long.

"Dance schools are high risk businesses. Drina knew that going in." Dad put his toiletries bag on the top of his perfectly packed suitcase and zipped it shut before turning to smile down at me. "But, don't worry. I've helped save entire divisions when their keystone product market share disappeared. I think keeping a business open that has a lot of community goodwill and a very good track record for turning out successful students is definitely not impossible compared to that."

"But being practical is easier?"

"Always. Planning and practical decision-making are the cornerstones of success. Like I told your aunt, love doesn't pay the bills." He picked up his suitcase and plopped it on the ground. "Speaking of, I'd love to keep talking, but I need to get to the airport."

The word 'airport' made my heart drop into my stomach. Flights usually meant more days away and Dad already had been away most of the past two months.

"You just got back. Mom won't be happy about it," I pointed out.

He gave me an "I know" look. "Mom never is, but she'll have to deal. I'll get an earful about it later, but she doesn't understand this is important. Success requires sacrifice."

I'd heard that a million times, and even though I agreed with him, it didn't make the worry in my gut less. He and Mom had been fighting so much lately, this wouldn't help.

"Where are you going this time?" I tried to keep my voice as perky as possible, even though the thought of another bunch of days without him around wasn't an exciting prospect.

"Indiana, Ireland, then Italy," He said while checking the packing list taped in his passport case.

"Three 'I's in a row, huh?"

He laughed. "What can I say? I'm an efficient traveler."

I wracked my brain for another "I" place. "No India?"

"That's next month. I just need to find two more 'I' places to keep up my track record."

"I hear Iceland is nice this time of year. You know, they'll have sunlight again." I got up on my tiptoes to give Dad a kiss on the cheek. "Have a safe trip and have fun. I'm going to go get ready. Can't be late to school if I ever want to take over the world."

He smiled and reached over to ruffle my hair as if I were still eight. "That's my girl."

Imitating him, I reached up to ruffle his hair, too, laughing as he pretended to duck away. "Like father, like daughter."

Things to remember when designing for people:

1. Not everyone thinks logically
2. Most people never read the instructions (Why?!?! WTF is wrong with people?)
   a. Instructions and labels should be your last pick for controlling risk
3. Once it's in their hands, it's out of your control
4. Human beings come in a lot of different shapes and sizes...
5. ...And different levels of education...
6. ...And different capabilities...
7. ...And from different cultures with different things they'd consider normal or common...
8. So you can't just design for the most common user, you need to make sure you design for the full range of users
9. Everyone makes mistakes. No one is perfect.
10. If you actually take the time to understand the end user in the beginning, you'll have a better and safer product in the end
11. <u>It's not about you, it's about them.</u>

☑Chapter 18

The physical therapy clinic hadn't changed much since I'd been there as a patient in eighth grade for rehab for my knee. A few new pieces of equipment littered the room, but the same row of four therapy beds lined the back wall, each filled with a patient doing exercises with rubber therapy bands or getting ice and stim. The weird part, though, was seeing it from the non-patient side. "Thank you again for letting me come here and talk to you and your patients," I said to Annie, the physical therapist Dr. Aubrey had suggested I contact, as she led me to a little table behind the clinic's check-in desk.

"No problem. I'm excited to have you here. It's not often people ask our opinion," she said, gesturing me towards a chair opposite hers. "I think it's great that you're taking the time to talk to actual patients for your project. And I think some of my patients might enjoy having someone to talk to, too. I know you can't wave a wand and fix their problems because this is just a school project, but sometimes it's nice to feel like someone is listening."

I nodded, unsure of what to say, instead pulling out my notebook and the set of questions Oliver and Mr. Newton had helped me put together and tried not to look self-conscious while doing so. I'd thought I was only going to talk to the therapists, not actual patients.

Annie folded her hands on the table and smiled at me. "So, what are you working on?"

"*Your job is to look for problems, not solutions,*" Oliver's words echoed in my brain as I took a deep breath and said, "My grandmom had a stroke a few years ago and when she was recovering, she used a glove to help her use her hand and uncurl her fingers. I remember her complaining about that glove and I thought maybe I could come up with a better design?"

She nodded. "Okay, so she had an assistive glove. Have you asked her exactly what she didn't like about it?"

I shook my head, wishing I had been clearer. It had been over a year but it was still a little hard to get out. "She died last year, so no."

The physical therapist cringed. "I'm sorry. Was it another stroke?"

"No, pneumonia." That was one of the things that had

hurt the most about losing her and made me the maddest, that she'd died from a common infection in the twenty-first century. It was frustrating how we carry supercomputers in our pockets but can't figure out how to keep people breathing through a simple illness.

"Sorry." Annie took that moment to turn around and dig through a drawer before putting a few gloves on the table that looked a lot like the one Grandmom had used. "We're getting a lot closer to switching to robotic gloves to help with daily tasks—"

"I saw journal articles like the study that was done for the Department of Veterans Affairs for the hand assistive glove. And didn't the FDA just come out with a guidance for neural interfaces?" I couldn't help but feel a little spark of pride at being able to show off some of my research.

"You know more about that than me," she said, with a laugh. "We're on the treatment end, not the design side. But, anyway, we already have some great gloves for rehab for spasticity, which is when patient's muscles can't relax after a stroke and they have trouble unclenching their fingers. We even use a special kind of glove and computer program that turns rehab into a game using virtual reality so patients can retrain their brain and muscles to function again." She slid a bulky black glove with springs and linkages on it across the table at me and I automatically picked it up to turn it around and move the fingers. "The springs provide resistance so, as the patient goes through their exercises, they retrain their brain and muscles to work together again.

I like using it with orthopedic rehab patients, too, because it's really good for retraining fine motor skills."

I played with the glove some more, ideas popping into my head for my own design, and I resisted the urge to tune Annie out and draw them immediately. "And the other kind of gloves?"

She pushed a different one my way, a glove that had a few straps and not-so-obvious springs built across the fingers. "What these kinds of gloves do is help patients get through their everyday tasks by helping to counter the contracting muscles." Seeing my tilted head and confused look, she curled her hand into a fist, then splayed her fingers wide. "It's like an active splint that keeps the hand open but still lets the patient close it when they work against the springs. That's probably what your grandmother used."

I nodded, not looking up from the glove I was turning around in my hands. I glanced down at my notepad for my first question. "So, what are the problems with what you have right now?"

"How about we ask Julia? She should be finishing up in a minute or two." Annie stood and gestured me towards a younger woman who was seated in front of a computer. She was dressed in one of my favorite workout clothing brands, and her dark hair was up in tight ponytail. She didn't look like a patient, but maybe she was there with one of her grandparents.

"I probably should talk to another PT instead of patients and their families, right?"

"Therapists see and hear patient challenges but it's good to get feedback from the patients, who actually have to live with the thing you design," Annie countered in a good-natured tone, "and Julia is probably the perfect first patient to interview." She turned her attention towards the woman. "If she has a few minutes to spare, that is."

Julia looked away from her computer screen and grinned at us. "Just call me specimen number one. I'll take any excuse not to do my trig homework."

Annie seemed to decide to help move us past my faux pas. "Julia, this is Grace. She's working on a project for school to design an assist for stroke patients, like you."

I blinked, probably looking a little bit like I was trying to imitate a fish, then tried to smooth the surprise off my features. Up until that point, all of the patients had been older and had really visible symptoms.

"Aren't you too young for this?" Looking at her a second time, I noticed something bulky under the long sleeve covering her left elbow and how, on her left hand, she was wearing the white glove-like thing that was connected to the computer. "I'm sorry, I didn't mean to imply—"

She waved off my apology. "Don't worry about it, no one ever expects someone as young as me to be a stroke patient. It's actually super common for young women, but lots of doctors ignore our symptoms." She let Annie help her out of the white glove attached to the computer and into a bulky black glove before following us to the table. "My roommate figured out something was going wrong and

I was really lucky she rushed me to the hospital. Everyone said I probably would have died if she hadn't."

I could feel my jaw tighten. "Are you kidding me? That's completely unacceptable," I said, then quickly added when I realized what had burst out of my mouth, "The part about doctors ignoring symptoms, not your friend saving you. It's ridiculous."

"No kidding. In fact, when she got me to the ER, all the nurses at the desk just thought it was just stress until she forced them to listen to her and triage me." Julia rolled her eyes and said, "You know, because, in their heads, the only things girls do is stress and overexaggerate our symptoms."

"'I know the feeling. Not the almost dying part," I said, realizing how silly I had to sound compared to her experience, but pushed on, "but I went through three doctors and a bunch of tests before someone realized that I had real food sensitivities and IBS and I wasn't just making stuff up. I mean, stress actually plays a real factor in my problems, but it's not the root cause."

"That sucks."

"Yeah, but compared to what you're going through, avoiding foods that give me stomachaches is nothing." I couldn't help but give her face and arm a once-over again, though. Unlike my grandmother, there was no sign of drooping in her face and she'd walked without help over to the table. "So, um," I said, trying not to sound like I was prying into her health problems, "it's just your hand that got affected?"

Julia aimed an amused smile at Annie and then turned it on me. "I look pretty healthy, don't I?"

"I'm sorry, I just—"

Annie patted me on the arm sympathetically. "She's messing with you, Grace. But," she said, tapping on my notebook with one fingernail, "a piece of advice. If you want to go into designing things for people, the first thing you need to do is let go of any assumptions about what typical patients look and act like. If you can let go of those, you won't end up just designing things for the loudest or more visible or most assumed group of people." She shrugged, then said, "And with that soapbox speech done, I'm going to leave you two to it."

"Thanks," I said to Annie's back as she made her way over to one of the therapy tables.

"She's right, I was messing with you a little bit. Sorry," Julia said with an impish smile. "But, anyway, I have what doctors call 'spasticity' in my left hand and elbow. My brain isn't talking right to those parts of me and, since it's not bad enough to need surgery, they're trying to retrain my brain and muscles to work together in a new way, instead."

"Then, I'd definitely love your feedback," I said, flipping my notebook to a clean page and clicking my pen. "Okay, first question—tell me about the problems you have with," I gestured at the glove Annie had put on Julia after helping her out of the computer-glove, "that?"

"You mean other than standing out everywhere I go with this thing on? I've got the 'you should see the other guy' jokes down pat when people ask if I got in a fight or something," she said, good naturedly.

I snorted. I'd used the same comeback when I had a black eye from a misplaced elbow from one of my teammates at a cheerleading competition. Cheer was rough. "I've definitely been there with wrist braces."

"Let's see. Outside of looking like I smashed my hand into a wall, it's a pain to do things with it and not get it wet. I like that it's soft and I know people didn't like the old plastic gloves because they were too hard, but I use this all this time and the soggy glove thing is such a pain. They're so expensive, it's not like I can just get a second one to trade out when this one's drying." Before I could ask another question, she added, "Also, it looks like something a guy would design for an older guy. I'd love something a little more—" she gestured at her outfit.

"Stylish?" I prompted, and, when she nodded, I added that to my list.

"Or as close to invisible as possible," she said, holding up her hand to give me a better view of the glove. "You know, maybe if you took the material out of the middle here," she pointed at her palm, "and moved this strap, it probably would be better."

I kept making notes, but remembered what Oliver said about how people would also talk about solutions when we were interviewing them, but that we should look for the problem they were trying to solve. Maybe what she really wanted was something that felt less restrictive or was cooler. I watched as she tugged at the wrist strap as she talked, running her finger under it every now and then like it was bothering her.

"Do you have anything you like about it?" Annie prompted as she passed us on her way to one of the leg machines with another patient.

Julia scrunched her nose. "I was getting to that," she said in an aside to me. "I like how it helps to keep my fingers extended but doesn't take too much work for me to curl my fingers back to pick something up."

I wrote "low actuation force" in my notebook under the pros section of the table I'd drawn in there, right under "soft." "What if—" I started to say, but stopped myself. Ideas were swirling in my head, but I was supposed to listen, not offer solutions. Which was turning out to be really hard. Leia was right about my habit of wanting to give people answers right away for everything. "I mean, what else?"

"It's not too heavy, so that's a positive. The loaner one I got at first was even bulkier and heavier. And I like that this doesn't cover up my fingertips, because my sense of touch is already weird right now and that would make it nonexistent." She thought for another minute. "That's about it, I think."

"Thanks," I said, as soon as I finished writing up my notes. She'd answered a lot of my questions without me even having to ask them. "That was a big help."

Julia reached out to shake my hand with her gloved one. "You're welcome. Good luck with your project. I'd love to see what you come up with."

"Thank you, Julia," Annie said. "Grace, I have an appointment with another patient right now and she's going to be working with the VR glove today. If you want, I can ask her permission for you to sit in and observe?" She made a gesturing motion towards one of the treatment beds where an older woman was seated. The woman's lips and eye on one side drooped slightly, just enough to be noticeable, kind of like Grandmom in the first few weeks after her stroke.

I had to hold back from eagerly nodding my head like a bobblehead doll. "That would be so great."

"Great. Let me check with her before I bring you over."

As I waited, I stared at my notes, energy building up in me as information and ideas started colliding in my thoughts. This was interesting, like collecting puzzle pieces, and, even though I wasn't supposed to, I couldn't help but imagine the perfect final puzzle. I knew I could design something better and easier for someone like Julia to use, and I couldn't wait to dive in further.

May

☐ Chapter 19

I closed my locker door and turned towards the hallway, jumping with surprise to find Alec looking right over my shoulder. "Damnit, Alec, creeper much?"

He stepped back into the middle of the hallway, ignoring the mutters of some of the people he cut off in the process. "Oh, guru of physics, I've come to beg a favor of you," he said.

"'Guru of physics?' That's not dramatic or anything." I leaned against my locker and waved at one of the JV football freshmen who passed.

"If I were you, I'd take the praise while I still could. Next year, you're going to have so many physics geniuses around you, it's doubtful anyone would consider you the best at anything."

"Harsh. Especially coming from someone who apparently wants my help with something," I pointed out.

"Me needing help doesn't make that any less true."

"You're so lucky I like you, or you'd be screwed." I checked my nails, adding 'make an appointment at the salon' to my to-do list. My sparkly pink manicure was looking really rough. "What do you need, oh anti-guru of groveling?"

"You know how Newton wants us to make prototypes of one of the working assemblies from our projects?"

"Yeah?" I tilted my head at him. "I have mine printing right now."

"Rub it in, overachiever." He narrowed his eyes at me and snorted. "I'm stuck. I can't get the gear teeth to line up in the assembly for my design. Can you take a look at my model and see what's going wrong?"

I arched my brows at his request. "That's not physics, it's CAD."

"Whatever," he said, an impatient note in his tone. "Do you have a few minutes? I really need to send this to the printer tonight to get in tomorrow morning's queue if I want to clean it and put it together in time to show Newton in Friday's class."

I checked my phone for the time and tried to keep my expression neutral. "I was supposed to meet up with Leia before dance class, but," I cringed, realizing how many times I'd been late to stuff with Leia lately, but said, "I can spare a few minutes." I pushed away from the lockers. Moving helped mask the worry as I tried to figure out how to be in two places at the same time. There was a theoretical physics equation for that, right?

"Thanks." After a second's thought, Alec arched his eyebrow and said, carefully. "Are you sure she's not going to be mad if you're late?"

I threw off a quick text to Leia and shook my head. "No, it's okay. Don't worry about it." I tossed my hair back and drew up my spine to give myself a confident look. "Besides, I'll probably figure this out in minutes and I won't be late at all. I'm a CAD guru, after all."

"Ok-ay," he drew out, shutting my locker for me and gesturing towards the multimedia lab. "I'm not coming to your funeral if she kills you. I like my life."

"Leia's not like that. She'll totally understand."

☑

Leia was at our old table at the little French bakery in the same "upscale" strip mall as the dance school. We used to hang out there all the time when we started dating, before our parents knew about us and while I was still dancing. That table had a lot of good memories, but this didn't look like it was going to be one of them. Leia pointed at her half-eaten *pain au chocolat* without even bothering to hide her annoyance. "You're late again."

"I know. Alec had a CAD emergency." I dropped my bag on the empty chair and hurried up to the counter. "*Un chocolat chaud fait avec lait d'amande, s'il vous plaît.*" I cringed after doing it—Leia always called me out for sounding pretentious by insisting on ordering in French, and I could practically *feel* her eye roll from across the bakery. Instead of heading back to the table and waiting for them to call me up, I paid and hung out at the counter until they handed me the wide teacup-like mug. Maybe, just maybe, she'd forgive and forget in that time. I picked up the saucer and slowly made my way back, willing the almond milk hot chocolate not to spill.

Leia looked even more annoyed by the time I got back to the table. "Is it even possible to have a CAD emergency?"

"If he wants to get an A on his final project, yes." I picked a rose macaron off her plate and tried to sound like being late was no big deal. "He messed up when he calculated the base circle diameter for one of his gears and that all went back to getting the diametral pitch wrong. It all took a little longer than I thought because we had to start practically from scratch."

She didn't even make one of her usual jokes about all the technical terms I'd just dropped, just shredded a section of her *pain au chocolat* into little pieces as she said, "You could have texted me. I was getting worried."

"I'm sorry. Between Alec and you and helping my aunt, maybe I was just a little busy today and couldn't keep track of everything." I heard the edge in my voice and, as soon as I saw her eyes widen, forced myself to take a deep breath before continuing. "I'm sorry," I said, in a much calmer tone, "I just lost track of time. You know how it is when I get started designing something. I'm really sorry."

Leia pursed her lips like she wanted to say something else, but paused, instead, to sip some water.

"So," she said evenly, "Brooklyn's at it again, talking about how great the Academy's prom was and how she heard Pine Central's prom sucked. Now she's campaigning to put our post-graduation party on the same day as your graduation, but that's been scheduled so long that even her parents can't get it moved." She took a bite of lemon macaron and waved the other half around as she added, "That girl wants to ruin every good thing about senior year for me."

I wanted to march over to Leia's school and kick the snot out of that little maggot, but I just kept my expression neutral. "Why don't you—"

She cut me off, sticking her hand up in the air in a "stop" gesture. "I don't need advice, I need you to listen to me."

Maybe I was tired, or maybe Leia's own annoyance had rubbed off on me, but I found myself snapping out, "You know, every time I try to offer you a solution, you practically bite off my head, telling me that I'm trying to fix things instead of listening, but things will never get better with Brooklyn because you just won't take my advice. You're never going to get off this ridiculous merry-go-round of problems with her if all you do is let her keep being a jerk to you." I pressed my lips together to force myself to pause and think before adding, "You know what? In a few weeks you'll never have to see her again if you don't want to, so why do you let her bother you so much?"

"If you don't want to listen, why do you even bother to make plans with me?" Leia shot back, putting her mug down with a little more force than necessary. "Since apparently, everyone else is more important, anyway."

"I said I'm sorry. It's the end of the year, people need help. I can't just say no to them."

"But you can say no to me, right? It's always me. I'm always getting bumped for everyone else. Phoebe needs clothes for a trip a month and a half from now and you drop everything to help her, Alec needs help with his homework and you cancel with me, Em needs..." she floundered for a second to come up with an example, then just waved it away and pushed on, "whatever Em needs and you go out of your way to help, but you haven't even spent one stupid hour in the past month helping me or *my* friends or even just asking me if I need anything. You always put me last and I'm getting tired of that."

That hurt. I was trying to be everything for everyone, and the only thanks I got was being told I wasn't doing enough. Before I could say anything I'd regret, I finished off my hot chocolate and stood, swinging my bag onto my shoulder. "I have to go change so I'm ready for the junior prep class." I hoped she'd say something to smooth things between us like she always did, but, instead, she just pursed her lips again and dropped her eyes to the table. I shook my head as if trying to shake off the negative atmosphere. "Sorry I was late," I said as I walked away from the table.

☐ Chapter 20

Avoiding my girlfriend all week was exhausting.

I dropped onto the ground, slipped off my Keds, and dug my feet into the sandy dirt at the edge of the lake in my backyard, my toes just barely touching the water. It was still cold enough to raise goosebumps on my arms and threaten to turn my toenails blue, but I ignored the cold, instead leaning back against the tree trunk and focusing on the reflections in the lake. The tree hid me from the house so that the world was just me, the pine needles poking me in the butt through my jeans, and the lake.

And there was the earthy cedar water smell, which my mom hated—but I loved, because it reminded me of the science experiments we did in middle school to measure the acidity of the water in the environmental center. The acidic tea of these iron-oxide filled lakes fascinated little biology-loving me, but Mom, who grew up in New York City, never understood the appeal of the smell of decaying plant matter. Outside of the summer, when she and dad would hang out on our private beach, I had this place to myself.

"Grace?"

And Leia, who loved this place almost as much as me. Crap, I hadn't expected her. I closed my eyes and shoved my toes deeper into the water. Maybe if I sat really still, she wouldn't notice me and would go away.

A gentle hand touched my arm right before a warm body settled onto the ground next to me. "Your mom said you were out here." She looked over at me with a hurt expression. "We might have been fighting, but I can't believe you bailed on me and my best friend again. I promised Emily that you'd be there to help." Her voice had taken on her disappointed teacher tone, like I was a little kid who needed a lecture on how to behave in class. "We had to rush to figure out how to handle all the kids with only two people."

I pushed my hair out of my eyes with a huff. It hadn't been my fault that everyone needed everything from me all the time. "I'm sorry. I didn't 'bail out' on purpose, but rehearsal ran over and Aunt Drina needed me to watch the rosebuds. What do you expect me to do, run out on my own aunt and leave her with a dozen four-year-olds, to help out in a garden that won't die if we wait another day to prune it, or whatever you wanted me to do today?" I tried to bite back the sarcasm in my voice but it still snuck through.

"I know you're stressed, but you have no right to take it out on me." Her voice grew lower and dangerously quieter as anger creeped in. "Don't you think I'm stressed, too? Don't you think I have finals and family things and senior stuff, just like you do? The only difference is that *I'm* not blowing *you* off all of the time and expecting you to say it's fine." She barely took a breath before diving back in again, fingers curling into the sand beneath her. "I'm always the one hanging out with your friends and dealing with your in-jokes, but you can't take a few hours out of your precious schedule to do something for *me*. It's not fair, Grace."

"You're the one who sided with my parents about helping out my aunt. And if I remember right, you're also the one who said I should push harder on my project. And now you're mad I never have any time anymore?"

"No, I'm mad you think I'm the only one you can blow off or snap at. I'm tired of being the one who gives in to things all the time," she shot back. I opened my mouth to argue but slammed it shut again at one warning shake of her head. "I'm tired and I have my own stuff to worry about. I'm just... tired." She looked at me, her expression both hurt and sad at the same time, and I could see the tears that were starting to form in the inner corners of her eyes. "I think I—we—need a break."

I tried to speak, but I couldn't pull in enough air to make a sound, lead filling my lungs.

Leia looked away from me before adding, "Not forever, but I think we both need a few weeks to get back to being unstressed. Alone."

"I—" my voice wouldn't go any louder than a whisper and I tried again, pushing against the cold that pulsed through my body—a definite symptom of shock, the semi-functional part of my brain unhelpfully pointed out. "I don't know what to do to fix this."

Leia shook her head and "Maybe you need to stop thinking of us as a thing or an equation or a machine that you can schedule and calculate into perfection," she said, her words biting hard. She took a deep breath, ran her hand across her eyes and said, "I'm sorry, that was unfair." She stood and paused mid-step without turning back to face me, her voice shaky and teary as she said, "I just need time. Bye, Grace."

Before I could even form the words, "I'm sorry," she was already out of sight.

□

A damp chill filled the air as the sun started to set and I tried to ignore it as it soaked into my clothes and hair, instead curling my arms around my legs and dropping my chin to my knees as I stared out over the lake. I hadn't moved from my spot since Leia left and wasn't ready to head inside and back to being perfect, unflustered Grace who always said the right thing and always knew how to deal with everything. I didn't know how to deal with this. There wasn't a handbook or a perfect equation to help me figure out how to fix something this big, how to take back control of the situation. Last time, I'd run to Aunt Drina because she knew everything, but I wasn't that little girl whose entire world revolved around a dance school and her favorite aunt anymore.

I didn't even know how to keep from feeling like I was just on the edge of choking on my own feelings, suffocating until I became a shell, a *wili* from the ballet *Giselle*, ghosts of girls who died from heartbreak, wandering around this yard among the fireflies and mist for the rest of my existence. And through it all, a thread of common sense rose up, making me annoyed at my own dramatics. I wiped my runny nose on my sleeve and hugged my legs tighter to myself. I just needed a few more minutes to pull myself together, just a few minutes, and then I'd be able to sit down and figure this out with a clear brain.

My phone ringing broke me out of my see-saw of competing thoughts and I quickly pulled it out of my pocket, the tiny ember of hope in my chest extinguishing when I saw Em's name on the screen. I intellectually knew it wasn't Leia—the ringtone hadn't been right—but that hadn't stopped my stupid, illogical heart from thinking otherwise. I inhaled, steadying and smoothing my shaking breaths before finally sucking up the courage to pick up.

"Hey, what's up?" I said, trying my best to sound upbeat.

"Hi, Alec and I were talking about the donations for the Noelle's Song raffle we're going to do at the farmers market and I was wondering if you heard—" Em stopped abruptly, her words hanging in the air, before saying in a concerned tone, "Grace, what's wrong?" Before I could respond, she added, "and don't say nothing, because I can hear it in your voice. Something's up."

I tried to force my voice to sound just a bit lighter. "It's not important." I really didn't need Em, of all people, trying to sweep in and dissect my relationship problems.

"Bull," she said in a rare, forceful tone. "You can't play that 'I'm an emotionless robot' act with me. I have a sixth sense for these things, you know. Grace—" her voice then grew softer, "—what happened?"

"Leia and I just had a fight and I think…" I took a deep breath to stop my voice from shaking and pushed through, "I think Leia asked for a pause." The inexactness in that sentence bugged me and I corrected myself. "Not think, I know she asked for a pause."

"No." She coughed as if trying to cover up the shock in her voice and, in a smoother tone, asked, "Pause as in pause or pause as in a breakup without having to say 'breakup?'"

I stared at the screen in horror. "I didn't know that was a thing." Great, an all-new worry to add to my list of problems.

Em was quick to clear her throat and say, "It's not. I mean, I'm sure it's not a thing for you and Leia. In fact, I'm positive. People go on breaks all the time and get back together again stronger than before." Rather than continue stumbling over herself in a spiral of bad platitudes, she went silent for a beat, then said, "Oh, Grace, I'm sorry. How are you feeling?"

For a self-proclaimed relationship expert, that was a ridiculous question. "Awful? How else do you want me to feel?"

"I don't know. Some people feel relieved, others get mad or sad…" she drifted off, leaving an opening for me to fill in the blanks.

I wasn't the bare-my-feelings-to-the-world type, and Em should have known that. Still, something about her tone made me want to say something. I dug my toes into the soil, the cold sand grating against my skin. "How about this? My stupid heart keeps telling me to fix this with Leia while my brain says maybe I should let it happen because it makes sense."

"What?" I hadn't heard Em sound that shocked in a while.

I shut my eyes, regret burning me for what had just come out of my mouth. "Look, what's been going on with me and Leia is hard to explain."

Em made a disbelieving sound. "Aren't you the one always telling the rest of us how Einstein said, 'If you can't explain it simply, you don't understand it enough?'"

This was a mistake. I pulled myself to standing, shoving aside the fog that had been threatening to choke me, and tried to center my brain around something a bit more concrete than talking about feelings and things I couldn't fix. "Okay, Einstein, enough about me. You were calling about the raffle baskets for Noelle's Song? Sorry, I have my list of stores I think will donate things back at my desk, if you give me a minute to—"

She didn't let it go. I shouldn't have expected anything less of Em. "Grace," she said, firmly, "we were talking about you and Leia. You're really good at dishing out relationship advice to the rest of us, but you can't take talking about your own problems?"

I felt my throat tighten again and I fought it back, throwing as much calm into my tone as I could. "The raffle is important and I know you need to get it done, so I'll worry about Leia later."

That earned me a disbelieving "pfft" from Em. "You *do* realize you're trying to stick things in neat little boxes and life's not like that."

"And you have to realize that I need to compartmentalize, otherwise, everything just falls apart."

Another "pfft" followed by a muttered curse. "That's ridiculous."

"Is it?" I said into the phone, feeling my hand start to shake as the words tumbled out of me. "Leia and I might be breaking up, my parents are fighting all the time, my final project is getting way bigger than I planned, I'm trying to get to graduation in one piece, I can't even eat one stupid thing without getting sick, and I need to help with things like the raffle and dance. How would you handle it? Just mush it all together and pretend everything is okay?" I realized I was on the verge of yelling and tried to steady and calm my voice. "I can't let one part of my life screw up the others."

"The eff you can." Em said. "Nobody can just randomly

turn off different parts of their lives. You're not superhuman."

"No, but I can focus on the things I need to get through without being distracted by other things. Be as perfect as possible in the things I can control." I felt my spine straighten up at those words, like I could pull myself up just by repeating that sentence.

"Perfect is for Photogram posts. No one has a perfect life, they just pretend like the rest of us."

I stared at the phone for a second, feeling like I'd just stepped into some sort of inspirational self-help talk. "I really don't know why I dumped this on you."

"Because I'm the love expert? Look, I can help you fix this, you know."

Now I understood why Leia always asked me to just listen and try not to fix things. "Please, no, we need to work it out on our own. She asked for time." Plus, I added without saying out loud, I knew what Em's fixes usually entailed and I already had enough chaos in my life at the moment.

"Are you sure? I could call her and—"

Before she could start weaving one of her elaborate plans and tangling me and Leia into it, I cut her off and said, "Positive, Em. Leave it alone."

"Okay," she said, sounding a little skeptical, but at least appearing to finally listen to my wishes. "Fine, but I'm here if you need me. I'll even get Alec to drive me over if you realize you need a hug."

I tried my hardest to ignore the part of me that really wanted to take her up on that offer and instead, said,

"Thanks. Now, about the raffle?"

"Oh, yeah. It was about the cheese shop in Millbrook where you said your mom knew the owner? Any chance she was able to talk to them yet?"

I breathed a sigh of relief, glad I could go back to something I could control. "Yup. He sent a list of what he can give us. Just give me a minute and I'll pull it up." I turned towards the house, towards my planner and notes and problems that were easy to calculate and solve.

I'd worry about Leia later.

Pros	Cons
• We're opposites. She keeps me from taking myself too seriously. I'm better because of her	• Only 2% of marriages in North America are high school sweethearts
• That last bullet point sounds really selfish, doesn't it? Yes, it does.	• We're opposites—Leia would be a better match with a liberal arts major and she'll probably meet someone "perfect"
• She keeps me from being selfish, too, because she's always volunteering and doing stuff for others because she's practically a saint. And this is yet another selfish bullet point...	• We'll be almost a 4 hr drive apart
	• Most couples break up freshman year at Thanksgiving (Turkey Dump)
• We support each other	• Which can completely mess up 1st semester and maybe 2nd semester, which are all the base classes
• ~~When we're not fighting.~~	• My future job will probably take me overseas or to Alaska, Leia wants to stay in NJ
•	
•	
•	~~• And I don't know how to fix this~~
• I love her	

☐ Chapter 21

I stared down at the list I'd made at 3 in the morning, when sleep was impossible because of the spiraling thoughts and nervous energy that buzzed through me like a storm. Thoughts of the future, of Leia meeting someone cuter, a liberal arts major with a matching passion for teaching little kids, haunted me. It was easy to imagine myself getting turkey dumped—the national statistics I'd found online were pretty damning for the survival of our relationship—then failing my first semester exams, spiraling into me getting kicked out of the engineering school and into a lower-earning major. All my plans falling apart like a game of Jenga when the person pulling the block didn't understand basic structural requirements.

It was so clear on paper. A geometric if-then logic exercise that always came to the same answer. Small fights led to big fights and big fights lead to breakups. And breakups when the two people were going to be long distance from each other had a statistical chance of nearly zero of unbreaking up. If I couldn't fix this, there was only one logical next step to this word problem. And I didn't know how.

My list haunted me Monday morning as I showered and blew out my hair into the perfectly straight style I always wore. Over again as I tried to line my eyes with a shaking hand I blamed on not enough sleep before I switched to a pencil liner that would be a lot more forgiving than the gel pot and brush. Again as I picked out my outfit for the day, jeans and a bright pink tank that would just barely show through my thin black cashmere sweater. People thought girls who liked girls couldn't be into fashion. I bit back a wild laugh at that thought and pulled on a pair of designer flats I'd gotten at a sample sale in New York. If that fashion thing was true, I wouldn't feel like someone was slowly choking me to death.

I met my eyes in the mirror, running a quick assessment of my whole look. Grace Correa, practically perfect in every way.

Right.

☑Chapter 22

"Can you explain to me why you need water ice so badly?"

"Osoba made us run through the graduation march, like, forty million times until we got it perfect." Em said, pushing open both of double doors with each hand. "I swear, it's going to start playing and I'm going to have flashbacks at my own graduation."

Phoebe caught one of the doors before it shut in her face and shook her head. "You're exaggerating. It wasn't that bad."

"You're right. It was only thirty-nine million times," Em said with an exaggerated eye roll. "I gave her an extra million for all the times she made the french horns re-tune."

The entire part about having to play the graduation march just didn't compute. I looked from Em to Phoebe and back. "You don't have to play at graduation, do you?"

"Oh, hell, no." Em gestured as if she were about to fling her flute case into the parking lot.

"It's for the class participation grade." Phoebe took the flute case from Em, then bumped her with her shoulder. "And we're supposed to be musical role models for all the people in the classes below us, Em."

"And that," Em said directly to me, "is why I need water ice."

"Hey, I'll take any excuse to go to Marranos." Alec came out of nowhere and pushed between Em and me. "Just listening to Em whine about having flashbacks is going to give me flashbacks."

I ignored him and turned my carefully cultivated raised eyebrow look at Em. "So, you're just being dramatic."

"And that surprises you?" Phoebe asked, before pointing towards the busses. "I'd love to come along, but I have to work this afternoon." She waved over her shoulder as she walked away and added, "Text me later, okay?"

"Have fun yarning, sell lots of wool," Em said, before turning back to me with a perfect imitation of my expression. "I'm not being dramatic. But I am concerned for the state of my soul in the dictatorship that is orchestra."

"That starship sailed a long time ago," Alec said with a cough to cover up his laugh.

Em narrowed her eyes and pursed her lips at Alec. "Please.

You're one to talk." She then turned her attention to me. "So, Marranos? You, me, Alec, and massive amounts of sugar?"

I thought about my schedule and lamented the lab time I'd be missing to work on the finite element analysis for my project. "You know I can't eat half the stuff there right now because of the lactose and fructose and—"

Em dug in her backpack, pulled out a little pill blister pack, and waved it at me. "I brought lactase tablets. No excuses now. You'll be fine." She reached out, grabbed both of our sleeves, and started pulling us in the direction of Alec's car. "C'mon. You know the place fills up on Wednesdays. We'll never get a table if you keep arguing, and I need some frozen custard and gummy bears."

"I thought it was water ice."

"Dealing with the two of you just got it upgraded to frozen custard if I want to restore my sanity."

□

Just like Em had predicted, Marranos was packed, even more so than usual. I squeezed past two guys in Haddontowne Academy uniforms on my way to the counter and threw a confused look over my shoulder at Em.

She didn't loosen her grip on my sleeve and the front of Alec's shirt as she wiggled through the crowd. "They had senior cut day today." She eyed one of the boys appreciatively. "These uniformed hotties are probably the senior delinquents."

"Or came to hang out with the delinquents after class," Alec pointed out. "You know, 'cause it's after school. And the people who cut probably didn't wear their uniforms?"

"Don't kill my fantasy, Kohen." Em grabbed my shoulders and pointed me towards the row of four tables that made up the bulk of Marranos' indoor seating. "Uniforms automatically equal hotness. I'm sure Grace agrees with me on that."

"Huh?" Suddenly, a familiar figure with short black hair with a blue streak came into focus. Even tiny, seated at one of the tables, dressed identically to most of the other girls, and looking down at her phone, Leia stood out in the crowd. My insides turned to ice and it was like the norovirus and a heart attack decided to hit me at the same time. My brain took an extra second to communicate to my legs, but when it did, I ground to a halt.

Em tripped the second I stopped, crashing into my back. "Oh, look who's here," she said in a deceptively innocent tone, her words muffled as she talked into my shirt. She might have been a good actress, but I'd had years of perfecting my Em b.s.-meter.

"Em," I warned in a low voice.

One look at my face and she dropped the act. "Fine, since you didn't want to elaborate, Phoebe got the details from Leia and told me. It's definitely fixable, so I invited Leia out for water ice. I thought you two could talk," she said. "Alec and I can give you some privacy if you want."

"Oh, hell no." I turned on my heel and prayed Leia wouldn't look up. This time, I was the one grabbing Alec by the shirt. "C'mon, Alec. Let's go. Em, outside. Now."

"Grace, you really need to stay and hear me out." Em

followed me back out into the parking lot. "I thought if you guys just had a chance to actually listen to each other, you'd fix this."

"*This* isn't how you fix things. Leia asked for some time and I'm not just going to waltz in and invade her space." I didn't even look back at her. At that moment, my hands were itching to reach out and strangle Em, even though I should have expected something like this from her. "And you have no right to try to trick me or to get in the middle of this. It's none of your business."

"It is my business because I care about you and Leia." Em came around me, blocking my way. "I know you can make it work if you just bothered to talk to each other."

"Just. Don't." I dodged around her with years of cheer and dance reflexes and headed straight for Alec's car. For his part, Alec just followed and watched us with a neutral expression.

"But—"

I resisted the urge to turn around and do the whole clichéd finger to the chest thing. "I know you're used to bossing everyone around and people listening to you, but I'm not one of those people. Stay the hell out of my relationships."

"You're throwing away the best thing that ever happened to you. People would kill for a relationship like yours and Leia's. You're being stubborn."

Her statement made me stumble, but I covered it up with a sharp 180-degree pivot. If I were a cat, I knew I'd be hissing my next words. "And you're being a meddling pain who doesn't know when her advice isn't wanted."

"Fine. If you don't want my advice, don't take it. Keep screwing up your life. I don't care anymore." One look at the hint of hurt that flashed across Em's pinched and angry features, though, and I had to resist the urge to take back everything I'd said. Instead, I looked over at my shoulder to see if Alec was still following. "Can you give me a ride back to my car?"

"Sure." Alec threw Em an apologetic look. "I'll be right back."

As soon as I was buckled into the passenger seat and Alec shifted the car into gear, I let out an exhausted breath. "Did you have any idea she was going to do that to me?"

"And ruin my chance at uninterrupted frozen custard consumption?" Alec took the turn out of Marranos' parking lot at a speed I'd normally complain about if I weren't in such a rush to get out of there. "No."

"I can't believe her. On what planet did she think that would be okay?"

"On Em planet." At my annoyed snort, he looked over at me before focusing back on the road. "C'mon, you know her. She was just trying to help. She only does stuff like this because she cares about you and Leia."

"I know, but," I gripped the door handle, trying to loosen the choking sensation in my chest, "I think we're fine, and that Em understands to stay out of things, and then, surprise—a sneak attack."

"You also know she gets really focused when she puts

her mind to something." He pulled into the mostly empty school parking lot and slowed to a stop behind my car. "You know I had nothing to do with this, right? Because it's not okay for you to take it out on me." He nodded at the video game sticker on his dashboard that I'd been worrying at with my nail. "Or my car."

I dropped my hands to my lap. "Yeah, I know. Sorry." I took a deep breath and reached for the door handle. "Just… the next time you hear her trying to come up with one of her 'plans,' can you, I don't know, distract her with community theater auditions or something?"

"Only if you promise to drive yourself to Marranos next time so if she does something like this, I don't have to put friendship in front of stromboli."

I stepped out of the car and closed the door, leaning in to talk through the open window. "Deal. I don't want to get in the way of you and food."

"You don't want to see me when I'm hungry," he growled.

I stifled a laugh at his reference. "Thanks for the ride, Hulk."

As soon as I stepped back, he waved and drove away. I slipped into my car, pushed the on button, and sat for a minute, trying to push back all the Leia-feelings. As soon as I started driving, though, my body went on autopilot and I ended up driving the opposite direction from home, towards Aunt Drina's studio. It didn't matter that my class wasn't for another hour, I needed to dance.

☑Chapter 23

I leaned forward in my straddle, my hips popping as my chest touched the floor. An indie pop ballad blasted out of the speakers and I rolled my body with the beat of the slow guitar until my nose was touching my left knee. My hamstring tugged, still a little tight, but didn't hurt. Class was starting in twenty minutes and I was taking advantage of every second to limber up. Technically, I was going to run my class through warmup, but the ritual of getting ready was just as important as a warm hamstring. Plus, the familiar routine helped focus my brain on everything but Leia and Em and everything that had just happened at Marranos.

"Mind if I stretch with you?" A pair of feet appeared right

under my nose and I turned my head to catch a pair of neon green legwarmers. Natalie didn't wait for my answer, just slid into a split next to me. "It's always more fun when you have someone to talk to."

"You're obviously not an introvert," I said. Between dance and cheer, I'd gotten so used to stretching with other people that it was actually a little comforting to have someone else in the room with me.

"Please. Drina told me about the whole cheerleader thing and how you have a million friends. I also heard about the time you gloriously told off the judge at the shore competition a few years ago." She leaned forward to touch her nose to her front knee and turned her head to add, "You're obviously not an introvert, either."

I stretched to the other leg, my side muscles hurting with the pressure of my laugh. The way I'd marched onto the stage and torn into one of the judges for giving "constructive criticism" about the weights of some of our senior girls was legendary at our dance school. Especially since I was only ten at the time and was defending people seven years older than me.

"No, definitely not. Touché."

She switched sides on her split. "Since I'm so good at reading you and your non-introvertness, I can tell something's really bothering you today," she said in a casual tone.

"Is it that obvious?"

She gestured with her chin towards the sound system, then back at me. "You've got Cyan Matthews on repeat, that's a real messy bun—not a 'I made it messy on purpose' bun, and your mascara looks pretty rough. I've been there, too. All you need is an empty pint of ice cream next to you and a spoon sticking out of your mouth."

"That's later," I admitted, glancing at my reflection and admitting to myself that she was ridiculously right. I looked like the most poorly pulled-together mess on the planet. I rolled my ankles and pointed my toes, debating my next step. Even though Natalie was still a stranger, at least she was neutral. "I got in a fight with my girlfriend. And then fought with one of my other friends." Go, me.

There always was a pattern, a beat, a series of moments after people who didn't really know me heard me say "my girlfriend." First, a nod while the information really didn't hit their brains, followed by a furrowed brow or a tilted head or a double-take widening of their eyes as they processed but didn't fully compute. After that, an expression would flicker across their face: surprise, disgust, confusion, slightly uncomfortable acceptance, disappointment—especially if it was a guy hitting on me—that would give me a hint to what I was going to have to deal with. My favorites were the people who gave the equivalent of a mental shrug as they gamely jumped to the next thought, like when I first came out to Em and seconds later she asked me where I got my earrings. Natalie did the pause-head-tilt-think, followed by an impossible to read think-some-more moment before reaching out to pat my shoulder, a sympathetic frown forming on her lips. "I'm sorry, that sucks."

She automatically won a spot on my 'good people' list.

The silence stretched on for about four counts before she quirked a smile at me. "So, cheerleading, huh?" Her tone was a cross between slightly awkward, teasing, and curious. "You don't strike me as the rah-rah type."

"It's an art and a sport," I said defensively, "You should see some of the acro combinations my coach came up with for us. It's really hard."

"I'm sure it is. It's just that I saw you dance and I've watched you teach. I saw the look on your face those times. I'm surprised you gave this up for a set of pom-poms." She faced me in a side split and held out her hands for me to pull her further in her stretch. "Not that there's anything wrong with pom-poms, but I really don't understand how anything can beat dance."

Usually, I'd default to my 'dance took too many hours of my life' speech or 'cheer is a lot more fun,' but something about Natalie and the way she seemed to handle things made me want to be transparent. "It has a lot more social and scholarship potential than spending my life inside a studio." I shrugged and added, "Plus, there's nothing like getting thrown twelve feet in the air for a great adrenaline rush. I think that was when I really fell in love with the sport."

"I'll stick to jetes, thanks," she said, then looked up with a skeptical expression. "Social potential?"

I folded forward as she tugged on my arms to help deepen my stretch, feeling the pull in my hip flexors. "Never underestimate the power of a cheerleading uniform when it comes to getting what you need in high school. Teachers love the school spirit part, especially if you're a good student, you get to hang out with all the other athletes, and we do enough events at school that most people know our names." I stretched back up to sitting in my straddle and, at her skeptical expression, added, "Social clout isn't easy to come by, you know."

"Wow. You make it sound like a formula."

"It is. Take a designer wardrobe. Add social-circle expanding school activity. Mix with common sense, remove any meanness, and, there it is—" I snapped my fingers, "social clout."

Natalie stood and immediately folded over until her palms rested flat on the floor behind her feet. "From my experience, there are people who just naturally stand out. Getting others to like them just comes easy to them. They've got," she searched for a word, pausing until it came to her, "woo. Others are drawn to them. It's the first thing you notice about them. Grace, you're one of those people. You have woo."

"Please stop using that word." Word-nerd Phoebe would have fits over someone using a verb as a noun.

She ignored my comment and kept speaking into her knees as she bent even lower. "What I mean is, it's not all an equation. You could have done all that stuff, but without your natural draw and personality, you wouldn't own the room."

"If you're trying to flirt and make me crush on you, right after a breakup is pretty bad timing," I said. When she turned her head to look at me confusedly, I bat my eyelashes at her to let her know I was joking.

She made an inelegant snorting sound and straightened up, stretching her arms to the ceiling. "Cute."

Aunt Drina poked her head into the studio. "Grace, you're learning April's part in the duet, right? Otherwise, you two need to let me know what song you want me to cut."

"Duet?" A duet was way more effort than the usual teachers' number where I'd go on stage, do a few choreographed steps Aunt Drina and the other teachers, then flit back off stage.

"For the teachers' contemporary number," Aunt Drina said. "Unless you both want to jump into the hip-hop or tap numbers. I know how much Natalie *loves* tap."

"Oh, you're funny," Natalie said, padding over to the door. "Nobody needs to see me try to tap or do hip-hop. I'll teach Grace what we choreographed so far." I opened my mouth to protest that I didn't have enough time, between finals and teaching, to practice, but she kept talking, turning to me again. "You'll catch on fast. I don't think we'll need too much practice. And I bet it'll be good for you to take your mind off other stuff."

Instead of answering, I looked at my aunt. "Are you doing a teacher's number?"

"Actually," she waved a printed apron at me, "we have a few ladies in the adult ballet class who won't go out on stage without me, so you're looking at townswoman number three in *The Breton Wedding*. So, yes, I'm performing."

"We can practice before you have to go to school, maybe every other day? I'm okay with getting up early if you are," Natalie said helpfully. "I can't do the teacher's contemporary number alone and the recital won't be the same without it…"

I didn't want to think about losing some of my 4:30 a.m. study time, but at least she hadn't mentioned weekends. I closed my eyes, feeling a sense of resignation settle over me, and said, "You two are going to team up against me until I say yes?" A part of me suspected that the whole bonding-while-stretching had probably been a part of their plan. Catch me off guard, loosen me up—literally—with a few stretches, make me like chatting with Natalie, and then drop this other responsibility right before I have to teach.

"Pretty much," Natalie said, just as Aunt Drina said, "Yes."

I shook my head. There was no use fighting the two of them. "Fine, but I get a veto if the music sucks."

Natalie bounced a little and gave my aunt a high-five. "This is going to be fun."

Some of my class started filtering in at that moment, so I rolled to standing and walked over to the sound system to switch over to my class playlist. "Okay, you two. Get out so I can teach—and before you can talk me into anything else." I waved dismissively at them and they left, giggling and whispering like kids.

☐ Chapter 24

Dance hadn't helped much. Even though I stayed after class for an hour running through different combinations to push my body to sweat out every ounce of emotion, I still hadn't been able to get the terrible, itchy ache out from under my skin. Showering and scrubbing at my red and blistered feet hadn't cleared my head. And now, studying wasn't helping, either.

Usually, I could get lost in figuring out a problem—physics or calculus were like logical little puzzles that came with their own little roadmaps of equations that fit together so perfectly. Not like life with its messy wonky edges. But every time I blinked, I could see Em's hurt expression and the image of Leia sitting at the table and the equations would just run away from me in the awful squish of my heart.

I dropped my forehead onto my physics book. Maybe I'd absorb the calm through osmosis. When my phone rang, I didn't even bother to roll my head to the side to look at the screen, even though my nose was dangerously close to getting a papercut in this position. I blindly picked up. "Hello?"

The voice that came out of my phone was low and angry. "How dare you yell at Em like that?" Phoebe didn't even bother with her typical super-polite greetings. For someone who was usually so even-tempered, she could get like a momma bear when one of her friends was hurting.

"You talked to Em," I said dully.

"Yes, I talked to her," she snapped back. "She was upset and was talking so fast I couldn't even understand her at first. What the frack, Grace? You do *not* yell at friends."

Heat started crawling up the back of my neck, and I wasn't sure if it was anger at Phoebe for lecturing me or shame at what I'd done earlier or both. Either way, the feeling was new and threw me off balance as if I'd just messed up a new lift or tumble, making me fumble a second before saying, "Em needs to know to stay out of other people's lives. And it's not really your business, either, it's between me and her."

"It's my business when one of my friends starts acting like a jerk to *my* best friend. I expect that kind of behavior from other people. Not you."

"I'm the one going through relationship problems

and had almost become one of Em's well-intentioned but poorly thought through victims, and you're actually trying to make it sound like I'm the bad guy?" I blew air through my lips and got up to start pacing my room. That itchy, achy feeling was back and I couldn't sit still. "Look, Em screwed up by trying to get involved in my life, I blew up at her. It's done. Fight over."

"Badly done," she shot back.

I recognized that quote right away. "Don't start quoting Jane Austen at me."

"You know how Em is. She was trying to help," Phoebe said, her voice still hard.

The disbelieving sound I made surprised even me. "Everyone keeps making that excuse for her, but that's not acceptable. I don't need her help."

"I don't believe you."

Those four words cut through me and I shot back to avoid the heart-suffocating feeling again. "You don't believe me because you think the whole world is unicorns and rainbows and fairytales. Wake up, Feebs. Crappy stuff happens. People fight. Things end. Relationships end. That's life." My words grew tight and I added, "Besides, aren't you supposed to be comforting me? I'm the one with the relationship problems. Hell, you didn't even *like* Leia when I first started dating her."

"This isn't about you and Leia, this is about how you treat others, and what happened with Em was unacceptable." Phoebe was always too empathetic for her own good. Em and Alec were good at distancing themselves, but she was a bleeding heart.

I couldn't take another minute of lecturing on how much I sucked. "I'm hanging up in a minute." Peeling my forehead from the shiny textbook page, I finally looked at the screen and hovered my thumb over the "end call" button.

"You're better than this, Grace," she said, sounding just like a mom.

"You're sticking yourself somewhere you don't belong." I took another deep breath to steady my voice and said, "Call me when you want to be a real friend." I turned off my phone and tossed it onto my bed, walking out of my room.

Mom passed me on the landing and paused, squinting at my face. "Are you okay, honey?"

I schooled my features into my perfectly peppy cheerleader expression. Hopefully, I didn't have a physics equation pressed into my skin. "Perfect. I just realized I forgot to schedule my regular appointment for highlights. They're going to kill me at the salon if I ask for a last-minute appointment this weekend."

Her gaze flickered to my barely showing light auburn roots and back to my eyes, and she paused, looking like she was about to say something before reaching out and squeezing my arm, instead.

"Just don't do anything drastic today, okay? Hair grows, but chopping it after a breakup isn't the best move."

"I'm not cutting my hair, I promise I'm just getting a

touch up. Besides, you know I'd never risk messing up my graduation pictures." I fake-fluffed my hair the way Em did whenever she imitated silver-screen Hollywood starlets. "I'm too vain for breakup hair. Besides, we're on time off, not a breakup."

"That's…good." Mom let go then patted my arm awkwardly. "Are you sure you're okay, though? I have a pint of almond milk Rocky Road in the freezer if you need it."

I pulled away and started the rest of the way down the stairs. "You know what? I'm not hungry now, but tell the ice cream that me, it, and a spoon have a date tomorrow." At least ice cream wasn't going to yell at me.

☐Chapter 25

There was nothing worse than trying to design on only a few hours of fitful sleep. Phoebe's chiding voice had followed me into my dreams, resulting in a nightmare where everyone, including Leia, made an appearance and I had to keep dancing while all of them yelled at me and I didn't have enough breath to apologize. When my alarm had finally gone off, I'd rolled out of bed and headed straight for my desk, hoping that maybe focusing on my project would shake off the remnants of the nightmare. But, somehow, realizing I had no idea what I was going to actually design— or if I even knew how to design anything—just made everything worse.

I ran through my notes one more time, making sure I hadn't missed anything from my visit to the PT's office or from all the research I'd done both before and after talking to the PT and her patients. I had a list under the "user needs" column I'd turned into another list of more engineering-talk sentences under another column my teacher and Oliver called "design inputs," where needs like "fit" became inputs like "has to fit hands for 90 percent of the population." But, even with all of this information, my sketches and ideas kept coming out too close to things I'd already seen in my research, the opposite of innovative. I balled up another sketch and stared at the blank paper, doodling another really bad attempt at a hand and, after adding a few lines and straps, dropping my pencil and balling that sheet up, too. That one had looked just like the glove one of the patients had been using, too.

I groaned and dropped my head onto my arms. Maybe there were only so many ways to make this kind of glove, or maybe I just wasn't creative enough. Maybe fighting with Leia had killed my creativity and I was going to fail this project thanks to emotional burnout. I wasn't the super-creative type. I didn't have Alec's art skills or Phoebe's way of looking at knitting patterns and figuring out how to change things around to make something new. I'd been at the literal drawing board for two days straight and nothing was coming. A few little changes here and there, but not enough to count as something new or even remotely better than the existing product. And I had too much pride to turn in something that wasn't better or new.

Peeking at my notes, a growing sense of dread bubbled up from my stomach as I thought about starting completely from scratch and what that would do to my schedule. I picked up my pencil to try again, but then my alarm went off—6 a.m.—and I reluctantly stood and padded towards the bathroom. Project or no, a shower was non-negotiable, especially since I'd fallen asleep in my dance clothes and looked like a cross between the Bride of Frankenstein and one of the sewer rats I'd spotted the last time I'd been in NYC.

I'd grabbed one of my parents' shower tablets from their bathroom a few days ago for a morning like this and flung it onto the shower floor before turning on the water. As soon as it started fizzing, the air filled with citrus and eucalyptus, which Mom always swore was better than coffee for waking up. I stepped into the shower and tried not to think—not about my project or my schedule or Leia, but my brain wouldn't stop buzzing and jumping from idea to idea, refusing to focus.

"Be in the moment," I said to myself, immediately feeling stupid for trying to regurgitate one of the yoga mantras I'd heard when Leia had dragged me to one of her classes. The stretches and exercises had been nice, but if I heard one more self-help-y platitude from the instructor, I would have probably turned warrior pose into a real warrior moment.

And then...

I reached out to grab my shower pouf, and a line of shampoo on the back of my hand caught the light, the little bubbles sparkling like rhinestones. I stopped my hand midway to the pouf, slowly rotating and moving my fingers around in different ways as an idea started forming in my head. I remembered how my grandmom had complained about how ugly her glove was and so had Julia and the other patients, but what if…

What if it was meant to stand out, but in a good way?

What if I could make something not only functional, but beautiful? Something that would fit in on the runway at New York Fashion week but that would also let the wearer use their hand again to do everyday tasks, and maybe help rehabilitate them along the way. Swirls and joints played across a mental sketchpad and I hurriedly shut off the water even though I was still covered in soap and shampoo. I had to get this down before I lost all the small details weaving themselves together in my brain.

Everything else disappeared into the background as my thoughts coalesced into a coherent something that I *knew* would work.

The towel did nothing to keep me from trailing a series of puddles behind me from the bathroom to my desk. My hair dripped water and shampoo onto my engineering pad as I sketched out the idea and made tons of notes that I hoped would make sense later.

"This might actually work," I muttered to myself, adding a note about small springs and pointing to some of the linkages with neat pencil strokes. The sketches weren't much, but they captured the idea just enough that I'd hopefully be able to build on it as soon as I got myself to a computer loaded with CAD.

My phone beeped, breaking my train of thought, and I realized I was soaking the carpet and my engineering design textbook, and that I had less than half an hour to get my butt out the door and to school. Making one last note, I rushed back into the bathroom, still on a design high as the ideas kept tumbling from me. I still had a lot to figure out, but now it felt real, and different and possible. It definitely could work.

Independent study   3rd period
Final Project Concept:

swirly

needs
springs
or
flexible metal/
material?

RISKS:

Grace 6/6/04
Correa

• Lots of stress points
  at the joints

spring?

finger

ring bands

of course
make the
linkages
work

can these
be functional.

May

□ Chapter 26

Conversations at the 'cool kids' tables really weren't too different from my regular table, just with fewer comic book and *Star Trek* references casually thrown around. Plus, dissection of the latest parties or soccer finals took up more of the bandwidth than, say, if Auburn High school really had deserved to win first in the Science Olympiad nationals. I missed my band of misfits and I was dying to show them the design I'd come up with for my project, but Phoebe had made it clear the minute I'd walked past her locker that she didn't want to talk. Sitting at a table for twenty minutes with that sort of tension didn't appeal to me.

Just as I opened my lunchbag, Alec passed my table,

balancing a tray full of lunch trash, and Ashley poked me in the arm with a baby carrot.

"You know, your friend might actually be cute if you worked your magic and made him over one day. I'd even think of dating him," she said, pointing the carrot in his direction once she had my attention. Ashley was the Photogram influencer definition of hot—tanned skin, toned hourglass figure, perfectly flatironed black hair, light violet eyes she swore were real but we all knew were contacts. If Alec knew she was talking about him, he'd probably pass out on top of the salad bar.

"Be still my heart, is Cassie rubbing off on you?" I winked at Cassie, who just rolled her eyes and gave a little shake of her head before turning back to her phone. "Unfortunately, Alec really likes his doesn't-give-a-damn geek look, so it's take it or leave it with him," I said.

"Shame." Ashley followed Alec with her eyes until he got close to us, then bounced up from her seat to go talk to someone at the table next to ours. I narrowed my eyes and looked from her to Alec—if she weren't so high maintenance, I'd actually consider trying to get the two together. But the thought of subjecting him to someone who once made the whole squad late to a competition because she couldn't find her mascara stopped that idea in its tracks.

Alec slid onto the bench next to me, completely oblivious of the crush-drama that had just happened. Except for giving one of those guy-nods, he ignored the football team at the table and dove straight in.

"Look, I'm not in the mood to get involved in whatever drama you have going on with the others, but can you explain to me why you've abandoned me at a table with the hair gel king?"

Tyler looked up from decimating his third burger and snorted. "Let me guess who you're talking about." He faked a moment of deep thought. "Lambert?"

I held my hand in front of my nose to keep from spit-snorting my chocolate milk. "Please, let's be fair. Em confiscated most of Kris' stash." Even though he'd made major strides in the past year, Em's boyfriend wasn't the most popular person in athletic circles.

"Well, he must have hidden a tub in the student council office, because that hair isn't moving today." Alec picked some of the feta cubes off my salad and popped them in his mouth before I could intercept him. "Anyway, you three need to fix what's going on or I'm going to have to find a new lunch table for the rest of the year. Like this one." He looked over at Tyler and the others and was greeted with shrugs.

"Tell that to Phoebe. She's the one being unreasonable. Honestly, you would think my friends would give a crap about me and how I feel, not try to trick me or turn their backs on me when I actually need them." I blew air through my lips to settle the shaking that was threatening to turn into tears. I would *not* cry at school.

"Dude. It takes skill to get both Em and Phoebe mad at you." He pointed out.

"Em's fine." I said, waving in the direction of our table,

where Em was waving her arms around animatedly as she spoke. "She gets over stuff fast. But you know Feebs holds grudges."

"True," he acknowledged. "What if I broker a peace settlement? I could be like the UN of our lunch table." He leaned forward, propping his elbows eagerly on the table.

I raised one eyebrow. It was a rare but useful skill. "What are your proposed terms?"

"Lordy, you two've spent way too much time in model UN," Cassie chimed in from the other side of the table.

Alec ignored her and put on his 'negotiation face.' "One coffee at the bookstore café after school. Phoebe will feel like she has the upper hand because it's on her turf, but she'll be distracted by all the new releases since it's Tuesday."

I kept the eyebrow up but nodded slightly in appreciation. I liked his train of thought. "Diabolically good proposal. What do you expect from me?"

"Show up and actually hear them out," Alec said, his tone and demeanor the same ones he used for negotiations in model UN. Cassie hadn't been far off with her joke. "Let those two do their whole emotional dumping on you before you try to fix things."

I narrowed my eyes at him. "I don't try to fix things."

"Please, you're worse than me. Leia calls you out on that all the time." At my cringe, he added, "Sorry, forgot. So, are you willing to try?"

"Of course." I pushed him towards our lunch table. "Go see if they are."

He leaned into my push like he was lounging, trusting that I wouldn't pull back my hands and let him fall. "I kind of like this. It's like being a Jedi ambassador."

"That's *not* going to get you cool points at this table," I pointed out before giving him another nudge. "May the Force be with you, Obi-Wan."

He held up his hand in the Vulcan symbol, mixing fandoms, but, as he walked away, curled all his fingers down so he was just giving me the middle finger. Behind me, Tyler snorted.

"Really mature," I said to both of them.

"Hey, you lost cool points with that Obi-Wan thing, too," Tyler said.

"Cool points are overrated when you're the epitome of coolness," I quipped back.

"Ding, ding, another two points for using a word like 'epitome,'" Cassie said, making two imaginary lines in the air. "At the rate you're going…"

I tossed my hair over my shoulder and flipped my legs over the bench to face the table again. "I'll be the epitome of SAT-word-using cool people," I finished her sentence and winked, glad for the distraction from my friend drama. Alec would figure it out.

☐ Chapter 27

I was in the zone, so focused on my work that the media center around me disappeared. Curves and straight lines merged into each other on the 2-D sketching grid, shooting dimensions at me as I clicked away at the model and made it just a little bit thicker. With the change in place, it rendered back into the 3-D assembly: a shiny metallic image twirling on my screen. I rotated it to an angle where I could get a good look at how the change affected the aesthetic.

"That's really pretty." Cassie leaned over my shoulder to stare at my screen, then straightened up and stepped over to my side, hands on her hips in mock reproach. "But we have to go. Coach is going to kill you if you're late, you know."

"It's the end of May," I said, distractedly, adding another round to the main linkage. "It's not like we're cheering at graduation or anything, it's just a game."

"She'll still kill you." She reached over and flicked my arm with a finger. "And that would totally ruin graduation. It's less than a month away—they'll never be able to get the bloodstains off the field in time."

I looked away from the screen long enough to let out a little snort-laugh, and shake my head at her. "Okay, just let me save this. I'll meet you in the locker room."

Cassie didn't budge. "I know how you get when you're doing something like this. I'll wait."

"Thanks, Mom."

"You're lucky I came in here when I did and you'll thank me later when you're not doing an extra lap during warmups." She pushed her hair behind her ear and studied my screen again. "What is that? I'm not kidding when I said that's gorgeous. It looks like one of those hand-flower bracelets or something."

I checked the length of one of my linkages against the size chart in my notebook and added another two millimeters to make sure it would fit right. "It's for my engineering design final. It's a glove for people who've had strokes and have trouble unclenching their hands. Oliver is working on something like it for paralyzed people and when he showed me his design, something about it stuck with me. I thought it might be fun to mix function with fashion."

She looked from my notebook to the screen and over to

me. "It looks amazing. So tell me again why you're going to study oil and stuff?"

"You know I wanted something in engineering, so—" I twirled the assembly around on the screen one more time before reluctantly hitting save and logging out. I still had a few fixes to make if I wanted the design to look just right. "Highest median salary."

Cassie rolled her eyes. "Of course. I forgot about that." She tugged on my sleeve as soon as I stood, practically dragging me out of the computer lab. "It's a shame," she said absently.

"What?" I had to pick up my pace to keep up with her as she wove through the hallway.

"You could totally have been the Lebutton of medical-ish stuff for people."

Even though the idea gave me visions of people walking down runways at fashion week in gorgeous prostheses and baroque-inspired cyberpunk ambulatory aids, my common-sense side squashed it quickly. "I guess I just want something with guaranteed security, you know?"

"You sound like my dad." Cassie waved at the other girls in the locker room before tossing her bags into her locker and starting to change. "Just remember," she added, her voice muffled through her shirt, "nothing's really guaranteed." She yanked on her sports bra and tilted her head thoughtfully for a second, adding, "well, except dying, but I'm pretty sure nerds like you are going to figure out how to change that, too."

I wiggled into my shell and snorted. "Doubtful."

"All I'm saying is that you're really good at making things and people look good. It's too bad you're just going to stop doing it." Cassie glanced up at the clock on the wall and quickly finished tying her sneakers. "C'mon. We've only got ten minutes to stretch."

I pulled my hair into a high ponytail and waved at her to go ahead while I finished pinning it in place. "Be right there." As soon as she left, I took a deep breath and stretched my arms over my head, shaking out the last of my design ideas. Time to focus on cheers and tumbling. Another deep breath, and I headed out of the locker room and over to the side of the soccer field, where Cassie and the rest of the squad were stretching.

Coach caught my eye and pointed at her watch. "Six minutes before we start our group warmup, Grace. Do something."

"Got it." I dropped onto the ground next to Cassie and started rolling my ankles. "Made it."

"You're welcome." She winced as she rolled her shoulders. "My back is so sore from the Pilates class I took yesterday. I'm ready to just shake my pom-poms once at the crowd and call it a day."

"I know how you feel. Ever since I got back into dance, all of my old injuries have been popping up to say hi." I rocked from side-to-side slightly, feeling my right hamstring get looser with every rock. Ever since I pulled it in the fall, it always took the longest to warm up enough to do any acro for cheer. "I'll talk to Coach and try to convince her to pull all the flying parts out of our routine. It might be nice to be able to walk tomorrow."

She giggled and turned her straddle into a side split. "Good idea."

A little bit of silence and I tried to sound casual as I said, "Congrats on prom queen, again. You and Christian looked really cute together up there. And Mike looked like he was okay about the whole thing." I wasn't digging for info on how to deal with a breakup, I told myself, but a part of me was still hoping she would say something.

"It's been, what, four months? Mike moved on pretty quick. I think one of the monitors caught him making out with Bridget Leon under the bleachers a few days after we broke up. And then Alyssa Kingsley, Kylie Young, Nikki Shah…" She counted off the names on her fingers with a bitter little grin. "Trust me, he wasn't devastated or anything."

Considering he nearly killed a guy for doing the same with Cassie the last time they broke up, apparently not. "So, what happened, anyway? I never got a chance to ask. You broke up with him, right?"

"It was kind of mutual." Cassie stood and I followed her, the two of us balancing against each other as we stretched out legs into pikes. "He already was complaining that he felt trapped, like he couldn't do all the things he wanted to do with his friends because he had to spend time with me and so he'd do annoying things, like not show up for our dates or cancel on me to go do something with the guys. So I decided to give him the time he wanted and started hanging out with Christian, instead."

The cancelling thing sounded way too familiar and I held back the urge to scrunch my eyes shut. "He wasn't upset when you broke up with him?"

"Not for long. Honestly, we were already both checked out of the relationship before the actual breakup. Besides, we were so predictable. Football player and cheerleader? It was nice to meet more people outside this social circle." Cassie rotated her leg in front of her and behind her, grabbing her foot with both hands and arching back until it touched the back of her head. When she was upright and able to talk again, she added, "Like you. I always envied that group you always hang out with and how easy you and Leia make your relationship work." I cringed at that, but she didn't notice and barreled on. "That's what it's like with Christian. Easy. There's no drama or fighting with him, and he makes me feel so smart, like I deserve to date someone as smart as he is."

I forgot my own problems for a minute to grab Cassie's shoulders. The den mother in me wanted to shake some sense into her, but instead I said, calmly, "You *are* smart and you deserve to date anyone you want, do you understand? Christian is really lucky to have you as his girlfriend."

"Thanks," she said, blushing a little bit. "He said the same thing, actually."

"Good, then we're all on the same page. You're awesome

and don't ever demean yourself, okay?" I stared at her intently until she nodded.

"Hey, it would be really hot if you two kissed right now. We all know Grace would like it," one of the boys' soccer players called out on his way to the field and I resisted the urge to go over and knee him in the groin.

I didn't move my hands from Cassie's shoulders, just eyed him up and down with a 'you're so beneath getting an answer from me' glare. "Shove it, Nick. At least girls want to kiss me."

Cassie giggled and added, "Yeah. When was the last time anyone wanted your Neanderthal ass?" When he just gave us the finger and turned away to start his warmups, she actually collapsed into a real giggle fit. "What an idiot," she said between giggles and breaths. "You know he had a massive crush on you last year until someone clued him in about Leia, right?"

I snorted, looking over at Nick and snorting again. "Nice way to bounce back from disappointment, like a deflated soccer ball."

"By the way, with what's going on with you and Leia…"

I blinked at Cassie for a second in surprise. She was nice but tended to be a little bit self-focused sometimes. I hadn't expected her to pick up on what was going on. "Yes?"

Coach clapped her hands. "Line up, everyone," she called out, waving us over to opposite side of the field, where there were no bleachers. "Warmups."

"Word gets around, especially when your friends try to

fish for info and want to know if you told me more than them," she said with a wink as we both hurried over to get into our neat line to start jumping jacks.

I knew exactly which friend she was talking about. "Em."

She nodded, then kept her voice pitched low, keeping her eyes on Coach. "Yup, Em. Remember what you told me after I broke up with Mike the first time?"

I tried, and failed, to remember what she'd said. "I told you a lot of things."

Cassie broke the rules for a second to look over at me, her expression both serious and understanding. "You said I need to remember that the best part about being human is that, no matter how hard we fall—in love or out of it— eventually, we bounce and bounce until we find our balance. We don't break, even if it feels like we do. That helped a lot, back then and when I broke up with Mike again."

We bounce. Aunt Drina had taught me that after I came to her crying because I kissed Leia during my sweet sixteen party and I wasn't sure if Leia really wanted to date me or was just trying not to upset the birthday girl. The words rang so true even as Cassie repeated them back to me. We bounce.

☐Chapter 28

A twirl of my straw made the ice cubes swirl in my green tea latte like a little funnel cloud in the clear cup. The vortex settled and I gave it another twirl, watching the drink get lighter as the coconut milk mixed in.

"It really couldn't wait 'til after?" Em's voice made me look up as she and Phoebe made their way over to the corner table I'd grabbed in the bookstore café. Even though it was on the other side of the low romance novel bookshelves, where the occasional nosy bookworm would poke their head over to listen in, it was also in the least crowded part of the café.

Phoebe clutched a book to her chest with one arm while balancing a mug and saucer with her other hand. "It was the last copy. Someone else might have gotten it if I didn't."

Em shook her head and slid her mug onto the table. "So? We'd just go to the bookstore in Millbrook tomorrow. They always have lots of copies of the new stuff."

"But I have to read it tonight before people start posting spoilers." Her exasperated sigh carried an unspoken 'you should know that by now.'

Em's dismissive wave almost knocked over my drink. "Get the e-book."

Phoebe clutched the book tighter as she took her seat, not acknowledging that I was sitting next to her. "There are some books that just *have* to be read on paper. E-books aren't the same." She primly took a sip of what looked to be cocoa. "Besides, I have the book now, so I don't know why you're still going on about it."

"Because you're such a...book purist."

"Says the drama purist who dressed up like a pirate for a week to get into character."

As much as part of me wanted to chime into the banter with my own practically scripted role of the voice of reason in this banana-pants friendship, the elephant in the room wouldn't let me. "Thanks for coming," I said, breaking in before Em could retort.

"Em and Alec made me," Phoebe said with a sniff, sitting up ramrod straight.

Em looked over at me and sympathy snuck over her features for the barest of seconds. "I'm not happy with how you talked to me," she said, her voice soft. "We've known you for a long time, and you're not the kind of person who hurts others."

"At least, you weren't," Phoebe said, peeking over the top of her mug before her gaze dropped back to the saucer. "What you said to Em is wrong."

"I screwed up too, Fee," Em told her. It was weird seeing Em being the super-mature one out of the group, for once. Usually, that was my job. "I just wanted to help."

I forced myself to keep from snorting or making any other scoffing sounds. "By trying to orchestrate something behind my back? *And* Leia's?"

Em waved her hand dismissively at that comment. "I think you're giving up too easy. You two can fix this."

"I don't know." I went back to making my latte tornado. "I hope so, but it won't be with surprise meetings over water ice."

"It might, if you just talk," she retorted forcefully.

I shook my head, not looking up at either of them. "It can't, because it's all my fault."

Em started coughing, as if some of her latte had gone down the wrong way. As soon as she could breathe again, she choked out, "What do you mean, your fault?"

"It was all me. I kept missing some of our dates, being late when we were supposed to get together, that kind of stuff, and it got on her nerves. Whenever I wasn't late or didn't have to cancel, we'd fight about not being able to spend time together. I can't fix my schedule and I don't know if I can fix this."

"You can fix this because she loves you, stupid." Now, *that* was our Em.

The comment made my heart twist and made me want to vomit. I dropped my chin into my hand and started rubbing my temple. "Maybe love's not enough." I really didn't have to explain anything to them, but these were two of my best friends. I took a deep breath, feeling incredibly old. "And maybe I don't want to fix it."

"Excuse me?" Phoebe said, her eyes growing super wide.

I pressed my lips together and nodded before saying out loud what had been bouncing around in my brain for the past few days. "It's probably going to end, anyway. We're going to be too far apart to see each other next year. It's only fair that we both get a chance to meet other people. The timing's perfect—school's ending, we're at this transition point in our lives, anyway, and both Leia and I have GPAs high enough that a little emotional turmoil right now really won't impact our final grades. Besides, a breakup during freshman year at college can really screw up the whole four-year plan." I took in their wide-eyed stares and added, "And our entire future."

"That is the stupidest thing I've ever heard from someone who is supposed to be smart," Em said, while Phoebe said at the same time, "Oh my God, Grace. Life's not some sort of chemistry formula."

"Actually, carbon, oxygen..." I trailed off when they both scowled at me instead of getting my science joke. For two very different people, they sometimes seemed to share the same brain. "Look, I'm probably not getting back together with her. And whether you like it or not, you have to admit that I had a right to be upset at you the other day." I aimed that last comment at Em.

"Yeah, but," Phoebe said, curling her fingers around her mug, "that doesn't give you a right to yell at your friends."

I nodded at her. "True, but remember that I don't get involved in your relationships, either."

"You and Leia love giving us advice." Phoebe pointed out.

"You ask for it," I countered. "And I don't try to trick you into doing anything you don't want."

Phoebe closed her eyes for a second and nodded. This time, she was the serious one. "Fair enough."

Looking from one to the other, I felt myself just… deflate. As if any energy I'd had left for the rest of the school year had just evaporated out of me. "Honest to goodness, I really didn't plan on any of this."

"You can't plan other people's emotions. They're not computers or science experiments." Em sounded a little like my mom and I had to avoid rolling my eyes.

"Yeah. Emotions are messy. I get it." I said, taking a sip from my drink to give me a second to center myself and steady my voice. "Trust me, this thing with Leia sucks for me, too."

Phoebe scooted her chair next to mine and dropped her head on my shoulder, wrapping her arm around me and patting my arm. "You know this doesn't mean you're one hundred percent off the hook, right? This isn't like some Hallmark movie. I'm still upset about what you did."

"*Quelle surprise*," I said, softly.

Em shared a long look with Phoebe, then turned to me. "But we're not going to bring this up anymore. Because we're *friends*. And friends don't beat a dead horse into a pulp." She looked back at Phoebe on the last sentence, who sat back up and stuck her tongue out at both of us.

I could feel the corners of my lips curling up at their antics. "Thanks, Em."

"And friends don't replace friends with eye candy when they go off to their fancy new universities, even if it's to help further their GPAs or social standing or whatever other ridiculous thing you've calculated out," Em added. "No breaking up our friendship, got it?"

I should have seen a comment like that coming from Em. I faked a serious nod. "I'll remember that."

"Good, because I might need your help understanding any science stuff in my biomedical ethics class next year." Em took in my reaction and laughed. "Oh, yeah, you missed that at lunch the other day. In addition to nurturing my fledgling but illustrious acting career at one of the best programs in the nation, I'm going to minor in leadership for social action, and I have to take an ethics class."

Leadership for social action. With all her new volunteer activities, our little Em was really growing up. "Kris had no influence on that at all, did he?" I asked, looking over at Phoebe, who shared my look of amusement.

A pout dramatically formed on Em's lips. "Why is it so hard for anyone to believe that I'm into helping people without my boyfriend talking me into it?"

I patted her hand. "I believe you. It's just that last year you we talking about not minoring at all so you could spend more time hanging in the theater district."

"And last year you were talking about all your great plans for this summer with Leia," Em shot back quickly.

That comment hurt. "What were you saying about a dead horse a minute ago?"

Em cringed, probably realizing what she'd said. "Truce. Let's pick on Phoebe, instead. Any bets on how many times she's going to miss her cues at our concert Thursday night because she's too busy staring at Dev?"

Phoebe narrowed her eyes at us and downed the rest of her cocoa in one gulp. "And, on that, I'm heading to the young adult section. There's a new Pamela Kaye book out today." She made a big show of grabbing her book and sticking her nose in the air as she left the table.

Em started laughing and I joined in, my laugh actually feeling real for the first time since the fight.

☑Chapter 29

"You need to be nice to Kris tonight," Alec said without pre-amble as he broke the silence in our Engineering Design class.

"I'm sorry, what?" I asked, looking up from a paper on stroke rehabilitation.

"At the concert. We're all sitting together and we don't need any unnecessary arguments because you won't have your buffer with you. Leia's not coming tonight, right?"

I stared at Alec for a solid minute, but he nonchalantly kept working on his sketch. "What do you mean, 'buffer?'"

"Leia. I'm assuming she's not coming to the concert, right?"

"You realize she's not talking to me?" I asked, pushing past the pang in my stomach at those words. "I'd assume no."

"Okay, no buffer. Definite chance for you to butt heads with Kris, then."

I felt a little bit like Alice talking to the Cheshire Cat in the analyses I did for my English paper, but no amount of geometry could make this conversation compute. "You're making no sense."

"You were the first to get a significant other out of all of us." Before I could say anything, he waved his hand and added, "Em's five-minute relationships with the leading man of the week didn't count. Technically, Kris is the first guy she let her dad put through the Katsaros third degree."

"Ouch." Em's dad was super sweet to all of us, and like a stand-in dad for Alec, but I'd seen him be ridiculously overprotective of her before, to the point where she never even let him know about the foreign exchange student she'd dated most of Junior year. Alec was the only guy regularly allowed over at their house. "Actually, I'm a little surprised the two of you never dated."

He nearly turned green. "Heck no. She's practically my sister. It would be like incest. We have pictures of us together in diapers. Our families vacation together. We even once superglued Chloe to her bouncy chair by mistake when we were babysitting her. I mean, I love Em a lot—like a sister," he added with hard emphasis on "sister," "but just because you love her like a friend, too, and have known her for years, would you date her if she were into girls?"

"Point," I said, trying not to laugh at the image of a younger Alec and Em trying to unglue a baby from a chair and resisting the urge to ask how they managed to free her.

"I'll never understand those stupid rom-coms that have people go from hanging out with each other in diapers to falling in love."

I noticed Mr. Newton's warning stare and dropped my voice. "It happens."

Alec shook his head, hard. "Well, not to me and her. But, anyway, what I was saying before you derailed the conversation was that you've never had to do the third wheel or single thing with us. I'm a pro at it, but you've always had Leia and you were always the one giving out advice." He then added with a tilt of his head, "You were kinda superior about all of it most of the time, too. Like you were the super adult one out of all of us kindly bestowing us immature mortals with your knowledge."

I cringed. There was no way I came across like that, otherwise, why did everyone always call me for advice? "That's not fair. I only give advice when people ask. And I don't act like I'm superior."

"Just calling it like I see it," he said with a shrug. "I know you don't do it on purpose, but it sometimes comes across like that. And, honestly, when it came to relationships, Feebs and Em needed to be slapped upside the head sometimes, anyway."

"I also never slapped anyone upside the head," I shot back.

"Mmmhmm. Not literally. Anyway, it's *my* turn to give *you* advice for tonight. Rule number one of third wheel-itude is to acknowledge that you're a third wheel, but don't let it get to you. Like, everyone really does want to hang out with you even if they seem kinda absorbed by their significant other, so don't think anything otherwise." He held up one finger, as if to emphasize his point.

"I don't," I said as patiently as I could. Alec giving me advice was cute and I didn't want to take away from his self-perceived Obi-Wan moment.

He then grew super serious, holding up a second finger. "And rule number two is that you should be friendly with the significant others because you can't hide behind your own significant other. Even if that significant other is in the running for Lambertfield's most obnoxious junior politician."

My lips mouthed a "huh?" and my forehead wrinkled. "I'm friendly with Kris." Sometimes he got on my nerves, but I didn't remember one moment where I was ever rude to him.

"No, *Leia* was friendly with him." Before I could argue otherwise, he said, "You sat on the other side of her every time we went out as a group. You literally sit on the other side of the lunch table to avoid him because she's not around to block him. No Leia buffer means playing nice with Kris or else you're going to look like the bad, unsupportive friend."

I didn't say anything, just gave him a noncommittal hum.

Alec continued without acknowledging my hum. "Also, a tip? When you're stressed, you become totally unapproachable. I know it and Feebs and Em know it, but if you want a decent lunchtable ecosystem, can you just try, like, deep breathing or meditation or something for the rest of the quarter?"

I resisted the urge to contradict him. I was always the

portrait of calm and common sense at our lunchtable. "You don't pull punches, do you?"

"With the others? Yeah. But you're super logical and it's stupid to soften the blow with you." He turned back to his sketch, adding a tiny detail to the page as if he hadn't paused to do the verbal equivalent of whacking me upside my head.

"Thanks," I said, dryly.

"Good, now, take a look at this and let me know what you think. I need some of your physics genius to help me figure out how to make this actually work." He pushed his sketch my way, pointing at a series of gears in his design.

I stared at the paper, trying to visualize his neat drawing in 3-D. So far, it looked good. "I thought you were okay with your project."

He tapped his pencil against a worm gear he'd drawn into the interface between two parts. "Yeah, except for making it functional, like Newton wants. Remember, I took this class for the CAD and design part, not the engineering stuff. That's really your thing."

I casually tapped my phone and glanced at the time while trying to look like I wasn't checking. I'd already lost a half an hour of my planned project work time for this heart-to-heart and couldn't afford to lose any more time, but I mentally shifted my bedtime up an extra hour after the concert to make up for it. I ran through a mantra, like he had suggested. Alec was a friend, someone who'd dropped everything to help me in the past, too, and sleep was for the weak. "Okay. Show me where you're stuck."

INDEPENDENT STUDY ENGINEERING DRAWING AND DESIGN

FAILURE MODES AND EFFECTS ANALYSIS (USE): MOBILITY GLOVE (USER GROUP: PATIENT)

TASK	POSSIBLE MODE OF FAILURE	POSSIBLE EFFECTS OF FAILURE	SEVERITY	POSSIBLE CAUSE OF FAILURE	OCCURRENCE	DETECTION	RISK #	RISK CONTROL MEASURES
Put on glove	Glove put on wrong	Glove not seated right. Puts pressure on wrong part of finger. Patient has minor pain	6	Used to other glove designs (familiarity)	8	1	48	Instruction leaflet. Make it sit at the base of wrist to always be in the same spot every time
Open hand	User can't open hand	User can't open hand. Needs to use a different glove. Annoyance ???	8 *5?*	Wrong/too weak spring strength selected by doc? *(figure out what else works here)*	3	2	48 *30*	*I have no clue... user training? Extra springs included in package?*
	User can only open hand partway		4	Too small glove size	2	2	16	Make a size chart for fitting. Multiple sizes

Relationship with Leia							
Break-up before 1st semester finals	9	*We might both fail 1st semester finals *Loss of a relationship *Might affect 2nd semester grades, too *Ruin Leia's break plans	8	-Long distance relationships have low survival rates -Growth (from change) -Meet other people -Statistics are against h.s. relationship survival	3	216	*Communication Plan *Stress test? *Preemptive breakup *???????
Drift apart	5	*Stress that impacts grades *Miss out on meeting new people	?	-Long distance -Can't fix fights over? the phone -Growth (from change)	6	???	*Communication Plan *regular meetups *Figure out how not to fight ????
Break-up 2nd year	10	*Could fail classes *Poor GPA/lower hiring potential for both *Hurts our chances of finding other people	?	See above? -I don't know how to fix this right now, how am I supposed to figure out how to fix the future?			*Communication Plan *Relationship checks *Uhhhhhmmm...

□ Chapter 30

Rules were great, but I never understood the school theater's rule about not allowing people into the auditorium unless it was between numbers, especially if the "number" was just a bunch of intro speeches for the orchestra concert. As soon as the usher gave me the green light, I hurried into the auditorium, making a beeline for the row on my ticket. Alec was already inside and I was positive the buzz I'd felt in my pocket was him texting to see where I was. I checked the little metal plates on the aisles and kept heading down until I reached my row. Phoebe and Em had scored us pretty good seats—not as good as their families, who were up a few rows, but really good ones—and I would have bet my

Physics grade that part of it somehow had involved Dev's and Kris' influences with the front office.

I looked down the aisle and my stomach dropped. Sitting next to Alec and right next to my empty seat was Leia. Part of me wanted to jump in front of her and demand why she was there—Em and Phoebe were my friends and I couldn't understand why she had to invade this part of my world—and part of me just wanted to apologize and make things better. I froze, staring at the empty seat, unsure of which way I wanted to go.

Alec mouthed "I tried to text you" when Leia wasn't looking his way.

Kris, who was sitting on the aisle closest to me, noticed Alec's expression and how Leia suddenly looked up, then dropped her attention to her program, and followed their eyes to me.

"Oh," he said under his breath as he studied my face, glanced out of the side of his eye at Leia, then gracefully stood and shifted over into the empty seat next to Leia as if that was the plan all along, leaving his old seat next to Alec for me. "Hey, Grace," he whispered, breaking the uncomfortable silence that had fallen on the four of us when I'd shown up, "You haven't missed anything, Osoba just gave one of her long speeches again. She mentioned Em and Phoebe when she talked about the graduating seniors, but nothing big." He had leaned in and forward to talk to me and I could tell that was his way of helping me by blocking my view of Leia.

I hoped my gratitude for what he was trying to do showed in my eyes. Kris was new-ish to our group and he didn't owe me anything, but he was still doing what he could to protect me. Maybe Em was a little bit right about him.

"Good, thanks. They wouldn't let me in the auditorium until her speech was over. I'm surprised to see you here. I thought Em said you didn't do school concerts."

"I say a lot of things, but I didn't want to miss Em's last concert." Kris looked up at the stage and a smile came across his face when the orchestra filed on stage. Em squinted into the audience as she sat down, her face breaking into a wide grin as her eyes reached our section. "And that's why," he said, raising his arm to wave at her. "That smile makes even handbells tolerable."

My chest grew a little tight and I resisted the urge to look over at Leia. I couldn't believe I was jealous of Em and Kris.

"I told you she has really good vision," Alec said in a whisper that was so loud, it probably didn't even count as a whisper. "Which means she'll know if you sneak out during the handbells and don't come back for the finale."

"Says someone who knows from experience," Leia said, poking him in the arm.

"I have no idea what you're talking about," Alec quipped. "I love handbells."

It was weird seeing Leia bantering with my friends like nothing had happened between us, or how she studiously didn't look my way when she responded, or when she did, it was like she was looking through me, like when she turned to Kris and said, "Last year, he tried to tell Em he went to the bathroom and they wouldn't let him back into the auditorium. She called him out faster than you can say 'handbell.'"

"It wasn't pretty, Em wouldn't let him live it down for weeks," I added, trying to stay a part of the conversation. These were my friends and my history first.

Leia focused on me for half a second, a frown flitting across her features, before she smoothed her expression into something neutral and turned to face the stage again. "They're starting." The unspoken "shh" hung in the air and both of the guys looked at each other uncomfortably before Alec gave a tiny shrug of his shoulders and tilted his chin towards the stage.

☑

The after-concert fries at the diner made the concert look like a giant cuddlefest. Leia and I sat on opposite corners of the table, and the fact that we weren't really talking to each other cast an awkward cloud on the whole group. Em, Kris, and Dev had managed an overly cheery conversation throughout, laughing a little too loudly at times, and trying to bring us both into the conversation.

And, all throughout, I felt terrible my personal life had messed up Phoebe's, Em's, and Dev's last post-high-school -concert celebration. I kept throwing apologetic looks their way, and Phoebe kept making 'it's okay' hand gestures between telling Leia about Trixie's wedding plans and dropping into my conversation with Dev about their trip.

I literally breathed a sigh of relief when first Em, then Alec, said they needed to go home. I pulled out my wallet and dropped my part of the bill plus a tip onto the plate where everyone else had put their money. "'Night," I said to her, trying my hardest to keep my tone light.

Leia put a hand on my arm as I passed by her on my way out. "Hey, stay a minute? We really need to talk."

I looked warily at her hand, then slowly sat down, nodding at Phoebe's worried look to let her know she and the others could go. "Okay." She'd been the one who had asked for time off, not me. "But I can't stay long. Homework."

"Yeah, me, too. I don't understand why they put these concerts in the middle of the week."

I shifted in my chair, trying to figure out where she was going with this small talk and trying not to let my confusion show. "It's dance recital season. I bet one of the schools has the auditorium rented for the weekend," I said, and resisted the urge to pull out my phone and confirm my guess.

"Good point." An uncomfortable silence settled between us before Leia cleared her throat and said, "So, um, do you have time to hang out next Friday? I kind of hoped we could—"

I cut her off before she could finish her sentence. "I can't. I'm busy next Friday." I wasn't lying—Alec and I had scheduled to meet with Oliver at the university after school to work on our projects and it wasn't like I could just call him up and reschedule.

Her expression shifted from uncomfortable to disap-pointed. "Next Saturday?"

I shook my head. I'd promised Phoebe that I'd help with her sister's bridal shower stuff and I had no idea how long she'd need me. "Busy."

Leia put her glass down on the table with enough force to rattle the plates, her lips drawing into a tight line. "You don't want to even try, do you?"

I took a deep breath and shook my head. "No." The word burned my tongue and it took every ounce of energy in me to keep from pulling it back. It would be impractical to try to do anything else. "You asked for time off to think, and I took the time to think, too. And, I think..." I couldn't believe the words coming out of my mouth, but they correlated so well with my lists and what I'd told Em and Phoebe the other night, "I think maybe we shouldn't try."

Leia looked on the verge of tears, which unfairly also made her eyes a million times more luminous. "Do you realize how much that hurts? That you don't even care enough to put effort into fixing this? Because you know, Grace, this time I'm not going to be the one who fixes everything."

Her soft words hit me so hard, it was like she just twisted a screw into my heart. I forced my expression to stay detached but compassionate. I could fall apart later, but if I softened at all at the moment, I'd be in danger of taking everything back. "I care about you, but you were right, I wasn't giving you the time you deserved and that's not going to change. There's no point in trying to make something work that's just going to fall apart later, so it's better to spare ourselves a really long, painful relationship death that would ruin it for both of us. Right now is the most logical time for this to end."

"Of course. How *practical* of you." She practically hissed out "practical," like it was some sort of curse.

"Practical is how I am. You know I'm not changing." The *not even for you* was unspoken, but it still hung painfully in the air between us. It took everything in me not to get up and leave. She deserved the right to yell at me or cry or whatever would feel better, no matter how much crappier it would make me feel.

"Apparently not." She didn't do any of those things, though. Instead, she leaned back in the booth and ran a hand over her eyes, before taking a series of deep breaths I recognized from her yoga class. "Okay," she said softly to herself, before looking straight back at me. "Well, these next few weeks are going to be weird with all of the stuff we already planned with everyone. You can't expect me to drop our friends because of you. You might have been friends with them first, but they're my friends, too." Her voice was firm, counteracting the tears I could see forming in the corner of her eyes.

"Of course." I took a deep breath to steady my own voice. "We can totally be adults about this. Relationships end all the time for totally normal reasons."

"Right. Adults." She seemed to mirror my inhale, then nodded solemnly on the exhale. "Agreed. It's not like we're kids or anything."

I dropped my eyes because it hurt too much to see how she'd rallied herself to come across as strong despite how much she was hurting. "We were friends before this. Plenty of people break up and stay friends."

"No need to be dramatic," she said in a distant tone that matched mine.

"So… friends?"

"Friends," she said, cautiously, but then added, "sort of. Not 'hang out together by ourselves friends,' though. I'm sorry, but I don't want that since you've made it clear you aren't interested in trying."

"Yeah, I can see how that would be awkward." I looked up and tried—and failed—to give her a small, shaky smile.

She folded her hands on top of the table, her eyes focused on them instead of me. "Okay, so that's what we're doing?"

I nodded. "I think it's the best solution for everyone."

Leia made an unreadable humming sound, straightened her back, and slid out of the booth. "Great. Now that it's settled," she reached into her purse, pulled out a ten, and dropped it on the table next to her untouched sandwich. "I gotta go."

I picked up the ten and tried to hand it back to her, "No, I'll pay. I can—"

"I can pay for my own stuff, thanks," she said stiffly, stepping a meter away from the table before I could push the bill back into her hands. "Bye, Grace."

The finality in her voice was what hurt the most as I watched her walk away.

May – June

☐ Chapter 31

The music flowed through me, my heart syncing with the slow beat. Even though I was supposed to only listen, my whole body vibrated with the need to become a part of it and my foot snuck out to make tiny circles and _tendu_s while my fingers rolled along the underside of the barre. For the first time in almost a week, I could feel my heart stretching with all the emotions I'd locked away after my conversation with Leia. The rough spot where Natalie and April had cut the music shook me out of my reverie, but I was pulled back in on the next breath until the music faded and I opened my eyes again.

"What do you think?" Natalie looked confident, like

she'd been watching my reaction the whole time and knew what I would say.

I took an extra second to start really breathing again. "It's…" I fought to find the right word, "heartbreaking." The longing and sadness of the song still hadn't seeped completely out of me and I needed a moment to come back to the now.

"I know. Isn't it perfect?" We dancers were unquestionably weird.

I found myself nodding. "Definitely." I stepped away from the barre, trying to ignore the need bubbling up in me to get sucked into the song. I hadn't wanted to do this teacher number thing, but just one listen to the song they'd picked pulled me right in. It fit my mood perfectly. "What do you have so far?"

Natalie pushed herself up to standing and hit play again on Aunt Drina's antiquated CD player. "We were right through the bridge, but I'm okay with changing things if any of April's original choreography doesn't fit you." She paced out to the middle of the studio and started to mark a pattern, hands moving quickly to imitate turns or jumps, and I followed her. "It's about two people who each just lost the people they loved. They're longing for human contact and lean on each other just to keep going. Their friendship becomes the mirror that lets the other person see who they are so they can pick up the pieces. So, we put in a lot of mirroring, too."

That premise sounded…perfect. "Wow."

"We mixed a little bit of modern dance into my part.

I get to use flexed feet a lot in contrast to your character which is good because," she pointed to her injured leg with a rueful expression, "you know."

"Right." I rolled my ankle a few times unconsciously before catching myself and firmly planting my foot on the floor, hoping she didn't notice. "Teach me, Miss Natalie," I said in imitation of the little rosebud class kids.

The music looped back to the beginning and she counted off the beats, marking and calling out the steps to my part while I followed. We repeated it a few more times until I was sure I had the choreography down, then she switched to doing her part alongside me. We didn't touch or partner, though Natalie called out tiny partnered lifts or movements. When my muscles were just starting to hit the edge of exhaustion from the two-minute bursts of movement, she stretched her arms over her head, turned to me, and asked, "Ready to try it full-out?"

I propped my heel on the floor and stretched my hamstring one more time before nodding, trying to push away the nerves about hurting her leg in any of the lifts or partner work. The song's first notes hung in the air and transformed my nerves into anticipation. I moved, hitting each step and turn and jump perfectly on beat, twisting downwards as Natalie rolled over my shoulders and up to standing, pulling me up with her. Everything from the past two weeks disappeared in the music and movement and, for a moment, I was free. Nothing but movement.

We ran out of choreography and both Natalie and I

collapsed in sweaty lumps on the floor. Natalie raised her head the tiniest bit and said, "I think this might work."

A little clapping sound came from the back of the studio. I rolled onto my back and looked into the mirror without getting up to see Aunt Drina squatting in the back corner of the classroom. She stood, using the barre to help her up.

"I didn't want to interrupt. It's looking good." Her feet stopped right next to my head, the short rubber heels of her teaching shoes making soft thunking sounds on the floor. "I just don't believe you yet, Grace."

"Wha?" Language wasn't exactly working yet.

"Mechanically, you're perfect, but it's like you turned off your feelings." The soft leather of her shoe tapped the floor. "Robots are all about perfect steps. Dancers are about emotion. You need to find whatever part of you connects to the story and draw from it."

She was right, but still I bit back the reflex to remind her that this was just a recital and I was just a substitute teacher. I nodded silently and used the rest of the moment as an excuse to sit up, rubbing my hamstring again. My muscles were only cooling the littlest bit and it was already starting to get stiff.

"And I was stellar, as usual, right?" Natalie said teasingly as she got up to turn off the endlessly repeating music.

"Are we now ignoring the fact that you've been working on this for a month and this is the first time Grace danced it?"

"Yup," Natalie responded with a bright smile.

Aunt Drina snorted and patted my arm. "You'll get it,

Grace." She glanced up at the studio clock and fixed her wrap cardigan. She was way too pulled together for someone up so freakishly early. "Now, I've got an hour and a half to prep and brush up on what I actually need before the guy comes to give me a quote on a new air conditioning unit." She shook her head ruefully. "I never thought I'd be so interested in BTUs, but welcome to life as a business owner."

"Glamorous," Natalie said dryly, giving me a look as if to say 'I've heard this all before.'

Aunt Drina leveled the same expression at me. "She says that, but wait how glamorous she feels when the AC cuts out during summer classes." She flipped her hand in a wave at us and shook her head as she walked out. "Mop all your sweat up before you leave."

"Horses sweat, men perspire, ladies glow," I quoted at her.

"Then wipe up the glow." Came the response from the hallway.

Natalie tossed me an oat bar from her dance bag and I rolled to standing with a groan, every muscle feeling like overcooked carrots. With a muffled noise of thanks, I alternated between my water bottle and the bar. Getting to the dance school by 5:30 in the morning didn't leave a lot of time for breakfast. I looked up at the clock—6:20. Barely enough time to get to school and shower before my 6:50 early mod class.

"I'll take care of cleaning up," Natalie said, as if she'd read my mind, "I don't have class until 11. You know, the perks of college." She slid back down to the ground, picking at a container full of berries she'd pulled from her bag and studying me. "Ever see *My Best Friend's Wedding*?" she asked.

I blinked at the weird change in subject, but answered anyway as I slipped off my foot undeez and wiped my neck with the towel from my dance bag. That was an old movie, but my mom and Aunt Drina loved it. Even Phoebe's mom had mentioned it the other day. "Yeah, why?"

"That was me and my best friend Drew." She said, popping a handful of blueberries into her mouth. "I didn't really realize I loved him until he proposed to this girl he met freshman year of college. They're getting married next year, right after we all graduate."

"Ouch," I said around a mouthful of oats.

She shook her head and continued, as if she was telling someone else's story instead of something really personal. "He was always there for me, you know? I was crushed when he introduced me to Ashley. They came home for winter break last year, this massive ring on her finger, and that's when I realized what I'd lost. I think about him when I'm choreographing and dancing this piece."

"I'm sorry," I said, resisting the urge to either look up at the clock again or to hug her. Neither of us needed any more sweat.

"Don't be. I'm actually okay. I wouldn't have met my awesome current boyfriend if that hadn't happened. But dance made me feel better back then and I can still pull up those feelings when I dance now." She looked sideways at me as I stepped out into the school hallway. "I bet you have something you can pull from, too." One eyebrow arched up. "Leia, maybe?"

"Too soon," I practically choked on the words. I shouldered my bag and headed for the front door. "I'll think of something." Before Natalie could come up with any other ideas, I pushed out of the dance school lobby and into the fresh morning air.

☐Chapter 32

The prototype was lighter than I expected. I turned it gently in my hands, trying not to tangle the cables leading to the linkages at the back of the glove, and squinted to get a better look at the tiny servos that connected to each joint.

"What do you think?" Oliver asked, dropping his elbows onto the work bench we had clustered around.

"It's pretty cool," Alec said, pressing a button on the glove prototype he was holding, making its fingers curl and uncurl.

"Definitely cool, but," I started to say, but then stopped myself before I could run my mouth and give any unwanted advice. Alec and I were Oliver's guests in the biorobotics lab, not fellow students or teachers.

A huge grin broke across Oliver's face. "But?" He gestured for me to go on. "I can tell you want to say something. Critiques are absolutely fine. I'm not made of sugar."

"Well," I began, making the glove into a fist, then pinching, and then curling my own hand. I watched how the bones in my hand moved. "Why did you decide to make the four fingers only rotate around one axis and the thumb around another? Right now, the pinching motion looks more like a lobster claw than a hand." I brought the glove closer to my face to look at the servos. "It looks like you should be able to add another axis."

"Good catch," Oliver said, making an imaginary mark in the air as if he were giving me a point. "Honestly, I haven't programmed that yet. Y'know. Punch cards and linear algebra and all that stuff."

"Oh," I said, feeling a little silly. Oliver had warned us that we were holding rough prototypes and not the final design.

Alec snorted. "You're kidding about punch cards, right? That's technology from my grandmom's time."

"Punch cards sound cooler than MathCad," Oliver said with a shrug. "But yeah, I had to do one of those my freshman year when we learned about the history of programming because my professor wanted to make us suffer." He took the glove from me and slipped his hand into it, laying the wires across his forearm. "But, really, I haven't exactly figured that out yet. I worked out where to tap into on the forearm to make the impulse from the muscle natural for rotation around the x axis for the fingers and the y axis for the thumb, but..." He shrugged. "I have a long way to go still. It's a little frustrating, because I'm not recreating the wheel. I'm definitely not the first person to do this."

I nodded. I knew how he felt. My little rehabilitation glove was nothing compared to the Iron Man-esque glove he was building, but imitating all the nuances of movement of the human body was *hard*. Another thought came to my mind as I watched him move the glove's fingers.

"You didn't machine those linkages, did you?" They weren't as detailed or swirly as mine, but they still had curves that I knew would be a pain to make if someone was cutting them from a bar of metal.

"Nope, I decided that I wanted to go with additive manufacturing—I think you guys probably know it as metal 3-D printing. If you look at these..." He picked up two unattached linkages from another prototype and handed one to Alec and one to me. "It's great because I can even change the density and porosity of the material within a single linkage. See how I added material where the stresses would be higher," he pointed to a slightly thicker section of a linkage, "and how I actually went with a thinner, slightly porous structure in the other spots where I needed a little more flex and less weight?"

Alec squinted at the linkage where Oliver was pointing. "Okay, now that's cool."

I felt a grin creep across my face as his words sunk in,

"Sort of like how bone naturally grows thicker where it sees stress… Someone's law?" It had amazed me how the body had this way of adapting to stress and how it could just change to make itself stronger.

Oliver's face lit up. "Wolff's law. Yes, something like that. Did your teacher cover that in class or something?"

I shook my head, dropping my eyes to the glove self-consciously as I tried to figure out how to communicate the real reason why I knew that without sounding like a total nerd. "No, I went down an anatomy scientific paper wormhole once when I started pointe in dance class. I was seriously convinced that law was the reason why my pinky toes got wider after pointe than before and wanted to figure out how to perfectly pad my shoes to share the load better so it wouldn't happen."

"And?" Oliver prodded.

"I just quit pointe instead. I wasn't into ballet, anyway, and it was definitely not worth the pain." I snorted at the memory, then went back to twirling the metal phalange between my fingers. "But, seriously, this is cool. I didn't think of doing that to give it more flex."

Oliver nodded. "Designing stuff for the human body has so many challenges, you need to be creative."

I couldn't look away from the prototype—his printing solution gave me so many ideas. "But it has to be worth it. I love these challenges, and it has to be cool to know you can make a difference in someone's life with something you designed."

"Tell me again why you're not looking at programs like this?" Oliver asked with a grin. "It sounds to me like biomedical or mechanical might be perfect for you."

"Because it's not a part of her twenty-year plan," Alec jumped in. "Grace is a little obsessed with being practical."

Oliver shook his head. "If I were practical, I would have stayed in Ireland for grad school. My university had an amazing program, but from the minute I heard about Dr. Aubrey's work, I wanted to study under her. Practical would have meant I probably wouldn't have gotten to do some of the really awesome research and design she's challenged me with as my advisor."

"I'm not wired that way," I said, shaking my head. "Everything needs to make sense. I can have fun and take risks after I know I have a stable career."

"Have fun now." I looked over my shoulder to see Dr. Aubrey walking over to join us, a wry smile on her face. "Take it from this old woman, life loves sending you curveballs. The second you plan something, I promise it will fall apart." Before I could reply, she added, "And I've found that the most interesting things in life come when that happens." She then glanced at Oliver's tablet. "Have you been able to figure out the sensitivity issue yet?"

"I didn't almost break my fingers the last time I tried to use the glove," Oliver said with a shrug, "so, progress?"

"I think that might be a good acceptance criteria," she said with a grin. "And, with that, I'm really curious to see what you three have been up to. Grace, how's your project going?"

To Do

☑ Recital costume options w/Aunt Drina & Nat

☑ New foot undeez (check out dance socks?)

☑ Appt with dietician about new reactions

☐ Pre-write thank you cards for graduation ← (ask Mom for guest list)

☑ Break up with Leia ←

☐ French: dissertation sur Louis de Funes

☐ Finish 3d model for glove linkages

☐ Add linkage .stl files to queue

☐ ☺ Help Phoebe with bridal shower!!! ♡☺

OMG, I can't believe you put your breakup in your planner. That's extra even for you

Stay out of my planner, Em!

☐ Chapter 33

My Physics teacher once told us astronauts didn't really feel gravity slam into them upon reentry into Earth's atmosphere. Instead, their bodies just gradually got heavier and heavier as the heat shield burned bright orange around them. Like sitting inside a giant, barely controlled fireball tumbling towards the Earth while gravity tried to squeeze their insides to mush.

Maybe I wasn't as melodramatic as Em when it came to describing emotional things—this time, she was midway through a retelling of her "devastating" short plays rehearsal—but the second I saw Leia sitting at Phoebe's kitchen table, I swear I felt that gravity slam into me. Even

Em screeched to a stop mid-sentence the moment she stepped through the doorway behind me, throwing me a not-so-subtle worried look.

Leia hadn't bowed out like I thought she would. Of course she wouldn't—she was the most dependable person in the world and knew that Phoebe's mom needed all the help she could get. I tried not to let my steps falter and went deeper into Phoebe's kitchen, propping myself up against a shelf full of cookbooks and ignoring Phoebe's apologetic look.

Phoebe's mom was pacing in front of the sink, muttering to herself as she went through a checklist attached to a very familiar rose gold clipboard—my mom's signature color. She tapped the list a few times with her pen before closing her eyes, taking a deep breath, and then looking up at us with a big smile.

"Thank you all so much for coming. With all of our family up in Massachusetts and Petur's family in Iceland, this is going to be a huge help for me and Phoebe."

"No problem, Mrs. Martins," Alec said, dropping his backpack and just missing my feet in the process. "We're lucky Em stole Grace's planner during lunch and penciled this in, or else you'd be one person short."

I elbowed him and studiously ignored the amused look that ran across Leia's face for a second, so faint that probably I was the only one able to see the tiny scrunching at the corner of her eyes or how the corners of her lips twitched upwards ever so slightly.

"Where's Trixie, anyway? Isn't she home this week?" I asked.

Phoebe maneuvered past us with a giant cooling rack full of cookies, looking like she'd just stepped off the set of *Leave it to Beaver,* hair in a high ponytail and wearing a fifties-style cherry print ruffled apron covered in flour.

"Your mom has her and Petur busy tasting cakes and then they're checking out some spots in town for pictures." She gently nudged aside a pile of books on the kitchen island to make room for the rack. "Trix just texted that chocolate chip with mocha filling or funfetti with vanilla are neck-in-neck right now."

Mrs. Martins cringed at the word "funfetti," but just pressed her lips together, consulted the clipboard, and said, "Okay, they're not due back for another four hours, so I'm hoping we can get all of the favors, table decorations, and place cards done and put away by then. I picked a vintage tea time theme—" *That* explained Phoebe's choice of outfit…"—and little imperfections are charming, so don't feel like you need to be perfect, okay?" At our nods, she pointed to a pile of place cards set in two neat piles on the kitchen table next to two handwritten lists. "Grace and Leia, since you both have beautiful handwriting, can you write up the place cards? I thought it would give it a more personal, vintage-y touch than something off a printer."

Phoebe's brows drew together as she looked at both me and Leia. "Mom, I don't think—"

Leia was the first to cut her off, "Sure, Mrs. Martins. No problem."

I nodded, shaking my head at Phoebe's confused and

worried look. "We can definitely do that."

"Great. The list is there, and I have an example I made," Mrs. Martins waved over to the table and added, with a little laugh, "though you'll probably have to redo it, too, because my writing definitely isn't beautiful." She then turned to Em and Alec. "Do you two mind making the centerpieces? They should be pretty easy to put together"

"How about Alec decorates and I'll be quality control? He's the artistic one." Em asked, poking at one of the china teapots lined up on the kitchen counter. "Unless you want the centerpieces I make to look like the stuff Monet painted when he started going blind."

"How about you sort the flowers and butterflies into piles to make things easier for Alec?" Phoebe shot back, pointing at a pile of fake flowers, fake butterflies, and mini umbrellas. "No artistic skill needed, Monet." Part of me realized that Phoebe had taken over my usual problem-solving role, but since my brain was still trying to process the situation, I couldn't even think of anything to add.

"Aye-aye, boss-lady ma'am," Em said with a jaunty salute.

"And Phoebe and I will be working on decorating the chair and wishing well in the family room," Mrs. Martins nodded at the half wall dividing the kitchen from the living room, where fake flowers were scattered all over the floor, along with a lacy parasol and a giant laundry basket half-wrapped with poster paper. "So just yell out if you need anything."

"Got it," Alec said over his shoulder. He slipped behind Phoebe's mom to plug in the glue gun and then dropped onto one of the island stools.

"Great. Thank you all again," Mrs. Martins said with a grin before dropping her clipboard on the counter and gesturing to Phoebe to follow her into the family room. "You kids are fantastic."

Leia tapped Phoebe's arm before she could leave. "Um, I wanted to let you know I can only stay for about two hours because I'm meeting up with my friend Abby for dinner over in Philly, if that's okay?" Leia had mentioned Abigail a few times before, a girl from her middle school who she'd had a crush on, before meeting me. The way Leia smiled and said "Abby" reminded me of the smile she used to just save for me. In that second, my stomach seized as if I'd eaten hot boulders. I couldn't even hide the hurt I knew had to be all over my face. Awkward wasn't even the right word for the whole situation. Gut-wrenching and awful were more like it.

Phoebe glanced over at me, seemed to notice my expression, then shook her head the tiniest amount before turning her full attention to Leia and saying, "Of course it's not a problem. I'm so thankful for any help you can give."

"Definitely. I just wish I'd planned better. Dinner in Philly on a Friday night wasn't my smartest move. I panicked when I realized I'd be competing with commuters," Leia said with a bright laugh.

Before Leia could turn around and see my expression, I tried my best to paste on a detached, friend smile. Em wandered over from the island, pretending to check out the list in my hands, and whispered in my ear, "I know I'm not taking sides, but, if that's the competition, I bet one hundred percent that you're prettier and smarter."

It was such an Em thing to say that, despite the ache that lingered in my chest, I had to resist the urge to laugh.

"Thanks," I whispered back, then, at her concerned, searching look, I added a nod to let her know I was okay. I was *not* jealous, I told myself. I didn't have the right to be.

Before anyone else could decide to join in the "pity Grace party," I took a deep breath and headed over to the kitchen table. "So," I said, sitting next to Leia and shifting my seat slightly to give us both a little bit of room. I stared down at my list, which was thankfully written out in Petur's neat handwriting. "You came to help out?"

"I keep my promises," Leia said, her tone light but definitely clipped. She picked up one of the fancy fountain pens Mrs. Martins had left for us and bent over her first place card. Out of the corner of my eye, I saw her worrying at her lip in the same way she always did before tackling a new task. It was one of the unconscious habits I had found incredibly cute when we'd first met.

I answered her minor jab with a humming sound, then picked up my own pen and tried to focus on my list. At the same time, I realized I was close enough to smell Leia's perfume and shampoo, and my annoyingly illogical heart clenched over the familiarity of it all. This was going to be a long afternoon.

□

"Is that an accent or a dot?" Leia whispered to me, pointing at one of the names on the list in Mrs. Martins' handwriting. Phoebe's mom hadn't been kidding about her writing, which was a far cry from the list I was using in Petur's super clear, boxy handwriting.

I squinted at the "i" in question, trying to puzzle out the name like Agent Carter deciphering a coded letter. I was at a severe disadvantage since I'd taken French and this was nothing like any of the names I'd seen in my textbooks. "Accent, I think? You're the one who took Spanish, what do you think it should be?"

"Spanish and Portuguese are two totally different languages."

I had no idea why she thought I might know the answer, but at least an educated guess was better than no guess at all. "Yeah, but the languages share a peninsula in Europe and the continent of South America, so I bet the names aren't too different?"

Leia gave me one of her exasperated looks, then, biting her lip, drew an ambiguous dot/line over the i with her calligraphy pen. "We're switching lists after you finish that name. At least *you* learned how to write the little doodle under the letter c in French class."

"*Cédille,*" I muttered the French name for the little mark under my breath, then focused on carefully copying the little p-like letter in the last name I was writing from my list. "Icelandic has accents, too. And really different letters."

"But those names are on a legible list, unlike mine," she said, jabbing her finger at a scribble on her list that looked a little bit like it was supposed to be "Maria."

I made a hushing sound, glancing over at the living room, where tufts of tulle were apparently being cut. "Don't let Phoebe's mom hear you say that."

"Her writing's worse than my dad's, and he's a doctor," she shot back, then reached over to try to swipe my list away from me.

I held it behind me, out of her reach. "And that's why you should keep it. You have experience deciphering parental hieroglyphics, unlike me." She lunged and I slid my chair sideways. "Nope."

Leia narrowed her eyes and I knew, from that look, that I was in trouble. "Really?" She leaned in close enough that we were nose to nose. "Don't mess with me. I'll take you down over a cedilla."

My eyes widened and my heartbeat picked up so much I was positive she could hear it. "I—" Heat crept up my neck and I knew it would hit my cheeks at any moment.

"Are you two okay over there?" Phoebe's mom asked as she walked in with armfuls of fake flowers. Behind her, Phoebe stared at us with incredibly wide eyes.

Leia plucked the paper from my hand and dropped back into her seat as I froze in place. "Perfectly fine," she said, hopping away from me and casually sliding her list over to my side of the table. "Just switching up lists." Her own cheeks seemed to be a little pink, too, but then she dropped her head and her hair swung forward in a dark curtain, blocking my view.

I cleared my throat and nodded, picking up my pen again. "Perfectly," I said in a exact echo of Leia, then clamped my lips shut before I could do anything even more embarrassing.

As they stepped down the stairs to the family room, I could hear Mrs. Martins whisper to Phoebe, "Is there anything I'm missing here?" Phoebe's hushed "Breakup," and Mrs. Martins' surprised, "Ohhhh."

Behind us, Em added, in a purposely loud whisper, "They can hear you, you know. You're making it awkward."

Alec couldn't seem to resist chiming in, but didn't bother to whisper. "*More* awkward."

Leia and I shared an amused look and both cracked up at the same time at everyone's antics. "Fine, guys, we get it," I said, waving my hand in the air like a truce flag.

"This is now officially a no-awkward zone," Leia said, scrunching her nose over her shoulder at Alec and Em. "Promise."

"Kiss and make up?" Em said, dropping her chin into her hands and watching us like she was a kid waiting for a tv show to start.

"No," Leia and I said in unison, then dissolved into laughter again. She bumped me with her shoulder, then turned back to her place card.

"Nice try, Em," I said. "Now, leave me alone so I can figure out if this person's name is Lidia or Ligia."

☑Chapter 34

A knock came at my bedroom door and I pulled the quilt over my head. "Still sleeping," I called out. Since mom and dad were supposed to be at some charity golf thing down the shore in Galloway, it was probably the cleaning service. My room was clean enough, anyway.

"No, you're not." Phoebe's voice came through the crack I heard her open in my door. "You're not the sleeping-in type." I peeked over the quilt and saw a hand waving what looked to be a cupcake through the small opening. "Are you decent?"

"I'm not naked, if that's what you're asking," I said, completely unable to keep the sarcasm out of my voice.

"Good." The door flew open and she barreled in, dropping on top of my bed and shoving the cupcake my way. "Cupcake?"

"Are you giving me a choice?" I gingerly took the plastic container from her and sat up. My quilt bunched around me like a wall between me and Phoebe-on-a-mission. I patted my hair down so I'd look a little less like the Bride of Frankenstein. I really needed to rethink sharing the door code with my friends.

She dug into the teal canvas tote she'd brought with her and pulled out her own cupcake and a set of mini speakers. "Not really." She popped open her cupcake container and bit into the obnoxiously green frosting. "Yours is gluten free and they didn't use dates to make the cake, just eggs and regular stuff. No food issue excuses," she added after swallowing. "Eat."

"Wow, you're pushy today."

She didn't respond, just smiled and connected her phone to the speakers. Within seconds, twangy seventies music filled my room. "I saw your face yesterday when you heard Leia talking about Abby." She studied my face for a second before tentatively reaching out and patting my arm. "You still love her." Her soft words were a statement, not a question.

Instead of answering, I pulled my cupcake out of its box and studied it. Cookie dough, from the gourmet cupcake place near the yarn shop where Phoebe worked. I popped the little nugget of cookie dough from the top of the cupcake into my mouth. As soon as I could talk without choking on the words, I pointed at the speakers. Someone was singing about taking a train. "What the hell is this stuff?"

"Don't hate on the Monkees. They make perfect music for moping and eating cupcakes. Them and the Partridge Family." Phoebe stared me down with an only partly sympathetic look, as if daring me to contradict her. She then dropped her eyes and picked at her cupcake wrapper. "It might help if you talk to someone about Leia instead of trying to keep that whole pulled-together façade going. It's a little cracked right now, you know. The mascara gave it away yesterday after dinner."

Crap. I'd have to switch to waterproof for a while. I took another bite of the cupcake and spoke around it in a way that would horrify mom. "What difference does it make if I still love her? Talking about it isn't going to fix anything, especially not now."

"Sometimes, it's not about the fixing. It's about getting things off your chest. Trust me, it feels a lot better when you do."

The bouncy beat of the music was really distracting. "Says the girl who hid in the church when she was supposed to go to confession before our Confirmation."

"Whatever, I was thirteen and Father Lionel was a grump."

"Mmmhmm." The teasing wasn't helping, and Phoebe's silence, punctuated by a random off-key attempt to sing along, ate at me until the words just bubbled up. "I can't believe she moved on so fast. And with that girl, too."

Phoebe nodded, shuffling up on the bed until she was sitting next to me, squishing my protective wall of blanket. She didn't say anything, just polished off her cupcake and picked the chocolate crumbs off her top, popping them in her mouth.

"I mean, I'm not completely sure she's moved on but if she did, and with Abby? Really? Abby's a little trust-fund baby who can't do math. I heard she's barely scraping by to graduate this year."

"Don't be a study snob," Phoebe murmured.

I ignored that comment. "Leia's so much better than her, though. She deserves someone who wants to make something of herself."

Phoebe looked at me with a wicked little smile. "Someone like you?"

"Shut up."

She shrugged and changed the song over to one about words. "What about Natalie?"

I blinked at her, confused. "What *about* Natalie?"

"Aren't you two dating?"

"Um, no. She has a boyfriend." I emphasized the boy-friend part to get it into her thick skull.

Phoebe tilted her head, shook it slightly, and narrowed her eyes. "So she's—"

"A non-romantic acquaintance." The whole conversation had gotten so ridiculous, laughter threatened to bubble up through the ache. "We're friends. And we're dancing a duet at the recital. You actually thought we were dating?"

She straightened up and said, defensively, "You were spending so much time together and you just kept mentioning her all the time…"

"I'm allowed to make new friends. And I can be friends with a people without wanting to date them. Or do you think I'm hopelessly in love with you and Em, too?"

Phoebe made a snorting half-laugh sound. "If Em were here, she'd say yes."

"Well…" I really couldn't think of a retort for that. She *would* say that. "Em and her ego don't count."

"So, no rebound for you?"

I arched an eyebrow at her, even though she probably couldn't see it under the mess of hair that swooped right over my forehead. "Obviously not."

"Crud. This calls for a real wallowing breakup song." She scrolled through her phone until she found a song that was even bouncier than the last few.

"This is a wallowing song? Is it even a song?" The song sounded like people goofing off, not even a professional thing. I never understood Phoebe's affinity for music from cheesy seventies TV shows.

"Shh, just sing along." She dove right in, totally off-key, into a song about buying a dog. For someone who played the flute, she was shockingly tone deaf.

The singer started making weird sounds. "I refuse to pretend to snore."

Phoebe elbowed me and I narrowed my eyes at her before halfheartedly trying to sing the most ridiculous chorus on the planet. Just when I thought the torture was over, she put the song on repeat, bouncing against me with a grin as I tried my hardest to sing along so she wouldn't make us do this a third time.

"See?" She asked during the instrumental break the musicians had inexplicably filled with random conversation and noises. "Best breakup song ever, right?"

I actually was starting to feel a little better, but I wasn't going to admit it. "It's the most ridiculous breakup song ever."

"You like it. You're just not going to admit it, but that's okay." Phoebe said. "And I promise, *you're* going to be okay."

I closed my eyes, the goofiness of the past few minutes fading a little into the ache that never really had gone away. "You're right. I wanted this. She can date whoever she wants, she'll be happy, I'll get over it." In a deadpan voice, I added, "It was the most logical choice."

She caught the imitation. "You're not Spock." She stopped the music and hugged me. "I know you guys make fun of me for quoting books sometimes, but, you know, they have the best truths. And *Cradled* had the best quote about logical stuff."

I leaned into her hug, pushing back the tightness behind my eyes and at the back of my throat and focusing on her weird little line of conversation. "Hit me with the quote, book nerd," I said, trying to sound light.

"Kaylie had to pick between going to this big-deal music intensive or staying on PEI with Evan, and her aunt just hugged her, like this," Phoebe squeezed me tighter, "and said: 'Sometimes, the most illogical choices lead to the most wonderful things, but sometimes the most logical choice is the one that's best for you, regardless of what anyone else might believe. In the end, it's your decision.'" She let go and reached up to smooth down my hair. "'If you think you did the right thing for you, I support you. And even if it's logical or right, it doesn't mean you're not allowed to cry.'"

Crap. She just had to say that last sentence. I couldn't hold back a sniffle. "How did you get to be the mature one?"

"Books. Books taught me everything I know. And my friends."

I poked her in the arm. "Nerd."

"Says the nerdy cheerleader." She got up from the bed and tugged on my sleeve. "Now, you need to get up, get…" she gestured at my sweatshirt and rumpled shorts, "…into something that's more Grace, and you're coming with me to Cupcake Heaven for another cupcake."

"I'm not going to fit into my recital dress," I protested, but let her pull me up anyway.

"And since you're not with anyone, there's a really pretty girl who works there…" Phoebe opened my closet and stared at my outfits, perfectly organized by color and type. She rifled through the blue section.

I pushed past her, pulling a pair of jeans and a pink tank from the closet. If I let Phoebe dress me, I'd probably end up looking like a reject from a fairy tale, even with stuff from my own closet. "Are you trying to set me up with her?"

She pursed her lips when I shook my head at the vintage

fifties designer sundress she pulled out to counter my choice. "She looks like Rei from *Sailor Moon*. She's got this amazing hair and wears the cutest outfits and the other girl who works there said she was available and into girls…"

I headed into the bathroom to change, saying over my shoulder, "I sense an ulterior motive. You just want me to become your cupcake dealer by proxy."

Phoebe tossed a sparkly belt my way. "I'd never do that to you. But if you do end up dating her, remember that my favorite flavor is mint chocolate chip. Or s'mores. Maybe you can talk them into making mint chocolate chip s'mores cupcakes all year round?"

"I'm not dating anyone, I just don't want to hear any more seventies ridiculousness." I pulled the brush through my hair and yanked it up into a ponytail. I threw cold water on my face, hoping it would freeze away the red in my nose and eyes before changing. With a little dab of concealer under my eyes and over my nose, I poked my head out the bathroom door. "But you did a good job making me feel less like crap. Thanks."

Her grin grew even wider and she made a self-conscious shrug. "I have a lot of practice. Do you know how many times Em's called me about her emotional disasters?"

Satisfied with not looking like I'd been crying for days, I headed back into my bedroom and struck a half-hearted 'ta-dah!' pose. "Lead me to the cupcakes."

Phoebe gathered her things and followed me down the stairs. "And the cute girl."

"You suck at playing matchmaker. Please stop," I said.

She put her hand to her heart as if she'd been wounded. "Fine, but you just crushed my mint chocolate chip s'mores dreams."

"You'll live."

June

☐ Chapter 35

I picked the last of the gooey support material out of one of the swirls in the right metacarpal linkage and slipped the prototype onto my hand, twisting and turning my hand to admire the fit. There was something magical about seeing an idea go from my computer screen and into a real 3-D printed prototype, and a little part of me felt like an archeologist uncovering a treasure, washing away the support materials and pinning the pieces together until they became a real, tangible thing.

"It looks like that fits like a glove," Mr. Newton said, laughing at his own joke as he came over and leaned closer to look at the glove. "That came together really well."

"Thanks," I said, hinging at my wrist and nodding at the light tug that accompanied the movement, forcing my fingers to curl. "The SLA isn't strong enough to really support testing it out, but, look," I tilted my wrist back, relaxing my hand, and smiled as my fingers opened back up to straight. "At least it's proving the concept. I'm thinking of doing a sintered metal prototype once I'm sure I've gotten the fit right." The University had a 3-D printer that laser sintered metal powder into actual parts, and Oliver had promised to find a way to sneak me into the queue for my final prototype.

My teacher nodded, gesturing at me to take off the glove so he could get a better look. "I'm impressed." His hand was too big to fit in the glove, forcing him to cup the prototype in his palm, instead, and I had to resist the urge to cringe as he manhandled it. "It really doesn't have to be this thin, though. Something thicker would be more robust. I also don't understand why you added the decorative features. That only weakens the structure."

"I wanted to make a support that didn't look like a support. Something I'd want to wear, you know?" I pointed at one of the joints, and added, "Besides, I ran a finite element analysis and reinforced any high stress points before printing this out. I'm pretty certain the metal version will hold up to testing."

He handed the prototype back to me and then pushed up his glasses, his face morphing into his 'patient teacher' expression. "You wouldn't have to worry about that if you went with a more practical design. Right now, your design would be very expensive to manufacture compared to one with straight linkages, and you're limiting yourself to only a portion of the population with a…" He paused, twisted his lips as he looked for the right word, and then continued, "Honestly, Grace? It's a very feminine design, which is beautiful, but isn't very universal. You're really limiting your user population by making it like this. I'd suggest streamlining the design so it can be used by a broader population."

I took in his criticism, took a deep breath, and nodded, "But I think that's the problem. There's a population of patients who aren't being served, patients who want to have beautiful things instead of a one-size-fits-all design that's usually designed by men for stereotypical men. And I think there's nothing wrong with making things functional and beautiful—no one said you can't have both."

"Not everything is a gender war thing, Grace," He pointed out with a frown, and tapped on my desk to emphasize his point. "Part of your grade includes taking into account the most efficient manufacturing methods and evaluating the market for your design. You have an uphill road on that if you insist on keeping this design."

"Challenge accepted," I muttered under my breath as he walked over to praise Nick's glorified spaghetti strainer. I set my prototype gently down on my desk and pulled up the manufacturing methods chapter in our textbook, jumping ahead past traditional manufacturing methods like milling and turning and over to casting. It wasn't 3-D printing, but, on a large scale, at least it was less expensive. People mass produced metal jewelry all the time, so I wasn't trying to reinvent the wheel.

An image of a final, testable prototype popped into my head and I grinned. It wasn't part of the project, but I had two weeks until the final presentation and I had plenty of time to make it work.

☐Chapter 36

"Okay, take a look at this and let me know what you think," Mom said, slipping off her reading glasses and pushing a list into my hands the second I walked into the study after school.

I glanced down at the paper, which was filled with names of different foods broken up by appetizer, main meal, and dessert, then looked back up at Mom. "Fundraiser?"

Mom dropped down into the spindly chair at her desk and gestured at a thick, accordion-style folder that sat open on the desk. "No, your graduation party. I really should have started planning this in December, but since you said you wanted something casual…"

"Caviar canapes are not casual," I said, pointing at one of

the appetizers on her list. I wasn't surprised, though. Casual for my mom was semi-formal for the rest of the planet.

"It's just a starting point. I used that list for Alice's baby shower last month and everyone loved it." She quirked a smile at my disbelieving look. "Fine. We'll do philly cheesesteak rolls, mini calzones, and mini tacos, and if Uncle Eduardo has a heart attack at your party, it will be on your conscience."

"Letty's studying to be a cardiologist, right? Just make sure she RSVPs and we're okay."

Mom pulled up something on her tablet. "Speaking of, I need to figure out what size tent we need to rent. The party company needs to know next week, so I wanted to get a final number. Do you know if Leia and her parents are coming?" She whipped off the last sentence a little too casually, then looked up at me with an innocently curious look. Mom-Prying 101.

"No."

She casually jotted a note onto her tablet. "Do you want me to leave spaces just in case they find time on their schedule to come?"

"Mom," I said, flatly.

"Grace," she said, imitating my tone.

"We're not together anymore," I said, the words cutting painfully at my throat as I said them. "You know that."

"You're so much your father's daughter. He also tries to hide his feelings, but I can see right through the both of you, and I hate it when you're hurting." Mom put down her tablet and dropped her hands delicately to her lap. "I really wish you would let me help you drown your feelings with a junk food binge or a shopping trip."

"Phoebe brought cupcakes?" I said, weakly, plopping into one of the overstuffed worn leather armchairs. "They were nice and carb-y?"

Mom rolled her eyes. "Can we please let me live out even the tiniest bit of my *Gilmore Girls* fantasy for once in my life?"

"I think going to New York City to buy expensive shoes and purses, and then getting high tea at the Plaza isn't very Gilmore Girls-like. They were more into coffee and bad takeout, I think."

"Yes, but good shoes and purses last forever while bad takeout and coffee just give you heartburn. I don't like mixing heartbreak with acid reflux."

"I was the one who did the breaking up, you know," I said pointedly.

Mom gave me one of the epic side-eyes she probably developed after years of dealing with corporate executives and PTA parents, then dropped back to a super casual expression and tone as she said, "You know, I know what it's like to break ties with your past to try new things. Sweetie, you might be a lot like your dad, but you have my heart. Dad is good at making quick decisions and clean breaks. You can try, but you can't just turn off the things you love. They'll just keep haunting you until you really face them."

"You're going to tell me the story again, aren't you?" Every once in a while, Mom pulled out her 'leaving New York for a new life' story, complete with the very rom-com-esque decision to hop on a train to Philly without knowing if Dad was going to be waiting for her in the station when she got there.

Mom arched her brows at me. "You haven't heard this part."

"I think I've heard all of your stories, Mom." I remembered years of sitting on Mom's lap or next to Dad as we flipped through yearbooks and photo albums, laughing through all their bad haircuts and ridiculous school stories. Mom's had been the worst—as someone always on the cutting edge of fashion, she had some gloriously bad nineties pictures that always made me laugh.

She shook her head, a small smile playing across her lips. "You know I was dating someone else when I met your father, right?"

"No." This was news. I'd heard about how she and Dad had bumped into each other on the L train one day and how their chance meetings had turned into a classic New York romance straight out of a movie, but not the other boyfriend part. I'd always thought the "other guy" in her stories turned up later.

"His name was Doug. We were the artistic power couple of the school. Everyone, even our professors, thought we were going to take the art world by storm." She laughed at that last sentence. "That sounds so ridiculously dramatic now, but everyone thought we had a lot of potential, especially together."

"Okay…" I tried to figure out how she was going to tie this story to my present situation and came up blank.

Mom held up her hand in a "wait" motion, as if knowing what I was thinking. "Doug and I had the same really tight group of friends. Looking back now, I think I stayed with him so long because everyone expected it. I think, somewhere along the way, I fell out of love with him as a boyfriend, but since we were such close friends and everyone told us we were the perfect couple, I just assumed that was how relationships evolved. I was young and stupid and I trusted everyone else before trusting my own feelings, you know?"

"And then you met Dad?"

"And then I met Dad," she echoed me, with a grin. "He was the exact opposite of all the rest of my friends. Super practical and knew exactly what he wanted in life, just like you. But when I realized I was falling for your dad and that he had fallen for me… I made the more logical choice, which was to stay with Doug. We had the same friends, the same dreams, and even came from the same borough. It just made sense. I even made a pros and cons list to make sure."

I cringed a little on the "pros vs cons" part. That hit a little close to home. "Obviously, you didn't stay with him."

"Obviously." She said, "If I'd trusted my heart the first time around, I wouldn't have hurt Doug and lost most of my friends when I realized I'd made the wrong decision. And I deserved losing them all, because of the way I handled things. Some people burn a few bridges, I managed the equivalent of setting the GWB on fire when I ran out in the middle of Doug's first art show and got on that train. But, honestly, Grace? The first time I felt free and happy was when I made that ridiculously illogical decision and ran straight towards something that was completely uncertain." Mom twisted her hands together as she added, "But I lost a lot of people I loved because I didn't trust myself."

"Wow." It was hard to picture my oh-so pulled together mom doing any of those things. She'd been a little vague sometimes about why she didn't have a lot of friends left to visit in the city, but this put a whole new light on everything I'd always believed about her and her life.

She leaned forward so we were practically nose-to-nose. "I wasn't happy when I took the logical way out, I wasn't happy when I refused to confront my own feelings, and I can tell that you're not happy, either."

I backed up and shook my head. I wasn't my mom and Leia wasn't my dad. There wasn't going to be a dramatic reunion in front of 30th Street Station for us. "I'm fine. And this isn't you almost staying in Manhattan because of that other guy in that weird love triangle thing you had going on before you realized you wanted to be with Dad. This is me. It was just time for things with Leia to end, and I really don't appreciate you trying to turn my relationships into a mother-daughter bonding ritual."

"I'm not pushing you to do anything. I just know how you are. Make sure you don't logic all the joy out of your life. I know what that feels like and I don't want you to have to learn from your mistakes if I can help it." There was a sad, nostalgic note in her voice that she covered up by pressing her lips together and further straightening her already perfectly straight back. She tucked a nonexistent loose strand of hair behind her ear and turned back to her folder. "Now, are you sure you want a red and orange cake and not just red and orange accents? Sweet Eats said they could make the whole cake PCHS orange with red piping, but if you want buttercream, everyone is going to end up dying their tongues, and that's not a great look."

That hint of sadness in her last statement before she'd switched to her perfect planner persona tugged forward all the arguments I'd been hearing coming from their room for the past few months.

"Mom," I asked in my tiniest voice and automatically hated myself for it. I was supposed to be an adult, ready to give support wherever I was needed. "Are you and Dad getting a divorce?"

Mom stopped in the middle of erasing and rewriting on her list for what seemed the hundredth time that afternoon and gently put her pencil down on her desk. "I'm sorry, what?"

I sunk deeper into the armchair, dropping my English textbook onto my lap. "You two have been fighting for the last two months. I hear you in the mornings."

"Oh, honey," Mom said, squeezing next to me in the armchair, half on the overstuffed arm. "Couples fight. You can't live with someone for over twenty years and agree on everything all the time. Dad and I are okay." She poked me gently on the tip of my nose and then She leaned over to cuddle into my side. "Are our fights that bad?"

"Awful. Dad even left the other morning without saying he loved you."

She squeezed my arm. "You noticed that, huh?" At my nod, she said, "I'm sorry for making you worry, but we're okay. People fight. It's how we act and what we do after the fight that's important. Dad and I make sure we keep talking through things, even if we don't always agree. We're going to be okay."

"Are you sure?"

"Positive. This is nothing compared to the great kitchen remodel fiasco from a few years ago. I swear, we risked almost twenty years of marriage over travertine." Mom went back to her list, looking up add, "One more piece of life advice, Grace. Never equate happiness with kitchen appliances, and always compromise on the backsplash."

☑Chapter 37

The line snaking out of Paris Patisserie brought back memories of every Monday before jazz class, when my entire class would basically line up to find out what flavor they were giving out for free macaron Mondays. From all the people in dance warmups on line and all the kids in Haddontowne Academy uniforms, it didn't look like things had really changed much, since the strip mall was close to their school, too.

I glanced at my phone—I had twenty minutes before recital practice with about thirty people on the line that stretched far down the sidewalk outside the patisserie. If transactions at the patisserie on macaron Monday still took an average of thirty seconds, I might still make it with time to spare, especially if I warmed up while on line. I technically could go after practice or just buy macarons another day, but they always gave away their beta test flavors first and I didn't want to miss out on the next matcha bubble tea macaron or whatever bit of sugary genius the bakers had dreamed up that week.

Slinging my dance bag over my shoulder, I hopped out of my car and jogged over to the end of the line, bouncing in place once I settled in behind a girl in a Haddontowne uniform. The line was moving as fast as I had predicted and I had finished two sets of ankle rolls, about twenty relevés, and a few plies before I was only a few people away from the front door. I looked through the bakery windows to check my posture in the ornate mirrored walls inside and froze when I saw a familiar face… belonging to the girl in front of me.

Apparently, Leia had decided to change her hair color again.

My heartbeat picked up to a rabbit pace and I mentally cursed myself for not even recognizing my own ex-girlfriend even though, in my defense, the Haddontowne late spring uniforms were figure-hiding crimes against fashion. She was focused on her phone, so I still had a chance to slip out of the line before she could notice I was there.

Someone behind me let off a massive sneeze, Leia looked up from her phone, and, before I could duck away, our eyes met in the mirror. Her already big brown eyes widened in surprise and recognition.

Crud.

I broke the gaze and, in front of me, I saw the shoulders of Leia's blazer heave up and down and then square up before she turned slightly to face me. "Grace." She had *that* look on her face, the pleasant but distant smile that she put on for people when she was trying to be polite and good even if she didn't want to talk to them. It killed me to see her using it on me. "I guess you're teaching today?"

I shook my head mechanically. "Recital practice. The junior preps needed an extra push, so Aunt Drina gave me their tap time." Before I could stop myself, I blurted out, "You changed your hair."

She reached up and, in the way she always did when she wanted to show off a new color or haircut, flipped her hair so the short red and black strands perfectly caught the sunlight. With her other hand, she propped the door open as she passed through, taking her hand off it within milliseconds of my own touching the metal and glass. "Change is good."

"It is," I said, finding myself unconsciously nodding like a bobblehead doll at her comment. Not everyone could pull off bright stop-sign-red highlights like hers, but she somehow—*always,* my traitorous brain whispered at me—made this vampire-mermaid hair look like something Botticelli would paint. I caught myself staring, forced a poor imitation of her unaffected smile onto my face, and tried to grasp at anything to sound as breezy and unaffected as I could. "I mean, my colorist talked me into changing my highlight color from butterscotch to dawn, and I feel like a totally new person," I joked, and tried to toss my hair in the same way she did, failing miserably as my ponytail flopped flatly over my shoulder.

Leia's eyes took on a little amused spark as she said, in a mock serious tone, "I can definitely tell." I braced myself for the inevitable teasing, maybe a comment like 'Are you sure she didn't just give you the same color and charge you more for it,' but it never came. Instead, she dropped her eyes to her watch. "Someone's messing with the wait time. We haven't moved for a whole minute." Something else was off, too. A sweet jasmine smell rose off her—she'd changed her perfume. That had been one of Leia's favorite tricks, to pick up a little bit of solid perfume and run her fingers through her hair, so every time she turned her head, she called it "whispering" the smell into the air. But, before, she'd always used a spicy smell, something that reminded me of her description of visiting a spice market on her family vacation in eighth grade, with bags of peppercorn and saffron scenting the air. Now... the jasmine and her hair combined made her seem even more painfully mature and distant. Like she was becoming a different person than the Leia I knew.

I craned my neck, glad for an excuse to look anywhere but at her. I caught sight of a guy with slicked back hair and thick black glasses holding up the line. "It's hipster guy. I think he's ordering one of his pretentious coffees again."

"Crud. We're going to be here forever." She narrowed her eyes at the front of the line and the expression on her face was adorable, like an angry kitten getting riled up. Leia was always freakishly cute when she was annoyed. "He's been coming here for years. Everyone knows you don't order stuff on macaron Mondays until they run out of macarons."

"Let's see if I can guess what he's ordering." I pretended to push invisible glasses up my nose. "I'd like a shakerato, but is your espresso single source fair trade picked by mountain dwelling monks under a vow of silence?"

"And none of that commercial white sugar. I need unrefined sugar hand scraped from a Moroccan sugarloaf," Leia added gleefully, imitating coffee hipster's current hand motions perfectly. "That sugarloaf is gluten free, right?"

"The ice has to be chipped by hand from imported Norwegian glacier ice." I pursed my lips, then added, "Oh, you don't have that? Fine. I'll *live* with ice made from filtered water. But you really need to look into getting some of that in. No one in SoHo would drink a shakerato made with *tap* ice."

Leia let off a delighted snort. "I'll bet you anything he's going to make us wait until he takes the perfect picture of it for his Photogram, too, just because the counter is a better offset color than the tables."

"I don't have to bet," I said as a grumble rose up from the front of the line. "Two years and that guy hasn't changed."

"Remember when he was writing his 'novel?'" Leia said, moving forward as the line started up again.

"'It's a literary thinkpiece about the brevity of our lives on this earth, with a misunderstood writer at the core. Is the man writing his story or is his story writing him?'" I quoted the synopsis he would force on everyone in listening distance for months.

"I'm a little scared that you remember that."

"Be very scared. I remember he also wanted to name his manic pixie dream girl character Sunshine, to represent the world outside that a true writer dedicated to his craft never experiences."

This time, Leia's laugh, punctuated with half-choked sounds she always refused to let me call a snort, came freely. "You're right, I remember that," she managed to squeak out. "And he wanted to name the main character after some biblical character thrown into hell and then rescued by an angel, right?"

"Yes," I broke into another round of laughter and, once I could breathe again, said, "I wonder if he actually wrote it."

"I doubt it. He carried that notebook around with him everywhere but I never saw him actually write in it."

"You know, someday, we're going to see him on TV with his book being turned into a movie and we're going to regret making fun of him," I said with a wicked grin.

Leia looked over her shoulder at me and echoed my grin. "Sure. And we can go to his book signings and ask him if he remembers us."

"We're the girls who knocked you over that one time when you were trying to Photogram your hand whipped goat milk Champurrado… can you sign our book?" I channeled Em and pretended to hold out an imaginary book.

She cringed. "Ouch, I remember that. Definitely not our best moment. Did Photogram exist back then, though?"

"I'm... not sure."

A tiny, knowing smile played at the edges of her lips. "You're dying to look it up, aren't you?"

"No," I said, but she had been right—I'd been seconds away from pulling out my phone.

"You know, you can look it up if you really want to. I won't judge," she said, folding her arms and watching me.

"Yes, you will," I shot back, my cheeks warming slightly under her teasing. I could search the creation of Photogram before class, where I wouldn't be under the scrutiny of her amused eyes. To change the subject, I craned my neck to check out the front of the line. "Okay, so the macarons this time are pink with greenish filling. What do you think the flavor is?"

"A good excuse for changing the subject?" Her lips quirked up higher on one side and I arched my eyebrow in return until she fake-sighed and said, "Maybe some sort of strawberry pistachio thing?"

"I didn't think of pistachio. Strawberry sounds too normal for macaron Monday. Rose?"

She thought for a second and her lips pressed together cutely as she nodded. "That actually sounds amazing. Now, if it's not pistachio rose, I'll be disappointed."

As we got closer to the counter, the line clumped tighter together and I found myself painfully trying *not* to bump into Leia as the girl behind me kept invading my private space.

Leia broke into a bounce, turning to me with a brilliant smile. "We were right."

"Aren't we always?"

She reached out as if to poke me on the nose, like she'd always do when she thought I was getting a little ridiculous, but pulled back before reaching my face, her expression dropping. "Um, yeah. We used to be."

I suppressed a cringe at that and added, flatly, "Right." Before the awkward silence between us could stretch too long, we reached the front of the line and the frazzled employee behind the counter handed us each a macaron. I cradled mine carefully in my hands as I followed Leia back outside, where she automatically went to our old spot by the giant stone planters in front of the bakery and propped herself on one of the planters. She scrunched up her nose and scrutinized the macaron the same way she always used to, sniffing it before taking the tiniest bite. I used to joke with her about that, how she acted like they were explosive, and she would always remind me of the pop rock macaron incident from a few years ago and of how I was way too trusting of the bakery and their experiments.

"Okay, this is amazing," she said, after a second's contemplation. She was smiling, her lips turned up wide enough that her long lashes nearly brushed her cheeks, her eyes sparkling.

A little strand of red hair had fallen in front of her nose and I almost reached up to push it away, catching myself halfway through as I not-so-smoothly pretended that I was reaching up to scratch my neck, instead. Her eyes tracked my movement and, before I could make a comment about her eating habits, she furrowed her brow, popped the rest of the macaron in her mouth and hopped off the planter. "Have a good practice."

"Thanks, good talking to—" but before I could finish, she had pushed through the line of people still waiting for macarons and disappeared.

I didn't like the feeling that flowed through my chest at that moment.

☐Chapter 38

My ponytail stuck to my neck and I wound it into a bun as I walked over to the sound system to start the song again. I didn't remember any of my dance teachers ever having to demo our recital pieces this many times, but my junior prep class just wasn't *getting* it. No matter how many times I ran through the recital dance, they just weren't hitting their marks in the same way they needed to if they were going to make their dance stand out from the fifty million other classes dancing to the exact same song in practically every recital on the planet. "One more time. I know all of you know this song, but it seems like you're not feeling it. Trust me, if you let yourselves really get into the song, the timing will be easy." I ignored the groans and the 'buts' and hit the back button on my phone. "Okay, just let go this time and try to feel for the beats. No counting."

I hit play and walked back to the front of the studio, leaning against the mirror to watch, a little voice in the back of my head warning me that I'd have to clean my sweat off the mirrors before Aunt Drina's ballet class.

A painfully popular song filled the room with upbeat male vocals and my class started to move. The no counting advice was a disaster as a few girls immediately came off beat, turning and jumping either earlier or later than the rest of the class. Sensing immediate danger as they all headed towards a group lift on the chorus, I clapped my hands as loudly as I could. "Stop, stop." I turned off the music again and used that minute to squash my urge to pound my head against the wall. As soon as I could think straight again, I turned back to the class and said, "Okay, we're going to try something different."

One of the girls in front wiped her sweat from her forehead as she said, "We've kind of been trying different things since you started teaching."

"Cute, Avery. Then, we're going to try another something-different. I know you guys can do this, you're all great dancers." *Well, most of you*, I almost said, but pressed my lips together and gestured, instead, towards the back corner of the studio. "Line up. We're going to ballet run, jété in the center of the room, then ballet run out. Really simple. Make sure to point your toes on the run and the jété. I want your arms to remain in motion, right arm front first, pinwheel to left arm front, always lifting up like so," I moved my arms to demonstrate, pulling up my chest and chin, "and eyes looking just over your fingers."

"We know this," another girl said, with a little eyeroll, "Ms. Drina makes us do it all the time."

"I know." This was one of Aunt Drina's favorite center exercises. Really basic, but the easier something seemed, the harder it was to actually get right. "Since you already know this, what I want you to do is focus on your arms and your expressions. Focus on the timing in the music for the jété—I don't care if you jump in the exact center as long as you hit the peak of your jump at the perfect spot in the music. I want you to imagine someone in that corner—girl, boy—who you love or have a crush on, and I want you to look and move as if you're running towards them. Got it?" Most of the class nodded tiredly and I walked back to the speakers to play their recital song again. Honest to goodness, I was going to set Aunt Drina up with a wireless system one of these days so she could avoid all the walking.

Then again, Aunt Drina refused to give up her CDs and record player, so it might be a lost cause.

One by one, the class went across the floor, trying and, except for about two of them, failing to look anything but mechanical. I was starting to feel like the entire class needed a lesson in emoting from Em. "Okay, good, but let's try that again with more feeling. How many of you are dating someone?" The two girls who had managed to do the exercise right raised their hands and I resisted the urge to facepalm. Of course. "Got it. If you don't have someone you're crushing on, think of something you love, like ice cream or macarons or—" I tried to dredge up the latest tween sensation currently playing on the speakers— "the guys from this K-pop group."

"HIJ," one of the girls muttered, and I nodded at her.

"Fine, them," I said, heading over to the corner, myself. "Anything you really want to run towards. And let it show in your whole body. You're yearning to reach whoever or whatever it is. You've come off an airplane after weeks or years away and you see them and you can't wait to reach them. Here, watch me."

As the music hit the chorus, I took a deep breath, rolled back my shoulders, and, right on the beat, started my ballet run. The last time I'd done this exercise as a student, I'd pictured Leia and my subconscious pushed the memory of her laugh to the front of my brain. Before I could stumble, the music rushed towards a peak and I pushed into a grand jété, letting the sensation of flying shove away all my feelings before I landed and used the momentum to finish my run to the corner.

I turned to the class, smoothing my expression into an imitation of what Phoebe called a teacher smile. "See?"

"Actually, you looked really sad." One of the quieter girls said from the back of the room, her big brown eyes studying me warily.

"Um. Well, I wanted you to see another option. I just want to see some emotion, okay?" Quiet girl looked at me skeptically, but nodded. At that moment, Aunt Drina waved from the open door and pointed at the clock. "Oops, we're running over," I said, gesturing at the class to move to the front of the room. "Okay, last time, start in the front corner and you can ballet run out the door. Before class on Wednesday, I want you all to listen to the song again and try to find something in it that you can connect to as you dance." Once they were lined up again, I started the music and let them leap out the door. A few more of the girls had gotten better, but most still stumbled through the exercise stiff-armed, their brains still focused on just the steps. We were *never* going to be ready for the recital.

"That was good advice, you know," Aunt Drina said, stepping into the studio as soon as the last girl jumped out, and handed me her homemade mirror-cleaning spray and a paper towel.

I started wiping the me-shaped sweat blot off the mirror and said, tossing a wry smile over my shoulder, "I learned that floor exercise from the best."

"Then you should take your own advice," Aunt Drina said while changing into her tan teaching shoes.

"What advice?" Natalie asked as she came into the studio still dressed in street clothes. She started stripping down to her leotard and tights without taking her attention off the two of us.

"The same advice I've been giving all of you for the past twenty years," my aunt said over her shoulder.

"Oh, yeah." Natalie turned her gaze towards me. "I agree with Drina and whatever it is."

I narrowed my eyes and scrunched my nose at both of them. "Whatever. Are you warmed up?" We were supposed to demo our recital piece for Aunt Drina and, thanks to my class running over, we only had fifteen minutes before the next class started.

"Yeah, I just ran out to grab a macaron. I managed to get one of their last ones." She pulled her leg into a perfect rifle to prove how loose she was, then dropped it down to an attitude. "Totally warm."

"Great, I can't wait to see how far you both have gotten," Aunt Drina said, walking over to the sound system and unplugging my phone. She pulled a CD from the top shelf and waved it at us, "I finally got everything cut today," before popping it into the player and pushing the forward button until it got to our track.

"Honest to God, we need to get you into the twenty-first century," I said, taking my starting position on the floor.

"When *you* own the dance school, you can do that. Until then, we do it my way." She winked at both of us, then, pushed play. "Shut up and dance, Grace."

"Cute," I muttered, then threw myself into the dance, trying my best to forget the café and the end of my last class and to focus on just getting everything right. Pointed feet, turn, push off the floor into the air, push into the floor with the weight of the music. Keep pace with Natalie. Four minutes later, the music stopped and we both dropped to the ground, breathing hard.

"The choreography is beautiful," Aunt Drina said.

"Thanks," Natalie puffed out between breaths. Even out of breath, I could hear the pride in her voice.

Aunt Drina started the music again and nodded along, pausing at the first chorus. "Right here, on the barrel jumps? You either need to get closer or try being on an angle to each other instead of straight across. The way it is right now competes with my attention instead of complementing, you know?" We both nodded, then she hit play again, stopping midway through the second verse. "And here. Make it more staccato. I know what you were trying to do, but you need to hit each movement," she demonstrated with her hands and feet. "Grace, you really nailed the precision there, but pull in your pelvis, it broke your line." She listened through the end of the song. "And Natalie, you really need to commit to that aerial-roll combo. I know it's a little scary…"

"A lot scary," she retorted, massaging her leg. "One bad landing and I'm done."

"…but if you're going to choreograph something, you either commit to it or take it out. And I know you well enough to know you're not taking it out."

Natalie muttered something about easy to say when you have two bendy ankles, but gave my aunt a good-natured grin. "Fair enough."

"Overall, I love it. You two really took this further than I expected and it's really beautiful." Aunt Drina said, and I tiredly reached out a hand to fist-bump Natalie. "But."

"Here it comes," Natalie said, and got a lip-zipping gesture from my aunt in reply.

"But, Grace."

I dropped my head to the ground. "Crap," I muttered into the grey marley.

"You're way too perfect. I could tell you were holding back on everything. You don't need to be that perfect. Perfect doesn't keep people watching." Aunt Drina knelt so she was closer to my back-flat-against-the-floor level. "I want to see some emotion from you."

"I tell her that after every practice," Natalie said, rolling to standing and heading to the side of the room to grab her water bottle.

"You were never like this when you were a student. I saw something on your face when you demo-ed for the last class. Is everything okay? Is there a reason why you won't let yourself connect emotionally to the music?"

I imitated Natalie's roll, putting some distance between myself and both of them. "You asked me to help out with your classes. That's what I signed up for. Not some psycho-therapy session."

Aunt Drina followed me, not taking her concerned eyes off me. "What happened to the girl who loved to dance, who opened herself up and let herself feel the music?"

I grabbed my phone, water bottle, and dance bag, and made my way to the exit. "She decided she wanted to have a good-paying job when she gets out of school, not tutus and debt." On that last word, I stepped out of the studio, saying over my shoulder. "See you Wednesday."

☑Chapter 39

"We were never that young, were we?" Cassie said out of the corner of her mouth as she stretched next to me, jutting her chin towards the group of eighth-graders gathered at the far end of the gym.

I looked over them and snorted in agreement. The girls and boys looked so incredibly unjaded as they bounced around anxiously, some of them trying to imitate us as we warmed up. "Never. I came onto this planet just like this."

"Your poor mom. That must have been one heck of a c-section," Cassie shot back, then rotated her leg into an impossible-looking stretch. Even though I knew it caused a lot of problems for her, and that Cassie needed to be extra careful when she stretched—among other things, the illogical part of me envied her contortionist-level hyper-flexibility. A low murmur rose up from the group watching us, things like, "woah," and "they're not expecting us to do that, right?" and I could hear Cassie suppress a giggle before twisting her leg behind her into a super-curved scorpion.

"Cute, Cassie. You're going to scare them away before they even try out."

"It'll weed out the weak and all the ones who only want to do it to become popular." She dropped out of her stretch and rotated her neck. "If I remember right, that's why you joined cheer, isn't it?"

"Younger me was smart beyond her years."

"Yes, she was, except for not believing this is a real sport." Cassie winked at me, "If I remember correctly."

I tried not to laugh. Younger me *had* been obnoxious, coming into tryouts and thinking that cheerleading would be a piece of cake after all my years of dance and acro. I learned I was wrong about two minutes into the routine they had taught us, and was lucky enough just to scrape by and get onto the JV squad. Cassie had been the first to give me a break and help me learn all the things she and most of the other girls had been doing since they were little.

"I have *no* idea what you're talking about."

Coach clapped her hands and we fell silent, dropping out of our stretches or giving our uniforms one last adjustment before stepping into hearing range. "Okay, everyone, welcome to the Pine Central cheer demo and workshop.

We're so excited to have some of you try out for our JV squad next year. I wanted to give you a chance to watch our Varsity squad, with some of our graduating seniors, go through one of their more complicated routines. After that, they'll help me lead you in a warmup and we're going to teach you a simple routine you will be expected to do in the tryouts in the fall. You're already one step ahead of anyone not here today, and I expect you not to waste your chance and really practice over the summer. As you're going to see, we expect only the best from our squads." She gestured towards us, but then her hand continued up to point to the row of championship pennants lining the gym wall, years' worth of first place cheer pennants sharing wall space with our football, field hockey, lacrosse, and field awards.

"Don't be afraid to ask questions, either," Cassie piped up, earning a smile from Coach. "We've been exactly where you are, too, so we get it, trust me. I almost threw up during my orientation." At my elbow in her side, she grinned even wider and pointed to the gym entrance. "The trash can is over there, by the way, if you need it."

Coach shook her head. "I don't know if I'm going to miss any of you," she said, just like she always did during orientation to whichever senior piped in with a silly aside during her opening speech. Tradition died hard at Pine Central. "Okay, demo. The routine you're about to watch got fourth place in States this year…"

"We were robbed!" One of our junior girls yelled out, and I joined in on the sounds of agreement and mumbles about judges always giving North Jersey schools preference.

"...and it's a great example of the kind of routines you'll see from our varsity squad here. Our JV squad had a similar routine this year, and, if you have limited time to devote to either squad, we also hold tryouts for our pep team, who cheer at some of our less attended sporting events and are still a good way to get involved." Coach was failing miserably at sounding excited about the pep team, but I could imagine how hard it was to convince anyone that cheering for the bowling team and at random badminton games was exciting. Her words drifted off, then she turned to get the sound system ready. "Have fun," she said, smiling our way before hitting the play button on our last time performing our routine.

We moved into position seconds before our music filled the air. Cassie looked over at me with a wide grin and did the cheesiest double thumbs up before we broke into our choreography. This wasn't competition, so, like when we did our routine at a home game, we let loose, jumping higher and moving through our routine with more bounce than our nerves usually allowed. I threw myself into an aerial and could hear the whoops of the rest of the squad as I stuck the landing, then added my own cheers as two of our guys crossed the floor in a matching series of back handsprings, each catching more air than the handspring before.

Even though I was tall, Coach had pegged me for a flyer Junior year because of my flexibility and ability to hit mid-air poses. She told the bases that they had to suck it up and deal with my extra weight compared to the five-foot-zero girls, and with each practice, we really learned to trust each other. I stepped into my teammates' hands and was up in the air, taking a second to find my balance before pulling my leg up into a scorpion. One, two, three seconds, and, as I dropped my leg, I was flying, the familiar rush of dropping through the air flooding through me just as I was caught and pushed back up again to a liberty position. It hit me hard that this was the last time I was going to do this and my heart got stuck in my throat just before my bases pushed up and I pulled my body into a twist as I dropped into their arms.

It was just an extracurricular activity, something to look good on my applications and boost my social standing, but, at that moment, I didn't want it to end. I choked on my words as the music paused and we started yelling out our Muskrat cheer. "We are P.C.!" got a few giggles from the eighth graders watching, breaking my mood. The first time I had to say that, I had dissolved into a laughing mess, taking the entire JV squad with me to the point where we couldn't finish our cheer. I snorted as we yelled, "We are P.C.!" again, then jumped back into the complicated choreography. The music ended and we held our final formation for a few more breaths before my teammates dropped me back down to the ground.

Even though we were out of breath and sweating, all of us were grinning. Cassie bumped me in the arm and said, "Admit it, you're going to miss this."

I opened my mouth to say no, but, at Cassie's skeptical smirk, I said, "Okay, fine, yes."

"Then, don't give it up."

"It's not that easy," I said.

She rolled her eyes. "Dating someone who keeps trying to make me debate whether or not the Enterprise could beat the Death Star isn't easy, either, but I do it. Anyway," she said, gesturing me to get off the mat, "time to inspire our future replacements."

"Right." I reluctantly followed, pasting on the cheeriest cheer smile I could. "And tell Christian that his question makes no sense because they aren't even in the same galaxy or time period. *Star Wars* is a 'long time ago in a galaxy far, far away' and Trek is in the future in our galaxy. They'd never meet."

"You are both a bunch of nerds."

"And you're lucky to know us." I widened my smile a little more and took my position for the easy routine Coach wanted us to demonstrate. "Come, join us. We're going to rule the world in a few years, anyway. Nerds always do."

☐Chapter 40

I flipped to the last page of my notebook, finished copying out my history notes for the third time, and, taking a last swig of my double-espresso iced coffee—heartburn be damned— triumphantly dropped my pen on my desk. "Done," I muttered, slamming my history notebook shut. Other than a last-minute review of the flashcards on my phone that I planned to do in the hallway right before the final, I was ready for anything my teacher could throw at me.

And I was officially done studying for finals, which gave me the rest of the week and the weekend to focus on finishing my engineering drawing and design project.

I expected the usual rush of accomplishment from

finishing a task—early, too—but, instead, a sense of emptiness filled me as I crossed "study for history final" off my planner to-do list. I...didn't have anything to do. Cheer was over, I couldn't stand hanging at the dance school while Aunt Drina freaked out over last minute recital details, Em and Feebs were at the Project Graduation planning meeting, and Alec was at the end-of-year party for the science team. I could have started working on my presentation for my design class, but I needed something to distract me for a few minutes.

I opened up Photogram and started scrolling through the pictures, laughing at a video of Em trying to shoot with Phoebe's bow and bulk liking all of my cousin's baby spam without reading any of her captions. All her captions were ninety percent "Six months, I can't believe how big she's gotten" or "Smartest baby in the world!" anyway. Right after liking a photo of a pouting Alec holding up a joke medal for "worst science jokes" at his party, I scrolled down and my heart dropped like lead in water. Leia smiled up at me from my screen, arms stretched wide and hugging her three sisters as they smushed together for a selfie at her oldest sister's college graduation. She almost never posted on Photogram and never posted selfies, but there she was, practically glowing and looking like she was on the verge of breaking into laughter. I'd seen that expression a million times before and it never grew old.

Item number one hundred that I'd forgotten to put on my to-do list: unfollow Leia on all social media platforms.

Em's voice popped into my head, defending her own

reasons for not unfollowing her ex-boyfriend this past fall after they broke up and, before I could start making excuses like that to myself, I opened up Leia's page. My finger hovered over the blue unfollow button and I shut my eyes as I hit it. The practical part of me wanted to snark at myself for being so dramatic about a social media account, but it couldn't push away the overwhelming feeling that I was slamming a door on the past.

So many things were coming to an end at the same time—cheer, dance, school, time with my friends, Leia, that I could barely catch my breath. I should have been excited. There were so many new, interesting things and places and people ahead of me, but at that moment, I was drowning in loss. My fingers instinctively went over to my design project, tracing every familiar curve in the prototype. Even this was going to end, a chance to have fun making beautiful things in favor of, well, calculations on oil flow and turbine design.

A part of me wondered if everyone went through this growing up moment, putting away the fun, childish things of the past in favor of success in the future. I shook my head, trying to shake away the weird reverie that had come over me—I just needed to remember what I was working towards—goals always made everything easier.

I reached for my notebook and wrote "Pros" across the top, not bothering to divide the page in two. I didn't need any cons at the moment. The list of pros flowed out of me out of sheer habit, everything from a secure salary and job marketability to world travel. But, all of it felt hollow.

Especially without Leia, that evil little voice came back at me, and I pushed it away again. "Relationships started after college have a higher chance of surviving," I added to my list, bolding and underlining the words. "I won't be the same person when I'm thirty that I am today, and people grow apart," I added with a flourish. All the same arguments I'd written before, all still statistically true, no matter how much I still hurt.

I opened up a search engine and typed in "highest paying majors," the familiar list popping up on screen. The list of highest earning careers changed positions a bit every time I'd searched, starting freshman year, but they were still basically the same ones. Steady, reliable, exactly what I needed if I wanted to succeed in the world. This time, Anesthesiologist was at the top, but, after a minute, I pushed that thought away—too many years of school and too much time spent in scrubs. Hospitals didn't bother me, exactly, but I didn't want to spend every waking hour in one. Plus, I liked making things and I didn't see that happening a lot in a job like that.

Engineering had always been the most practical, perfect fit for me. All my teachers said so, and I liked my physics and engineering classes at school. And even though it wasn't the most dynamic or sustainable industry, the world's over-reliance on petroleum would keep me employed and travelling probably up until I retired.

I put down my pen and stared at the list. Everything on it made sense, but the certainty and security behind them still didn't fade away the feeling that my world was turning into ghosts. Something that would soon be just memory and then not even that, just a past-me captured in things, like Em's favorite antiques.

A text from Phoebe popped up on my screen, punctuated with sparkle hearts, "*We were arguing over the best way to hand out tickets, and *someone* actually said, 'WWGD-What would Grace do?' You're apparently now Em's compass for common sense stuff* ☺" followed by another emoticon filled text from Em, "*Whatever Phoebe is texting you right now is a lie. But if you have any ideas on how to give out ride tickets without total chaos, I'll take them.*"

I opened up a new message window and group-texted them. "There's so many ways to do this. I'll make a list. Stop by after."

"*Grace-lists to the rescue!*" Em texted back, and I could picture her turning and sticking her tongue out at Phoebe in the middle of their meeting. "*Thanks.*"

I took another deep breath and tore my original list off my notepad, slipping it into my planner's "future plans" section. After I moved past this malaise, it would all make sense again.

☐

I sunk deeper into the soft leather of the armchair, legs slung over the arm of the chair and my planner propped on my knees. The clicks from Mom tapping away on her laptop were my background music as I wrote out list after list of ideas for Em and Phoebe. The room felt so cozy, the late afternoon light and the challenge of solving someone else's problems helping to push away the worries I had left behind in my bedroom.

"Grace, what do you think of an empanada food truck?" My mom asked, sliding her reading glasses down her nose as she turned to look at me.

I tilted my head confusedly. "For my graduation party?"

"No, for Trixie's wedding." Mom waved her own notepad in the air as she spoke, "They said they didn't want a sit-down and I know how trendy food trucks are with you kids, so I thought maybe they could get a few food trucks to cater. I'm not sure about the quality of those things, but at least the trucks would be a talking point. And everyone loves empanadas."

Her idea sounded right up Phoebe's sister's alley. Between that and talking the art gallery in Millbrook into allowing them to hold their reception there, Mom had totally captured Trixie's laid-back style. "Trix would love that. She also really likes the pita truck and the dumpling truck, in case you need a few others."

"There's a dumpling food truck?" She asked, skepticism lacing her voice. To be honest, I'd thought the same thing when I heard about it.

"Yup. Everyone says it's amazing. The chef trained at Nobu."

Mom's eyes widened in appreciation. "Nice. I'll add them to the list." She turned back to her laptop with a pleased hum. A few clicks and she turned to look at me again. "Can you help me with something Friday?"

I flipped from the notes pages to the actual calendar part of my planner. "You mean before or after helping with the Noelle's Song table at the farmer's market?"

"Actually, during. Since Trixie loves vintage so much, Ana Martins and I are going hunting at the farmers market for some vintage things to use at the shower and wedding." Mom flipped through one of her binders to show me the sketch of her hot chocolate bar, complete with pictures of different styles of vintage coffee and tea cups pasted in the top corner. "We thought we could put you and Phoebe to work finding some vintage tablecloths for the shower if you have a break or two from the table."

I pictured rows of tables with different tablecloths fluttering in the wind, like something out of a magazine. "That sounds really cool."

"I can't take credit. It was Phoebe's idea. And I thought since you're already going to be there, you can help. You have a good eye for these things."

"Sure." I watched her return to her work. She was in her element, deftly adding numbers to an excel spreadsheet and sketching out seating in her sketchbook for a silent minute before saying, "You know, Mom, you really should look into turning this into a business. Everyone asks you to help plan their parties, you might as well get paid for it."

Mom turned towards me, her brows drawing together in reproach. "I'm not going to charge your friend's sister.

I volunteered to help her plan this and I certainly will not suddenly start sending her bills."

"I don't mean starting with Trixie, just maybe think about making yourself an official party planner. You're really good at it." I remembered back to all my birthday parties and all of the family parties she'd planned. Every single one of them had been perfect and unique, better than any of the professionally planned parties I'd ever attended. And she made it all look so effortless, even though I knew how much organization and planning she had put into every one of them.

Mom's expression softened and she let out a small laugh. "I don't know. This is just a fun hobby for me. I haven't had a paying job in years, I wouldn't even know where to start. Plus, things change so much with your dad's job that I can't start something with all that uncertainty."

I knew a lame excuse when I heard one. "Dad's been in the same company for twenty years and they haven't moved him anywhere in that whole time. I think things are stable enough for you to try doing something for yourself. When you're good at something, you shouldn't just waste it."

"What should Mom try to do?" Dad's voice preceded him into the room. He paused in the doorway for a second, smiling at both of us before heading towards his own desk.

"Start her own party planning business," I said, grinning back at him. "She's amazing at it."

"I agree with Grace one hundred percent. You're amazing at everything you try, Inez." He dropped his laptop case on his desk and turned to face us again.

Mom twisted her lips up and crossed her arms in mock skepticism. "I don't hear either of you talking about how it's a high-risk business that's subject to market conditions or whatever other things you usually say. Or how I'd probably be better off looking for a corporate planner job with greater potential for advancement." Her imitation of Dad was spot on and I cringed a little bit when I realized I sometimes sort of sounded like that, too.

Dad laughed good-naturedly at the imitation. "Okay, that's fair. But I'm starting to learn that sometimes there's more to a job than if it makes business sense."

"Did Aunt Drina kidnap and brainwash you?" I asked, slowly closing my planner and scrunching my nose at him to let him know I was joking.

"Funny, Grace," Dad said, dryly. "And, no, she still has an awful business model, even if it makes her happy."

"You're in a really good mood today." Mom pointed out. She was right—Dad usually took a half hour to wind down from whatever work drama had preceded his drive home, but this time, he was practically bouncing in place.

He looked from her to me, clapped his hands together dramatically, and said, "They offered me a chance to head up European operations for the company. They've been very impressed with all the extra work I've put in these past few months to get the Taiwan project back on track and I ended up at the top of the short list for the position."

"Oh." Mom's voice was subdued. I watched as she forced her lips into a smile that didn't touch her eyes. "That's wonderful, David." It was almost like she'd just shut down, the excitement from earlier extinguished like someone had blown it out.

Dad either didn't seem to notice her lack of enthusiasm or was ignoring it. "It's a great opportunity. Another step on the ladder to CEO."

I didn't understand Mom's reaction, but stood up to give him a hug. "That's amazing, Dad."

He took the hug, but then held up his hand to let us know he wasn't done yet. "Tons of executive perks. Corner office, executive VP title, French and German lessons, oh, and relocating to Geneva and something along the lines of seventy-five percent travel."

That last sentence made my heart drop straight into my stomach. "Um, Geneva?"

"David—" Mom shared a long look with Dad and then, suddenly, her lips quirked up into a real grin and she started shaking her head. "You didn't take it."

Suddenly, all the fighting the past few weeks made sense. It wasn't just all of Dad's extra hours working on the Taiwan project. Dad must have known about this and Mom's relief meant she had known or suspected something.

"Nope." He dropped into the other armchair opposite me. "I didn't. I thanked them for considering me, but let them know I had too many important obligations here. A really smart person reminded me of that." He looked Mom in the eye and said, "They were outlining the salary and the entire position and I kept thinking how I should be happy.

But what you said about missing all the important things happening here just wouldn't get out of my head. Plus, I would have had to start right away, which probably would have meant missing Grace's graduation."

She perched herself on the arm of Dad's chair and started rubbing his shoulders. "It was the seventy-five percent travel that did it, wasn't it?"

"You know how much I hate flying." He said, picking up one of her hands and dropping a kiss onto her knuckles. "HR needs to learn how to better pitch a position, though. If they hadn't mentioned relocation or travel, I might have bit before realizing what they wanted."

I dropped back down into my own armchair and gave Dad my best owl impression. I hadn't expected any of that. "Seriously? Dad, you've been talking about positioning yourself for CEO my whole life."

He grinned at me, looking happier than I'd seen him in a long time. The faint wrinkles on his forehead and around his mouth even seemed to have relaxed a bit. "I know. I probably lost my chance, but life is way too short not to spend it with the people you love. I'm tired of fighting because of things that aren't important," he squeezed Mom's hand as he said that, "and I don't need to keep chasing after something better when I already have something amazing right here." He and Mom shared a long look, then he leaned forward to tap my arm. "I miss enough as it is. And, besides, I think Mom would kill me if I took her even further from New York. Geneva isn't exactly 'the boonies,' as you like to call this place, but I didn't want to risk it."

"That's not very practical, you know," Mom said, teasingly.

Dad started laughing. "Screw practical. Besides, that means I get to keep working with the team I just spent a long time getting back on track." He then joyfully slapped his hands on the armrests and said, "Now, let's talk about this potential business opportunity, Inez. It would be nice if at least one of us gets to be a CEO."

☐Chapter 41

"I look like a Disney fairy reject," I said, watching as a cloud of gold glitter floated to the stage's black marley floor with just the slightest tug at the skirt attached to the equally sparkly leotard. That glittery scourge was going to follow me for weeks, maybe even years. "A glittery, half-naked fairy reject. I'll never understand why something with this little fabric costs so much." Natalie was in a matching design, except her simple contemporary dress was crisscrossed with silver ribbons, in contrast to my glittery gold dress. In response to my comment, Natalie waved her arms to mimic wings, and wiggled so she could drop a ton of glitter on my feet. I was used to getting my recital costumes weeks before the recital, so only getting it on dress rehearsal night meant I didn't have time to adjust—and shake off all the extra glitter—before having to actually dance full-out in it.

Aunt Drina, who was standing second row center in the audience seats, waved her clipboard at us. "Stop it, you look great from here. I can't wait to see how the dresses move." She settled back into her seat and picked up her walkie-talkie, ready to talk to the people camped in the sound and lighting booth at the back of the middle school auditorium. "Just have fun, okay? Don't worry about technique at this point."

Natalie and I took our marks and, just before the stage lights came back on, she whispered, "Dance pretty."

My heart stopped for a minute—Leia had always used that phrase after I told her that saying 'good luck' was bad luck for dancers. Since she refused to say 'break a leg' or '*merde*' like everyone else, she'd settled on 'dance pretty.' I knew it wasn't unique, but...

Just like when I demoed the jetés for my class, it was too late to shake those thoughts out of my head. The music started and I threw myself into the first pencil turn, the familiar tune slipping under my skin and twisting my heart and lungs. The longing in the lyrics pulled through me, mixing with memories I couldn't brush away. The electric feeling of Leia's hand touching mine for the first time, the breathlessness of our first kiss... I dropped into a roll and, as I reached for Natalie's hand to let her pull me up into my tour jeté, let the chorus wash over me. Leia's expression at the patisserie rose up in my mind and I almost stopped, but, instead, I whirled into chaînés, as if the little turns could help me run away from every bottled-up feeling from the past few weeks that tore through me, helped along by the music.

I circled Natalie and her eyes met mine, the split-second sympathy in her expression breaking me even more. I wrapped my arms around my waist in my barrel leap, just like I'd done a million other times before, but that time, I was trying to just hold back all the emotions threatening to break free. I dropped to the floor, curved my back and arms into our final pose, and used every last bit of energy in me to keep back the tears tightening my throat and threatening to break free. The stage lights dropped and I collapsed out of the pose, out of breath but also emotionally exhausted, like someone had wrung all of the emotions out of my body.

"Here," Natalie whispered, holding out her hand to help me up. "You okay?"

I heaved in a deep breath and nodded, afraid that if I said anything, I'd break down.

All of the lights came back on again and Aunt Drina stood, a huge grin on her face. "That's exactly what I was looking for. It's nice to see you finally let go, Grace. Natalie, your stag leap was gorgeous, just really stretch your finger-tips on it, okay?" Without waiting for us to answer, she dropped her reading glasses back onto her nose and checked the schedule. "I've got to run and make sure the ballet classes are ready, but good job, both of you." She rushed out the stage side door, leaving me and Natalie still trying to catch our breaths center stage.

Natalie reached over to gently touch my shoulder and met my eyes again. "I know," she said, her voice soft, before pulling me into a hug. "It'll get better, I promise." With that, she walked into the back wings, leaving me alone on stage, trying to compose myself before my crowd of giggling students could reach me.

RISK-BENEFIT ANALYSIS: Me + Leia

	INITIAL ANALYSIS	EVIDENCE & UNCERTAINTIES	OUTCOME
RISKS	*Break-up *Break-up affecting grades *Meeting New People *Change	...	I can't eliminate these risks
HOW TO ELIMINATE/ LIMIT RISK	*Communication Plan *Stress test? *Preemptive breakup *regular meetups *Figure out how not to fight!?!? *Relationship checks	* Anecdotal evidence that disagreements are normal and healthy, so not fighting is not realistic *Preemptive breakup was a complete fail *2% of high school relationships survive	Statistics are against the efficacy of these measures
BENEFITS	Love is good! And I love Leia!	...	"Life is way too short not to spend it with the people you love"

SUMMARY & DECISION (IS THE BENEFIT GREATER THAN THE RISK?)

There are a lot of risks and the statistics are stacked against a relationship surviving through college. Emotional turmoil in freshman year can impact the entire college career, especially GPA and future Masters or hiring opportunities. We might change a lot and Leia will be around a lot of people who are probably as creative and smart and caring as she is, increasing chances of her meeting someone else.

Additional uncertainty: Does Leia even want to get back together with me after this? Is she with Abby now? I know she had a crush on her in middle school.

But 2% make it? That's not 0%. Leia is creative and smart and caring and she makes me a better person. And I love her and can't make that feeling go away.

Decision: I ~~think~~ KNOW the benefit outweighs the risk.

☐Chapter 42

"Between the glasses and that green thing you're drinking, you look like some sort of celebrity coming off a bender," Em said as soon as I got back to the Noelle's Song table. It was opening day of Lambertfield's first annual farmer's market, and she'd convinced us to help run the charity's fundraising table.

I pushed down my giant Diore sunglasses slightly and gave her my best celebrity-esque glare. "I couldn't sleep because I was too wound up last night from dress rehearsal, if you consider that 'partying.' I think I got about two hours of sleep." I'd tossed and turned all night, mixing dreams about Leia with nightmares about our breakup and my parents moving to Switzerland, and with all that, the bright sunlight was just too much to handle, especially after a long day of school.

"Dancers gone wild." Phoebe chimed in with a laugh. Her hair was pulled up in a high ponytail and she already had sweat marks on her blue Noelle's Song t-shirt. "At least you still manage to look glamorous when you're tired and melting, not like the rest of us mere mortals."

"Thanks, I try." I took a sip from my iced matcha latte and took my place behind the table. "Where's Kris? Since this is his aunt's charity, why isn't he here to help us out?" I said to Em.

Em shaded her eyes and looked out across the library parking lot, then shook her head and turned back towards me. "He went to go find us an umbrella or something so we don't cook to death. His cousin usually has extras at his farm stand."

"How many cousins does Kris *have?*" Phoebe asked. She was busying herself rearranging the basket of signed books and advanced copies she had scored from a few authors for the raffle. Taking a cue from her, I started fixing up the hockey raffle basket on my side of the table and slipped the basket of local cheeses into the cooler under the table.

Em snorted, checked her cell phone, then shrugged. "Your guess is as good as mine. I just assume he's related to the entire damn town except for you guys."

"Thank God for that," Alec said under his breath. I elbowed him and he shot me an 'am I right, though?' look.

"Well," I said, getting up and pulling my purse out from

under the table, "I'm going to go buy a bunch of water bottles. We're not going to be any help to Noelle's Song if anyone ends up in the hospital with heat exhaustion."

Em pointed in the direction of another stand. "You don't have to buy any. The mayor said we could grab some from the town info booth. Just tell them you're with me."

"Taking government kickbacks, huh, Em?" I teased, dropping my purse back onto the ground and shoving it under the table with my foot.

"Oh, shut up. Town hall is providing water for all the people fundraising or volunteering today."

Em looked annoyed, so I resisted another jab and headed in the direction she had pointed, instead. The fact that Em, formerly one of the most apolitical people I'd ever known, was now practically on first name basis with the mayor thanks to spending so much time at political stuff with her boyfriend, amused me to no end.

On the way back to our booth, arms full of water bottles, I could make out Em and Kris arguing while trying to attach a big beach umbrella to the table, Em's big hand gestures visible all the way back to the Springfield Farm CSA booth. Kris' infuriating smirk kept growing until he finally handed her the duct tape and gestured for her to take over. By the time I reached the table, the umbrella was up, Em was gloating, and Kris took a moment to drop a kiss on her temple before adding a few more layers of duct tape to the connection Em had jury-rigged to keep it from falling over.

Sometimes relationships that didn't look like they'd

even be possible on paper worked out perfectly.

"The redheaded lady on the town council says hi, Em. Nice to see you're making lots of friends in high places," I said jokingly as I dropped the bottles on the table. "I—" my next sentence died in my throat when I noticed Leia standing off to the side of the table, chatting with Phoebe. The umbrella had blocked them from my view. This town was too damn small.

Em faux-preened. "Town council is nothing. I've met our governor three times already."

"And insulted her at least once," Kris said.

"Hey, my taxes are paying her salary. If she makes a dumb-ass decision, I'm allowed to criticize her. I didn't sweat my butt off in Colonial stays for half the summer to have those taxes wasted on something that only helps a big corporation." Em shot back at him.

"Tax credits to incentivize corporations to come to our state…" Kris started to say.

Em cut him off. "Is corporate welfare. Economic fairy dust."

"Tell that to the economists who—" Kris said, and I tuned them out and turned my focus over to Phoebe and Leia.

Phoebe had Leia's phone in her hands and was typing something into it. "I know this range has a great JOAD— junior Olympic development—program, and it's not too far from Rowan if you like your lessons and want to continue with it. And if you want, I can lend you the bow I used when I first started," Phoebe looked at Leia critically and nodded, "I mean, the coaches should check, but I think it will be a good fit for you."

Leia took the phone and stared at the screen. "I can't believe I'm letting you talk me into trying to become Maeve." She quirked her lips up as she mentioned one of Phoebe's favorite book and movie characters.

I took a deep breath and stepped towards them. If Leia could do this, so could I. "You know Phoebe's an enabler," I said, forcing a light just-talking-with-friends-smile across my lips.

"Yes, I am," Phoebe said, making a cutesy anime-esque gesture with her free hand, some sort of cross between an okay sign and a victory sign. "And I think Leia would be an awesome archer. She really takes time to think through stuff and focus."

She did—Leia was the most level headed and thoughtful person I'd ever known. A feeling of pride rose in my chest, but was then squashed as Leia graced me with her super distant polite smile. I ignored the lump of ice that dropped into my lungs and said in an exaggeratedly fake conspiratorial tone, "Soon, she'll have you flying out to compete at Nationals with her. You'll be bow buddies. You'll never get out from her archery cult clutches."

Phoebe let out a giggle at that. "Who knows? Maybe Leia will be the next archery superstar."

"You both are being ridiculous," Leia finally said, breaking our chain of banter.

"If anyone can become a superstar, it would be Leia," I

said, adding, "You are amazing at succeeding at anything you decide to do."

"Says the girl who is going to take over the world someday," Leia shot back with a smile.

"We make a good pair, don't we?" The words slipped out of my mouth out of sheer habit, then, like a punch to my stomach, I remembered, and I added, weakly, "Not 'together pair,' but I mean…"

Leia stared at me for a second before her phone buzzed, breaking the silence that seemed to spring up around us. She glanced down at her phone. "Gotta go. Looks like Mom bought a chest from the Amish woodworkers and now needs help getting it into her car." She shoved her phone into her pocket, muttering, "How many chests do we need, anyway?" before turning her smile back on Phoebe, Em, and Kris. "See you later. Good luck fundraising."

I caught her purse strap as she turned to walk away. "Do you need help? You know I'm a pro at figuring out how to drop the seats in your mom's car."

Leia's smile was sad as she gently tugged the strap from my hands. "No. Thank you, we're fine." Without another word, she hurried down the row of booths.

Em leaned on the booth and looked at me with a curious expression. "Was that flirting between the two of you?"

Far down the aisle, I could see Leia meeting up with Abby, and I could practically hear her laugh carry our way. It stung, but I turned my attention back to Em and shook my head. I hesitated and took a moment to open up a bottle of water and take a sip before answering. "I need your advice."

Phoebe and Em shared a look. Phoebe put down the ribbon she'd been fussing with, crossed her arms, and put on a serious expression. "Okay, we're listening. What's up?"

"I think I screwed up," I said, slowly, as reality smacked me hard across the head.

A wide grin inched across Em's face. "I knew it. You miss Leia."

"Well, yes—"

Em cut me off, "And you want our help getting her back."

"Well, yes…"

Before Em could say anything else, Phoebe, who had been quietly studying me with a look that was a direct contrast to Em's smile reached out to put a hand on Em's arm to stay her and said, "Why did you change your mind?"

"I don't know." I was too blindsided to figure out a real response. "And… and…" I couldn't find the words to express what had been picking at me for the past few weeks.

"And Leia is worth the risk of failing and getting hurt later?" Phoebe asked, softly.

I closed my eyes and nodded, feeling the surety of that sentence deep in my bones. "Yes."

Em inched over and put an arm around my shoulders, giving me a one-armed hug. "Finally. We've been so worried about you. We'll help you fix this."

I wanted to hope, but I knew there were a few extra variables no one was acknowledging. "Assuming she's not so mad at me she never wants to see me again, or that she's not seeing Abby."

"She's not," Phoebe chimed in. "She told me so when we went to the cupcake shop the other day and I joked about setting her up with the Sailor Mars lookalike."

I froze mid pity party and did a doubletake at her comment. "You went to the cupcake shop with her?"

"Don't worry, Phoebe is a terrible matchmaker," Em said with another sympathetic squeeze to my shoulders. Out of the corner of my eye, I caught her mouthing "*What the hell?*" to Phoebe, who shrugged unconcernedly.

I held back a laugh. "It's not that. I thought you didn't like hanging out with Leia." Between cupcakes and talking archery with Leia, Phoebe had come a long way from barely tolerating her. It was like I didn't know my friends anymore. "Since when did you two get so close?"

"Since I realized she actually wasn't talking down to me all the time, it's just the way she talks." Phoebe said, unconcernedly. "And she helped me set up for the kids' knitting workshop at work so I bought her a cupcake as thanks. She's so sweet."

"And I majorly screwed things up with her," I said, returning us to the original point of our conversation.

"Right, but we can fix things," Em said. She untangled herself from me and slapped both palms resolutely on the table. "Step one, you need to apologize to her. Like, really apologize. You were the one who decided you didn't want to make this work, not her."

I cringed at that assessment but accepted it. "Fair criticism."

"I think we can still fix this." Em was in her element, and it showed in the way she practically glowed while the ideas flowed from her. "You two dated for two years and the only reason you broke up was, well, you being an idiot, so it's fixable. Now, what did you do in the past when you needed to apologize?"

I blinked at her in confusion. "Um, I said 'I'm sorry?'"

"No, I mean, what did you do? When Kris and I have really big fights and I know it's my fault, I usually get my mom to make this salted toffee I know he loves. And then I put up with letting him gloat about how he was right for about a day." Em smiled over at Kris, who was at the other side of the table talking with Alec, but, from the look of amusement on his face, had probably heard everything.

That sounded incredibly complicated and unnecessary, but I didn't say either of those things out loud. "We just said, 'I'm sorry' and moved on. We didn't need presents."

Em's eyes grew wide. "Not even flowers?"

"Nope."

"Huh. Weird. You're like my parents," Em said. She looked at me like I'd just announced I was an alien and added, "Wow."

"I don't think it would hurt this time, though," Phoebe said, breaking into the conversation with a smile and a shake of her head. "Presents don't fix things, but a little something would at least show that you put thought and effort into your apology. I think Leia deserves at least that much."

"Exactly," Em said, then turned back to me. "Think about it. What does she like?"

I thought of running into her at the patisserie and all the time we spent on that line over the years for free macarons and said, "Well, she likes macarons."

Em clapped her hands excitedly. "Perfect. Could the place write 'I'm sorry' on the macarons? That would be a nice touch."

"This is an apology, not a movie." Before Phoebe could chime in with a suggestion, I added, "Or a book."

"Fine," Em said, looking a little disappointed. If she had her way, I'd probably be doing a full production song and dance number on the front lawn of Haddontowne Academy. "Then get her favorite flavors, show up at her house, and, well, tell her you were absolutely wrong and that you'll never do it again."

"And that you're sorry, of course," Phoebe added.

"And I think—"

I stopped Em before she could continue. "I think I've got it."

Em ignored my waving hand and added, "Just be you, okay? Don't make a list and don't overthink it."

"Got it," I said, even though lists were definitely not off the table. "No overthinking."

Phoebe reached across the table to pat my hand. "It'll work out. Leia loves you."

The leaden feeling came back to my stomach. "I hope she still does."

☐Chapter 43

Haddontowne Academy's campus always looked exactly how I expected a cookie cutter private school campus to look. Manicured lawn, a pretentious carved stone sign, and ivy I could tell had been trained to grow artfully up the side of the main school building. The only thing they needed to be brochure-perfect were super preppy students in uniforms lounging on the front lawn. But the only people on the campus that Saturday morning were seniors heading out of the Senior Brunch. Based on Leia's car still sitting in her usual spot, I knew I hadn't missed her. I propped myself on top of one of the lions flanking the sign and waited.

I stared at the little box of special order rose and

pistachio macarons I'd picked up at the patisserie on my way over, feeling a little ridiculous about the whole thing. The girl at the counter had tied a sparkly red ribbon around the box and tucked a fresh flower from their display into the knot after hearing my story and handed it to me with a super sympathetic "good luck." I felt exactly like someone out of one of Em's favorite oldie teen movies, trying to clear up a misunderstanding with a boom box or flowers or singing a song on the school bleachers with the marching band playing background music. Those always had happy endings because they were perfectly scripted to end that way, while real life was much messier.

If I weren't more afraid of regretting not trying, I would have already been halfway home.

The school's heavy wooden doors opened and I hopped off the lion, scanning the groups of people in identical uniforms for a now-familiar red streak. As always, Leia stood out, gracefully picking her way down the stairs like a dancer, face tilting up to soak in the sunlight the minute she was on solid ground. Even in her ridiculous uniform shorts and blouse, she was pretty, pixie-like in every way possible.

I made my way against the flow, carefully holding the box of macarons to my chest so it couldn't get jostled or crushed by a stray elbow, and when I finally reached Leia, held it out with my most sincere expression. "I am so sorry. I was an idiot."

Leia seemed to take a minute to register it was me standing there and as her eyes travelled from my face to the box in my hands, I could see her facial features shift from surprise to dismay to resolutely polite. "Excuse me?"

"I screwed up. I thought breaking up would be the best for both of us, but I was wrong. I'm sorry. I want to try."

"So now you want to try? Like you just put me on pause and suddenly, because you've changed your mind, you want to unpause?"

"I…" I didn't really know how to respond to that, just tried to keep up. "Leia—"

She didn't stop, just kept walking towards her car at a pace that made me feel like I had to speed walk to keep up. "Sorry doesn't rewind the clock," she said, her words clipped and tight.

"I know. I was wrong. I forgot how much you meant to me. But I want to fix this. I love you and I want to fix us." When she didn't say anything, I pushed the box her way and said, "I screwed up."

Leia pushed past my arm. "You did. But people aren't equations. You can't just insert 'I'm sorry' plus pastries and get an unbroken relationship. In real life, people have real feelings and get hurt." She took a deep breath, then stopped just long enough to look me straight in the eyes. "You've always sucked at emotional stuff. Dating you is like dating a Vulcan with an ego who always thinks her way is the best way and I've always put up with it. I always had to put in the emotional effort. And you always had to be right because your stinking logic wouldn't let you believe otherwise. Always." Her lips slid into a straight line. "Maybe, just maybe, *I* don't want to get back together with *you*." With that, she turned away from me and headed straight for the parking lot before I could say another word.

I weighed my options, then followed her. If I could just catch her and explain everything, I could probably get her to forgive me. But, before I could make it even part of the way through the parking lot, a voice behind me broke my attention. "I'm sorry, but you're not a student here, which means I need you to leave the campus." An angry-looking teacher in a Haddontowne Academy cardigan passed me on the walkway and physically blocked my way towards the parking lot, looking a little bit like she was ready to kick me off campus, if necessary. I opened my mouth to argue, but she made a shushing sound and shook her head at me. "Students only past this point." Leia watched the whole thing from her car, a neutral look on her face before she slipped inside and started the car with a loud rattle.

"Fine," I said, stepping back and turning away before the teacher could make any more threats. This hadn't gone to plan. At all. I chucked the macarons in the nearest trashcan and pulled out my phone to text Em and Phoebe.

May

☐ Chapter 44

"We're late," Alec said for about the fifth time in the past four minutes.

I blew air through my lips and suppressed my instinct to hit the accelerator as I turned onto Phoebe's street.

"I know," I said, and also resisted the urge to say "stop reminding me." Instead, I scanned the street for an empty spot and parked in front of one of Phoebe's neighbors' houses. "The guests aren't supposed to show up for another three hours, so I think we're fine. It's just a bridal shower, so it shouldn't be too much work to set everything up."

"Since Em won't return my texts about this, I hope you're right." He opened his door and hopped out, adding,

"I try not to upset people who shoot pointy objects at things."

I hurried to catch up with him as he headed straight for the gate leading to Phoebe's backyard. "Phoebe never really gets mad."

"No, she just tries to cover up that she's about to burst into tears while saying 'it's okay' over and over again," he said as he opened the gate. Phoebe's parents had rented a big white tent that took up most of their backyard, and the space already looked pretty cute, from the tulle bunting hung around the perimeter of the tent to the big, white, wicker chair in the far corner, a lacy parasol hanging upside down over it. There was no way Trixie was going to miss it when she drove up to the house later.

"I swear, you and Em act like she's made out of porcelain sometimes," I said, trying to keep the eyeroll out of my tone. "She's not that fragile. She stands up for herself."

"Exactly. And with that, we're back to the fact that she's scarily good with a weapon."

I shook my head and laughed. I scanned the yard and tent for Phoebe or Em. "They're lucky the weather worked out. I can't imagine figuring out how to make this work in the rain."

Phoebe's dad, dressed in an apron and carrying an armful of grilling supplies, gave us a nod as he passed by on his way out to two long charcoal grills. "They're all inside. Head on into the kitchen," he said, nodding towards the back door. "Door's open."

Alec turned towards the back door and I followed him,

nearly tripping over the threshold as he stopped short with a muttered, "Oh, crap."

"What?" I tried to look around him, but he shifted so I couldn't see anything on the other side of the screen door.

"How about you stay out here and I'll go in and find out what they need from us?" Alec gestured towards one of the tables, which were all covered in the cute, faded vintage tablecloths Phoebe and I had picked up. "Like maybe the tablecloths need straightening or something."

I gently pushed him out of the way, then froze as I caught sight of the reason he'd stopped. Leia was in the kitchen, sliding mini quiches from a cookie sheet onto a pink china cake stand. Her smile wavered when she saw me, but she gamely nodded our way and went back to work.

I resisted the urge to bolt back to my car, swallowing back the nausea flooding through me.

"It's okay," I said to Alec, forcing a deep breath, "I can do this. If I want to fix things, I can't hide from her."

"Your choice," he said, under his breath, before opening the door and waving me through.

As soon as we got inside, Em saw us and flagged us over towards the kitchen island, where she was dropping little pigs in a blanket on the same plates as Leia. "Oh, Grace. Perfect. I need to go to the bathroom. Can you help Leia get the appetizers out of the oven and organized?" She looked over at Alec and added, "And Alec, you need to go help Phoebe and her mom carry out the wishing well and presents. We can't trust you around the appetizers."

"Excuse me, I'm perfectly trustworthy," Alec said in a faux-insulted tone. He looked as casually as he could over at me and added, "You'll back me up, right, Grace?"

"It's definitely true," Leia said in a teasing tone of voice. She looked up, but the minute her eyes met mine, she shifted them over to Em and exaggerated her nod. "I remember Em's birthday party and Appetizergate. We were lucky her mom had backups in the freezer."

"In my defense, my mom made the appetizers that time and she never makes her buffalo chicken potstickers for me," He said with a slight grumble. "Phoebe's family makes things with codfish and I don't eat that stuff. It's a totally safe situation."

"Still nope. Go, they're out in the garage." She reached out and grabbed Alec's sleeve to pull him with her out of the kitchen. "C'mon, they need your big, strong man arms to carry heavy stuff."

"I have no idea why I allow myself to be subjected to so much sexist stereotyping," he grumbled, but tossed me a worried look that I returned, before Em dragged him around the corner. The kitchen grew incredibly quiet, except for the rhythmic scrape of Leia's spatula against the baking sheets.

"Em's enjoying her unofficial managerial role way too much," I joked, breaking the silence as I joined her. "Watch out, she might try to take over the world, next."

Without looking up at me, Leia pointed at a baking sheet full of different appetizers on the stove, then to all the vintage and fancy trays laid out in a perfectly straight line on the counter in front of us.

"We have to evenly divide these up between all the platters." She said. There was no mention of the macarons, just a slightly flat tone in her voice as she focused on gently placing a quiche on a blue and white platter that I recognized from my parents' wedding china set.

"I figured," I said, my own voice tight. I kept looking towards the hallway, hoping Em would come back soon. The awkward cloud in the air was painful.

She didn't stop transferring the quiches, just waved at the second spatula Em had apparently been using. "Two of Trixie's college friends are working on planning out a few games and Amani, Trixie's friend—"

"I know who Amani is," I said, "I've been friends with Phoebe for a long time."

She ignored my comment. "Amani and Petur are keeping Trixie busy until the shower, and Mr. Martins is getting the grill ready. There's a lasagna in the fridge that's supposed to go into the oven in an hour and—"

This distant, super polite Leia was starting to get on my nerves. "What's with the Stepford wife act?"

She dropped the quiche pan with a giant clang, cursed, and crouched down to pick up the two quiches she'd let fall on the floor. "You can't blow up the world and then expect to be able to stick it back together again and have it exactly the same, Grace. I know we're doing this friend thing, but I don't need you throwing mixed signals my way every time we're in the same place. I can't take this rollercoaster," she said in a way that sounded calm and conversational but that carried a stressed note throughout. "And we don't want to ruin Trixie's shower arguing about things, do we?" she added in a half-whisper.

That last sentence was the last straw. "Of course I don't want to ruin *my* friend's party," I said, my voice sharper that it should have been, but I didn't care. "It looks like you have everything handled here, as always, and I don't need you telling me what I should or shouldn't do. I'm going to go clip the tablecloths so they don't fly away and *ruin* things." I dropped the half-full pan of codfish croquettes on the counter, grabbed a handful of tablecloth clips, and stalked outside.

I heard the slam of the screen door as Leia followed me outside. "What was that about?"

I whipped around and tried to keep my voice level as I said, "Why are you here? Phoebe's *my* friend." I knew I was being childish, but all the frustration from the past few weeks, everything I had to hold back so we could be "adults," and my own doubts about my decisions, all of it tumbled over me in a perfect convergence of factors and I had to dig my heels in to keep from walking away.

Her dark eyes narrowed and I recognized the spark of anger that ran across her features. I'd only seen it a few times, but I knew I'd hit on a dangerous nerve.

"Excuse me, but you don't have a monopoly on people or friendships. I can be friends with whomever I want. And

I'm not going to drop anyone just because you're acting like a spoiled child who never learned how to share." Angry Leia was like looking directly at a fire goddess, especially with her red-and-black hair blowing back in the wind. Beautiful and strong with a gaze that could burn you to a crisp on the spot. Except…I'd never really had that anger turned on me before.

Instead of making me back off, like most mortals did in the path of her wrath, it fueled my own fire. "We broke up. You have your own friends. Why don't you go spend time with them instead of monopolizing all my time with my friends, since you obviously don't want anything to do with me?"

"Em texted me last night and said Phoebe and her mom really needed my help setting up for the shower. Was I supposed to just ignore her?"

"Oh, Em texted you, did sh—" If my hands weren't full of clips, I would have facepalmed. Of course. Em struck again. "I'm going to kill her."

"Excuse me, is it so awful being around me that you'd rather I left one of *my* friends hangi—" she dropped off mid-word as her eyes widened and a little line of realization broke through her angry expression. "Oh. Em."

"We were played." I said, alternating between doing a little mental happy dance at catching something Leia had missed, and anger still bubbling up in me. "I'm going to kill her," I repeated. I dropped the tablecloth clips on the table and turned towards the house to go in and give that little meddling matchmaker a piece of my mind.

Leia reached out to catch my arm. "She was trying to help her friends," she said, "You can't be angry at her for that."

I tried to shrug my arm free, but she wouldn't let go. "Leia, back off."

"You're so angry right now at me and her and whatever the hell else, if you go in there, you're going to say something you might regret. And possibly ruin the shower."

I pulled harder, but for someone smaller than me, she had an iron grip, probably from pulling weeds and mulching things.

"Let me go."

"Breathe," she said in a supernaturally calm tone, "I know you're mad, but you need to breathe."

Force was an equal and opposite reaction. The more I pulled, the harder she pulled back. So, without giving her any warning, I stopped pulling and, instead, stepped towards her, catching her off guard. Without me providing an opposite force, Leia stumbled back and I instinctively reached out to catch her before she hit the tent pole, bringing us practically nose to nose.

"What if I don't want to?" I snapped back, my brain stopping and my breath—ironically—catching in my throat as her eyes met mine, fire meeting fire. We were so close, I could see each of her individual, long eyelashes as they fluttered towards her cheek.

Leia seemed to be short of breath, too, and, like something out of a sci-fi, we seemed to be frozen in time. She blinked, her eyes flickering down to my lips and them back up to catch my gaze again and said, so close that her breath whispered across my lips, "Then you'll suffocate to death." Her eyes scrunched the tiniest bit in amusement and any anger left in me dissipated with her next comment. "You know, science."

That broke the moment between us and I couldn't hold back the laughter that bubbled up like an overflowing beaker in Chem lab.

"You're ridiculous." I stepped back, letting go of her arm, and started self-consciously playing with the tulle hanging off the tentpole.

She still looked a little like I felt—somewhat dazed—but her lips had quirked up like she was internally laughing at me. "But, right." She stepped back a little awkwardly and pointed towards the back door. "I'm, um, going to go, though. I don't know if they need me anymore and it'll avoid more of…" she gestured between us, "awkward." She dropped her chin slightly and a lock of hair swung across her cheek.

I held back the powerful urge to push that strand behind her ear or to ask her to stay. "I'm still going to give Em a piece of my mind. She needs to stay out of this."

"Agreed." Leia took a deep breath and added, "I'll see you around," before heading back into the house.

As soon as she was inside, I dropped onto a chair to finally catch my breath. If I couldn't fix this soon, I was totally screwed.

☐ Chapter 45

"Thanks so much for coming," I said to Alec after dropping a dollar in the Marranos water ice window tip jar and heading over to one of the empty tables on their patio. After what had happened with Leia that morning, I desperately needed sugar therapy.

"You're welcome, but I'm surprised you didn't call Em and Feebs. They're better at this kind of stuff than I am."

"But at least I know I'm going to be safe from any kind of unsolicited relationship advice from you."

"True." He slipped into his seat and sat his milkshake on the table, taking a minute to wipe ice cream drips from the side of his cup before adding, with a conspiratorial grin,

"They *are* scarily dangerous when they conspire together."

"Yup." I tapped at the shell of chocolate on my frozen custard, then scooped a massive spoonful into my mouth, brain freeze and lactose intolerance be damned.

"You have to explain to me what the connection is with girls and ice cream after breakups."

I sucked air into my mouth, waiting for the initial pain from the brain freeze to wear off, before tapping at my bowl again with my spoon.

"Technically, this is frozen custard, which has a gloriously higher fat content than ice cream and therefore is much tastier and more comforting," I said, then pointed at him. "And don't pretend you didn't pull the same thing with a few bags of potato chips after you broke up with what's-her-face freshman year."

Alec feigned being hurt, slapping his hand against his chest as if I had wounded him. "Ouch, direct hit. You know, we're here to talk about you, not me."

"Sorry," I said, unable to hide the amusement I knew was pulling at my lips and crinkling my eyes. "But you brought up high-fat-content comfort foods."

"True." We sat in companionable silence for a few minutes, me picking at my custard and him poking at his milkshake to melt it down to the consistency he liked, before Alec cleared his throat. "I know you don't want relationship advice, but I'm going to give you some, anyway, because I hate seeing you miserable."

I put down my spoon and folded my arms, curious to

hear what Alec would come up with, considering his low track record of even getting to the point of asking someone out.

"Shoot."

"You know, your problem is," he said casually while pulling his straw out of the milkshake and waving it around like a conductor's baton, "is that you like being right. And lots of times, you are, but sometimes you're so focused on lists and facts and trying to be right and perfect that you miss the human part of it." He shrugged and added, "I suck at that, too, because humans really don't make any sense, especially girls."

I blinked at him for a second, taking in his admittedly accurate description of me, before snapping out of it and saying, "Sexist much?"

He ignored me and continued. "Thing is, we're used to facts being enough, but people are weird. They don't want to *hear* you're sorry, they want to see and believe it. At least, that's what my mom and Em want. I was kind of clueless about that, too, until Em's mom clued me in on that ages ago. I mean, unless you did something truly heinous, which you didn't, you were just really, well, Grace."

"I tried with the macarons and she didn't even want to talk."

Alec reached over and stole a piece of chocolate off my custard. "Because that was still you trying to say you were sorry. The macarons were an accessory to the words."

"Good point. But how am I supposed to show I'm sorry when she doesn't even want to talk?"

"I don't know. Everyone I know kind of wants to see me suffer just a little bit. Mom always listens more when I volunteer to do something I know she knows I hate, like the time I laid new insulation in the attic over the garage." He took another sip of his milkshake. "It's basically you showing her that you're willing to put in the hard work to fix things. Action beats words any time."

"Huh." I let his words sink in for a minute. "That... makes sense." What Leia had said about putting in the effort came back at me and I cringed reflexively.

"Anyway, now that I've dropped my Obi-Wan Kenobi-like knowledge on you, let's set the record straight. I did *not* eat that many chips after breaking up with Nina."

"Sure. Prince Edward Island called, your binge cleared out all their potatoes. They might not have enough storm-chips to last this winter."

He narrowed his eyes at me. "I'm not even going to pretend I got that reference."

"It's not really a reference, they're just known for their potatoes. You heard Phoebe when she went through her whole 'I need to move to Prince Edward Island because one of my favorite books is set there' info-dump last year."

Alec stuck up his nose in mock offense. "I didn't eat that many chips because I put all my energy into finishing the elven princess arc in my video game. I poured all of my emotions into my art so the world could see and benefit from my pain." He slapped his hand against his chest and pushed his lip out in an exaggerated pout.

He was being melodramatic, but that one sentence about pouring his emotions into his art struck a chord and, swirling it with his other bits of advice, I could feel a plan for a path forward forming. "You're a genius, you know?"

"Thanks. If any of this works, though, let Em and Phoebe think their advice is what saved everything. It'll make everyone happy. And if it doesn't work, the next frozen custard is on me."

"Deal."

☐Chapter 46

I stared at the converted Victorian manor that was Lambertfield's library and took a deep breath before heading down the paved path around the building. Alec's and Leia's words had stuck with me, and, as hard as it was to admit to myself, they were right—Leia had always taken the initiative in everything. She'd been the one who broke the ice between us, initiated our first kiss, and she had always gone to all of my activities from dance to cheer, while I never had *really* taken the time for her things. It was time to change that.

I stopped in front of the gate to the library's children's garden and peered over the fence. Leia was kneeling down next to one of the tomato plants, seemingly demonstrating whatever she was doing to a little boy, who nodded and then tried imitating her with the plant in front of him. Leia had been volunteering at the library's organic garden and cooking workshop since her best friend, Emily, had set it up freshman year and loved it. She was a natural with kids, and she said there was nothing more rewarding than seeing a kid light up when they ate something they'd grown from scratch and cooked for themselves. She had tried to get me to volunteer with her, but since I knew nothing about kids, gardening, or cooking, I always bowed out, figuring I'd just get in the way. I didn't realize it then, but it must have really bothered her—I remembered commenting on the little frowns she'd toss my way every time I declined, but she would always brush it off with, "It's okay. Next time."

My first thought had been to donate supplies to the garden, but Em and Phoebe killed that idea with a quick, "Don't try to buy yourself out of this," from Phoebe and "Kris tries to do it all the time. I get that you rich kids think it works, but it doesn't. It really feels ingenuine," from Em. Which was why I found myself, early on a Saturday morning, dressed in my grubbiest jeans and t-shirt and opening the garden gate.

As I stepped inside the garden, Leia looked up, brows drawn together and her lips turning down into a frown. "What are you doing here?" She asked, her tone flat. She pushed her hair out of her eyes with the back of her gloved hand, leaving a smudge of dirt on her forehead, and I resisted the urge to reach out and wipe it off.

On the other side of the garden, Emily, who had been

helping a kid pick string beans stood to her full height and stared me down, dark eyebrows drawn together tightly, like she was waiting for a signal from Leia to kick me out just like the teacher had.

I clasped my hands behind my back, straightened up, and carefully recited the sentences I'd worked on all night. "Okay," I practically inhaled the word, then continued, "I messed up, bad, and you have *every* right to tell me to leave, but I wanted to do something for you that's more than saying 'I'm sorry,' if that's okay." I watched her face for some change, then added, voice low, "I promise I'll stay out of your way."

Leia stared at me for a solid thirty seconds, her expression unreadable, but finally nodded. "Fine. We need extra hands to lay down manure in the back." Her eyes met mine and she dropped them before pointing to the other side of the garden. "The pile is there already. Make sure you put it down loosely. I hope you brought gloves."

"Yup," I pulled my new gardening gloves out of my back pocket and waved them with a cheesy grin, but she had already turned her back on me and was back to pointing out plant anatomy to the little boy. "Okay," I said, under my breath, before heading over to the fertilizer.

After only a half hour, my back and hands hurt, I was sweating from the sun beating down on us, was cursing the fact that I forgot a hat, and the stinking pile of manure was everywhere. But it wasn't as awful as I'd expected, partly because I had a front row view of Leia in action with the kids. She moved deftly from kid to kid, practically glowing as she gave advice and helped out as they worked on the garden. I hadn't seen her smile that widely in forever, and it made my heart hurt a little.

The youth services librarian walked back out into the garden from the library back door and straight to me, catching me in the middle of watching Leia. "I'm not good at gardening, but it looks like you're doing a pretty good job."

I quickly looked up at her, my cheeks growing warm at getting caught staring. "Thanks."

The librarian pushed her sunglasses up onto the top of her head, the hairs from her short, dark pixie cut sticking up a little, and stared me down with dark eyes. "Leia is a huge asset to this program. She's always ready to help out and is so great with the kids. Everyone loves her here. She's one of the best people I've met."

Somehow, it felt like she was testing my response, and I weighed a few answers before saying, honestly, "Me, too."

The librarian nodded, seeming to approve of my answer. "So, what do you think of gardening? It's a little late but the kids wanted to put in a pumpkin patch for Halloween and that plus some compost will make a great bed for the pumpkins."

"It stinks, but it's not as crappy as I thought," I said to her with a half-smile.

"Pun intended, I assume?"

I smiled up at her, glad we both could find some amusement in my predicament. "Yup."

She snorted, then she patted me on my shoulder before moving on to talk with Leia.

Turning back to my work, I scooped up another shovelful of manure and, trying hard not to breathe too deeply, shook it onto the still-empty part of the patch.

☑Chapter 47

"I left a box of macarons in the library kitchen, a box on her porch swing, and I talked one of her classmates into giving her a box after school yesterday. You don't think it's too much, is it?" I picked at my chicken salad and looked across the table at Phoebe and Em, feeling my brows draw together the smallest bit. Ever since the parking lot incident, I'd been doubting this entire plan.

Em shook her head, finished swallowing her bite of sandwich, and said, "This is possibly the most adorable thing I've ever heard."

My brows felt pressed together so tight that I was sure I was going to get worry lines etched into my forehead at eighteen. "She's not going to think it's stalker-y, though, right?"

"Well, it kinda is if you really think about it, but I happen to have intel that she's actually okay with the macarons," Em said. She waved her hand unconcernedly. "Keep up the adorable."

"By intel, Em means I texted Leia about it the other day right after you dropped off the first box and asked if she were okay with it," Phoebe added with a wry half-smile. "I thought she had a right to ask you to stop if she wanted to and this way she wouldn't have to talk directly to you."

"And?" I asked, bracing myself for the worst.

Phoebe scooped up a carrot-full of hummus before answering, totally oblivious to my stress. "She's still mad at you—"

Em scrunched her nose. "That girl can really hold a grudge."

"—but she thinks it's cute." Phoebe finished, then added, "I think it's because you're also putting effort into the garden and everything else."

"Which is really great. By the way, do you want to make me mad, too? Since you've started doing this, I've been craving macarons, too." Em poked Kris in the arm, pulling him away from a debate he and Alec were having over whether or not strawberry milk should be banned from school menus. "You should take notes."

I ignored Em's joke and went back to my lunch. "So. Not creepy?" I asked Phoebe.

"Nope," she answered. "Cute. Really cute. Those were her exact words. Right after 'Don't tell Grace, but…' I have the texts if you want to see them."

"No, I believe you." I let out a breath of relief. "Okay, good."

"It'll be okay," Phoebe said, softly, then gave me a little smile before popping another carrot into her mouth.

I took a deep breath, feeling my shoulders and lungs relax for the first time in a while. "I think you might be right."

☐Chapter 48

"The garden really looks nice," I said as I walked into the mudroom leading from the garden to the library's small teaching kitchen. The room still had its original beadboard walls and the people who had restored the kitchen for use as a teaching kitchen had added a deep slop sink near the door, where Leia was scrubbing her hands.

Leia gave her hands one last rinse under the tap before turning it off and grabbing a paper towel. "Thank you. The kids have been working hard on it since March."

"It shows." As soon as she moved away from the sink, I took her place there, turning on the water and grabbing the bar of really harsh-looking soap and the nail brush out of the soap dish.

"I'm glad you came again," she said, softly, as she started to make her way out to the kitchen. "Emily said you were here the other day, too, when I wasn't. I appreciate it."

Before Leia could leave, though, I pulled up all of my courage and said, "Hey, um, I have a question for you." She didn't say anything, but she didn't leave, either, just stood at the door to the kitchen, so I took it as a good sign and barreled on, fear twisting my throat so tight I practically had to push the words out. "Um. Well, you know how I've been helping out my aunt, right? I have to do a dance, too, in the recital on Saturday—tomorrow night, and I was wondering if maybe you wanted to come see it and maybe go for coffee afterwards?" I let the words hang in the air for a second before quickly adding, "You don't have to pay for tickets since I'm teaching and I wouldn't expect you to, anyway."

Her hands twisted around the paper towel for a moment before she softly said, "I don't know."

I took a shaky deep breath and nodded. "Okay. You don't have to let me know. The ticket booth will let you in if you want. And, um, I was wondering if it would be okay with you to keep helping out here?"

Leia leaned against the doorway, crossing her arms and shaking her head. "I told you. I'm not an equation. You can't just insert hours volunteering here and just expect me to be okay with you."

"I know. I still want to help." Those words surprised even me, but if putting up with manure and compost and sunburn meant spending more time with her, I would. "But only if you're okay with it. Otherwise, I'll stop."

She finally looked up at me, studying my face again with a serious gaze before unfolding her arms and turning away from me to grab an apron off the hook next to the door. "Okay," she said softly, before walking away.

☐ Chapter 49

"Customization, fit, individuality," I said aloud as I added those bullet points to my presentation. I hadn't needed Mom's essential oil diffuser this morning because the energy of finally finishing the project had given me enough of an adrenaline boost to keep awake. It was satisfying to lay out everything and see how it had flowed from concept to design. It had taken a lot more work than I'd expected and was way more evolved and complicated than the original idea I'd had when I first pitched the project, but that was okay—hearing patients who actually would use my design say they'd want to use it was magical. I'd learned so much from this swirly, sintered metal glove.

The project was coming to an end, but, for once, I was *excited*. I slipped my prototype onto my hand and smiled as it reflected the light from the desk lamp like a piece of incredibly complex art or jewelry. I didn't know how Mr. Newton was going to react, but I was proud of what I made. It was a not-exactly-perfect-but-close blend of practicality and style—a little bit like me. If this idea was feasible, maybe more things were possible, and part of me wanted to explore those possibilities. Maybe, someday, I'd actually make it real, and not just a prototype. Maybe, someday, it would help make a difference in someone's life.

Maybe I'd make more beautiful things that improved the quality of life for people who needed it, in a way that fit their lives.

I could also blame the energy running through me on recital day nerves—my body was practically vibrating, but everything was ready. My makeup case and recital dress bag were by the front door and Natalie and I had already done a final run-through last night. Like Aunt Drina always told us, recital day was too late to worry, it was now time to let go and enjoy the results of all our hard work. Like my engineering design class—there really wasn't anything more I could do for the project at this point beyond tiny tweaks to the presentation and polishing my prototype.

Like whatever was going to happen with Leia.

Whatever happened, I was ready to keep moving forward.

☑

A flash of red and orange caught the corner of my eye as I passed the dining room, and like a good PCHS Muskrat, I couldn't help but stop and check out what was going on. Mom had covered the table in piles of red and orange cardstock and was setting up rows of mini mason jars down the center of the table. It looked just like school spirit had vomited onto a crafty production line. She'd piled her hair on top of her head in a messy bun and was sticking her tongue out of the corner of her mouth as she concentrated on cutting the cardstock with her paper cutter. I hadn't seen her this focused since she was doing the Martins/Steffanson wedding layout.

I leaned against the doorway and smiled, watching for a second before saying, "Need help?"

Mom looked up from her paper cutter with a surprised look. "You don't have homework?"

"It's a Saturday morning at the end of the school year."

She smiled at me. "That hasn't stopped you from finding things to do before."

I pulled away from the doorway and conceded her comment. "And recital nerves for tonight are making me useless, anyway."

"Okay, that makes more sense." Mom wiped a stray hair out of her face as a nostalgic look came over her features. "You always had the worst nerves whenever you had to go up on stage. You know, when you were little, you'd get so nervous, you wouldn't want to eat. I even used to slip dry milk powder into your milk to get some more protein and calories into you."

That didn't even sound legal. "That's a thing?"

"At least according to your pediatrician, it was."

"Wow. Okay."

"Anyway, yes, I'd love your help if you're willing to make favors for your own graduation party." Mom gestured for me to take a seat.

"I didn't know people gave out graduation party favors, but sure." I pulled out the seat next to her and stared at her glue gun and stapler setup.

"They're a must-have when I'm planning the party. Plus, I think these will make great table decorations." Mom deftly rolled one strip of red paper into a loop, glued it onto a square of matching cardstock, and, after a few seconds, took the tiny cardstock graduation cap and slid it on top of one of the little mason jars. "Aren't they cute? I'm filling them with red and orange candy. I also found red, white, and orange tinsel piks that look like your pom-poms when I stick them in vases, so we're going with these jars and 'pom-pom' centerpieces instead of flowers."

I smiled at how she lit up when describing her plans. "Really cute. You should think about making a job out of this."

Mom attached a tiny gold tassel to one of the hats and held it up for me to see. "Maybe I will," she said, giving me a small wink. "But maybe after Trixie's wedding, because we still don't know if that's going to be a success."

"You managed to get Trixie and her mom to agree to

the same things even though they're exact opposites. Even Phoebe is calling you a miracle worker. I think it will go fine."

"I hope so." She handed me a pile of cardstock strips and a stapler. "Make circles out of these, please. I need about fifty tubes."

I pulled the first strip off the top of the pile and looped it on itself, trying my hardest to match the one Mom had just made. After a few loops where my only soundtrack was the swish of the paper cutter as she cut endless little squares, I took a deep breath.

"Mom, do you ever regret picking Dad and leaving NYC? You could have been this amazing events planner there doing movie premieres and stuff, or maybe doing something in fashion, instead of being stuck here."

Mom froze halfway through cutting. "That's a really loaded question for a Saturday morning."

"You wanted your Gilmore Girls moment and now you're complaining about my timing?"

She studied my face for a second, then cracked a smile. "Fine. Should I get us some ice cream or coffee or something?"

I raised my eyebrows and wagged my finger. "No food. Recital nerves, remember?"

Mom raised her own eyebrows. "Don't make me sneak milk powder into your smoothie."

"Also, lactose intolerant, remember? Which makes me wonder if your milk powder trick is the reason why I'm like this now."

She let out a short laugh. "I'll blend a lactase tablet in

there. You'll never notice."

This was a side of Mom I didn't get to see too much, and it was surprisingly fun. I tilted my head at her and cracked a grin.

"You're really taking that show's witty banter thing seriously, aren't you?" I always found it funny that Mom was more like the brunch-at-the-Plaza grandparents in her favorite show but kept wanting our relationship to be like the diner-and-takeout free-spirited mom and daughter.

"I got a daughter who was as smart as Rory but who never bothered to do the bonding thing until now. Don't kill my fantasy," she said, turning her nose up at me.

"Fine, we'll bond with banter."

"Good. To answer your question, I want to make it very clear in case I haven't been already these past few weeks—I love your father and you very much and I'd never wish for a different life for myself."

"But what about the city? I know you had so many plans. Do you ever wonder what your life would have been like if you hadn't left?"

"No." She put down the piece of paper she was holding and turned to look me straight in the eye. "Plans change, and it's okay. I wouldn't trade you or your dad for the best apartment in the Upper West Side. You're both worth putting up with living in the suburbs." She studied my face for a minute, then said, "So, what brought on this heart-to-heart?"

I twisted the paper in my hands. "I asked Leia to come to the recital tonight."

"Oh?"

"She didn't say yes or no."

Mom let out a soft "oh." "And you wonder if she's going to be your big regret if she decides not to come, even though you think being with her might throw off your plans?"

I looked down at my hands. "I don't know how to fix this. We were both fighting, but I was the one who decided we should break up. It made so much sense on paper. I'm trying to fix it, but now—" I shook my head and worried at my lip. "I think I messed up one of the best things in my life."

Mom reached over and wrapped her arms around me in a soft, lilac-scented hug. "Oh, my ridiculously practical girl." She smoothed my hair in the same comforting way she had when I was little. "It's not easy not being in control of everything, is it?" She ignored my snort, and added, "I wish I could fix this for you, but no matter what happens, you're going to be okay. You can't control everything or everyone. But life will hold wonderful surprises for you, regardless, I promise."

"That would have been really comforting if you hadn't called me 'ridiculously practical,'" I said, my voice a little wavery. Only the tiniest bit, because I was way too old to cry on my mom's shoulder.

"I'm a native New Yorker. We get to the point." She then gave me one last pat on the head before straightening up and pointing at the table. "Now, let's get these favors done. I'm not wasting any more of this free labor you offered."

"Yes, ma'am." I grabbed the stapler and started making loops again. Glancing at Mom out of the corner of my eye, I let out a soft, "Thanks."

"You're welcome," she responded, just as softly. "And I hope Leia shows up tonight."

"Me, too."

☑Chapter 50

Backstage was complete and total chaos. As the junior jazz class came offstage, I made shushing gestures at them before waving the senior jazz class onstage though the layers of curtains in the wings. Hairpins and pieces of costume flew through the air as the junior girls started half-changing while rushing to the classroom we'd designated as a changing room. I pushed the pins to the side with my feet as the seniors' music came on and I started swinging my legs to keep my hips warm. Natalie and I were up next, right before the finale number.

I patted my super-slicked-back low ponytail to check for last-minute flyaways, and rechecked to make sure the rhinestones one of the adult students had glued around my eyes hadn't fallen off, then ran my tongue over my teeth one more time to make sure I didn't have lipstick on them.

Even though the theater had told us not to, one of the ballet dancers had snuck rosin backstage and had set up a shoebox lid full of it in the wings. I rubbed my feet in the powder left behind after the ballet dancers had crushed the rosin to dust with their pointe shoes, all muttering about the slippery stage floor as they came on and off throughout the ballet earlier. Its sweet, piney smell brought me back to recitals past and rubbing rosin onto my heels and hands to keep my shoes in place or to keep from slipping in acro routines.

My phone buzzed in the pocket of my warmup pants and I pulled it out, tilting my screen to make sure it didn't shine onto the stage. "*Leia is here,*" Em's text read, super bright, and my nerves ratcheted up threefold.

"Put away the phone, Grace," a whisper came over my shoulder and I turned to frown at Natalie. "You know the rules: no phones backstage," she added with a grin, before plucking it out of my hands and dropping it onto one of the sandbags.

"Leia came," I whispered back at her, half in explanation, half-helplessly.

The music from the senior's number came to an end and Natalie grabbed my shoulders, looked straight into my eyes, and said, "You're going to wow her. We're going to be great. Just breathe and dance," before stepping between the last set of curtains and out onto the dark stage.

Taking her advice, I took a deep breath and stripped off my warmup pants and legwarmers before following her, padding out as quietly as possible onto the dark stage and trying my hardest not to squint out into the audience to find Leia. Still, as the lights came up, I finally caught sight of her sitting in an aisle seat next to Em and Phoebe, whose bright teal top was impossible to miss. My brain froze and it felt like every step in our dance flew out of my head in that moment. I was going to fail, be like one of the baby ballerinas who forgot their steps and stood stock-still on stage the entire number, and Leia was going to see, and Aunt Drina was going to be disappointed. But then, my body and weeks' worth of practice took over as the music washed over me and I let go, feeling everything melt from stiff to supple. It was the dress rehearsal all over again, except this time Leia was there and I bled my heart out in sweat and leaps that were higher than I'd ever leaped and turns that left me dizzy with their energy. Tears and sweat mingled on my face until I couldn't tell which was which. Natalie anchored me and spun around me and we helped each other up, two pieces in this musical puzzle until the music stopped and so did we, out of breath, staring into the audience as they applauded, some standing.

Leia stood, too, and, just as the lights went down, I managed to catch her eye for a split second before she turned and started hurrying her way out of the auditorium while everyone else sat back down for the next number. Throwing caution to the wind, I took another shuddering, burning breath and ran, leaping off the stage—thankfully, the middle school didn't have an orchestra pit—and followed her down the center aisle, ignoring all of the stares. I caught the lobby door before it swung shut and, just as Leia started pushing through the double doors to the outside, called out breathlessly, "Thank you. Thank you for coming."

Leia paused, her back straightening in familiar surprise, before she turned to look back at me with a hint of a smile on her face. "Your aunt is going to kill you."

I sucked in some more air, my lungs protesting at the abuse, and choked out. "Thanking you was more important." Another breath, and I added, "*You're* more important." One more breath, "Than anyone."

She ducked her head and started pushing through the door again, but just before she left, she looked up through her eyelashes at me in a way that nearly stopped my heart and said, so softly, "You were beautiful up there." And then she was gone, leaving me alone to catch my breath in the deserted lobby before Em and Phoebe came out to both wordlessly wrap me in a giant bear hug, smushing bouquets into my back.

A few minutes later, Natalie joined us, laughing as she added her sweaty body to the cuddle pile, then she reached over and flicked my hairsprayed-solid ponytail. "I told you we were going to be great, dummy. I'm glad you actually listened for once."

I just stuck my tongue out at her and squished all three of them even harder, holding back the urge to laugh in relief.

June

☐ Chapter 51

After sitting through over ten final presentations, my classmates' eyes had already started glazing over, like mine had been just before Mr. Newton called me up to give my own presentation. Since I knew most of them cared as much about my design as I had about theirs—which was pretty much not at all, I focused my attention on my teacher, who had seated himself in the front row.

I had already walked through most of my slides on the what and how of my design, and the prototype was making its round around the classroom. Just when I was sure Mr. Newton was about to pipe in with a question about financials, I pulled up a slide I'd made specifically because of his last digs at my projects.

"I also took some time to research price points of similar products on the market, as well as determining the potential market size based on knowledge of the target patient population. As you can see from this slide, utilizing the manufacturing methods I discussed in the earlier slide for mass production, we have favorable financials coming in already at year one."

"That's good," Mr. Newton said, half-frowning, "but aren't you concerned that your market size is a bit optimistic?"

"Not really. Not only do I have solid numbers behind these projections, but I decided to perform an end user design evaluation with my prototype and, while it's a small population size, the physical therapists I spoke to thought it was a good representative sample. It's a niche market, but people want it." I pulled up as many terms that Oliver had taught me as I could, trying to sound as professional as possible. "And what I also learned from this evaluation was that this is something missing from the market. There are a lot of functional stroke rehabilitation gloves out there that work perfectly well, or that patients can adapt to, but function and beautiful design are not mutually exclusive and shouldn't be. Good design that matches the user's style can give the user options, allowing them to take claim over the device. I had users comment that something like this would allow them to use their gloves in public without feeling like they're standing out too much, at least not as a patient. By designing something tailored to encompass the needs of all users, especially those with smaller hands, I did the opposite of many designers for, well, many products on the market, who tend to design using morphometric data typically collected from males or some squished generic numbers. This isn't a new concept, especially as we move towards a society that really values customization, fit, and individuality." I flipped to the next slide and nodded to Nick, who had kept the glove on his desk until that moment, finally passing it to Mr. Newton. "Why should we believe someone might want a customized cell phone cover but not a customized long-term medical accessory?"

My teacher played with the glove for a minute, taking a few notes in his notebook before looking back up at me with an unreadable expression.

"Good point. Grace, I'm really proud of your work. Your prototype, design, analyses, and test plan are, honestly, above and beyond what I expected for this project. And while I disagree with you on the viability of this from the financial side because, you're right, this is a really niche product, I appreciate that you did the legwork for your argument." He took his red pen and wrote a letter on the top of the report I'd turned in earlier in the week and handed it to me. "Good job."

"Thanks." I held back the urge to argue with him again on the financial part—especially since he wasn't really supposed to be grading us on that—and picked up my glove from his desk. On my way back to my desk, I glanced down at my report, letting out a little sigh of relief at the bold "A" he'd scribbled next to my name. It wasn't like this final grade really mattered much on the grand scale, especially since I wasn't in the running for valedictorian, but it would have been embarrassing to get a bad grade in the class that was supposed to prepare me for my future major. I took my seat and patted my prototype gently, tracing my fingers over its curves. It was going to be hard not to take it through some more iterations and testing to a final design, but I was glad I hadn't stopped at a plastic printed prototype and calculations, like most of my classmates. I slipped my phone out of my bag and, hiding it under my desk, I texted Oliver an "A" while the next person went up to do their presentation.

My phone buzzed and I looked down at the message. "*Congrats. Prof said to tell you she's sure you're going to be an amazing engineer someday.*" It buzzed again and a second message popped up. "*Everyone here is really proud of you.*"

I felt my smile grow into a grin.

☑Chapter 52

The lake water was finally getting warm, almost perfect for swimming. I splashed my toes in the shallow water and watched as the water rippled away from me in concentric circles. A turtle family had the same idea as me and were sunning themselves a few feet away on a fallen log, which my dad hadn't had the heart to have removed from our private "beach." I still had a few hours until I had to get ready for the graduation ceremony, so I had decided to come out back and just, as Phoebe liked to jokingly say sometimes, "commune with nature." The butt of my jeans was getting soggy from the patch of moss I was sitting on and I tried shifting over a little, to no luck. Soggy butt aside, I could have stayed there forever, waiting for the sun to set and the fireflies to come out, like I'd done a million times before. And while I knew I had to leave eventually to change, I let myself think otherwise and splashed my toes a little harder, scaring all of the tadpoles and making the turtles give me the turtle equivalent of a stinkeye.

"Hey, I was expecting macarons today." I jumped at the voice, this time really scaring the turtles off the log, and Leia gave a small laugh as she dropped down onto the ground next to me. "You disappointed me."

I clutched at my chest and fell onto my back dramatically, earning another round of laughter from her. After my heart rate evened out and I could breathe evenly again, I pushed my hair out of my eyes and looked up at Leia with my best attempt at a heartbreaker smile.

"The day isn't over, you know."

"I figured you'd be busy tonight—it's your graduation tonight, right?" At my small nod, she continued, "Since I haven't seen any macarons yet, I doubt you'll have time to hide any now."

"Who's to say I haven't hidden them already, and you haven't found them yet?" I said back, teasingly, and trying not to let her teasing get my hopes up. Things were getting better with Leia, but I didn't want to jump to any conclusions just because she stopped by.

"Because you're way too practical and won't put them anywhere where they could be missed and either picked up by someone else or where bugs could get to them."

"You know me way too well." I rolled onto my side, trying to look as adorable as possible by uncomfortably half-propping myself up on my elbow. I was thankful I'd worn my cutest shorts and the tank top she'd given me for my birthday last year.

"I definitely do." She picked up a flat rock from the pile I'd made earlier and flicked it so it skipped across the water. "I saw that glove thing you made on Photogram. It looks pretty amazing," she said in her most casual tone.

I nearly fell over, but fought it, using practically every muscle in my body to keep my balance. She was following me again on Photogram. "Thanks. It got an A."

"That's great," she said with a genuine smile, then it faded and her expression grew serious. "So, we really need to talk."

"I know."

"Macarons and the garden aside, you still kinda suck at emotional stuff, you know," she said while wrapping her arms around her knees and hugging them close to her like a protective barrier.

I forced myself not to straight-up disagree with her. "I'm trying. I think scooping layers of manure and compost for you has to count for something."

"Actually, it does. You are really cute when you're trying to hold your breath and not pass out."

I let out a weak laugh. "I honest-to-goodness have no idea why you enjoy gardening. It's dirty and smelly and my back still hurts from being hunched over so long."

She lit up, taking a deep breath and scrunching up her

shoulders in an achingly familiar happy movement. "It's amazing. There's magic in seeing seeds turn into plants." Her expression flattened again as she seemed to remember the purpose of the conversation and turned to meet my eyes straight on. "So, why did you break up with me and then change your mind?"

I shrugged. "I was afraid we'd get to our new schools, break up at Thanksgiving, and that it would destroy our first semester grades because that's right before finals. And that it would be a downward spiral from there into uncertain futures. So, I thought if we broke up now, we'd both have time to get over it and be ready for our new lives away from each other."

"You pre-emptively dumped me," she said flatly, but the corners of her eyes were crinkled like she was holding back a smile.

"Kind of?"

She rolled her eyes up to the sky and shook her head. "That is ridiculous."

"It made sense on paper," I said, realizing a little too late that my voice had taken on a slightly whiny tone.

"Correction, *you* are ridiculous. I can't believe you thought we weren't worth fighting for." She poked me in the arm, hard.

"I do now. I didn't think it would hurt as much as it did. I didn't realize how important you were to me until I lost you. I knew I loved you, but I didn't realize how much." I could feel sweat forming on my palms but I didn't dare wipe them on my shorts.

Her voice stayed level. "You hurt me. I had no idea why you just up and stopped trying." I stayed silent as she dug into me with her calm words, which hit harder than yelling ever would. "You know what the worst part was? You knew how crappy things were at school with Brooklyn and her minions and then, suddenly, I didn't even have you to lean on. Do you know how hard that was?"

"I'm so sorry."

"You better be. Because if we're going to try to fix this, I don't need you doing anything like it again. Or I'll head straight up to State College and kick your butt all the way back to New Jersey." Halfway through, she had cracked a smile, a bright, beautiful smile I hadn't seen in forever, and hope finally seemed like something feasible.

"So…you want to try again?"

Leia nodded. "We're not one hundred percent yet but, yes. We have a whole summer to try. Just don't overthink it this time, okay?" She reached down to the hand I had on the ground and tentatively intertwined her fingers with mine. "By the way," she whispered, looking straight into my eyes and letting her smile spread wider across her lips and touch her eyes. "I missed you, too."

□Chapter 53

I was going to sweat to death. Me, and the entire PCHS Senior class. If we didn't melt first, that was.

Someone seriously needed to rethink forcing hundreds of students to wear miles worth of unbreathable polyester in what was basically summer weather. At least our school had red graduation robes—I couldn't imagine wearing black, even for a late afternoon graduation ceremony. We were currently waiting to be lined up in the gym and half the kids had ignored the teachers and had pulled off their robes or were flapping their arms around to try to get some air circulating under the cheap material. I had unzipped mine because it had already started to suffocate me, and I was clustered with my friends under one of the air conditioning vents in the stands.

"Perfect," Em said as she finished pinning Phoebe's graduation cap to her head. "It's so much easier on your hair than mine."

Phoebe made a face and checked herself with her phone. "You mean because my hair is flatter than my singing." The humidity had plastered Phoebe's hair to her head, her waves only starting from the ear down in something that was more half-straight/half-curly frizz than any actual style. But with the cap, she looked cute, like she'd planned it.

"You said it, not me." Em pressed down on the top of her cap again and readjusted the bobby pins holding it in place. "At least you and Grace know yours won't move. Mine just doesn't want to stay. These caps were definitely not made for curly hair."

"You look smart and beautiful," Kris said to her, reaching over to flick at her orange tassel, and then bent over to give her a kiss on her cheek. "Which is exactly what you are."

Em's cheeks took on a slightly coral shade and waved him away with a grin. "As much as I could hear you say stuff like that forever, you have a speech to prep for and I don't want to be the reason you're not ready, Mister Class President." She reached over and pulled the folded papers out of his hands. "Do you want me to go over it with you again?"

He shook his head and took back the papers. "I think I'm good. I'd rather just hang with you guys. Matt is panicking about his speech and he's driving me nuts."

"That's what happens when you have valedictorians for best friends. Grace and Alec at least had the common courtesy to just graduate with honors. No nerves and speeches about how we're 'embarking on our future adventures,' etcetera." She winked at us and I reached up to touch my own "honors" gold tassel.

"Please don't tell me you're going to force us to listen to something like that, too," I said to Kris.

"Nope," He said, deadpanning. "Em nixed that about four drafts ago."

"Bless you," Phoebe said to Em, leaning over to prop her head on Em's shoulder. "Now I remember why you're my best friend."

"Ten minutes to line up," Dev said as he made his way over to squish next to Phoebe on the bleachers. His own hair was sticking out haphazardly from the bottom of the cap and Phoebe reached up to try and smooth it down. "Kris, MacKenzie asked me to remind you that you need to line up in front instead of alphabetically," he added around Phoebe's fussing.

"Got it."

"You know," Alec said, waving the air in front of him, "if they were going to stick hundreds of people in here in sweaty robes, the least they could have done was up the air conditioning. It smells worse than usual in here."

We all twisted our noses and nodded in agreement. "I'm actually going to miss this place," I said, looking around the gym I'd cheered in and suffered through endless PE in for four years. "I kind of want one more pep rally, you know? And a little more time hanging out here with all of you."

"Meh, you'll forget all about us when you're spending time around all the other super practical people going for degrees that the rest of us can't even pronounce," Alec said.

"Actually," I said, twisting the hem of my graduation robe so tightly that it was definitely going to have a major wrinkle, "I'm thinking of changing my major. Maybe practical isn't everything."

"No way," Em said, laying her hand across my forehead to mime checking for a fever.

"So, dance?" Phoebe asked, taking a moment to pull the robe from my hands before I could ruin it beyond any chance of ever getting my deposit back.

"Yeah, I'm not changing that much," I said with a smile. "But, I'm switching to an undecided engineering major and, at the end of the first semester, I'm going to audition and see if they'll let me take a dance minor. Working on that glove project made me see that maybe I might want to look into doing medical stuff. Or maybe there's some other kind of engineering I don't know about that is the perfect fit for me. I know I want to design things, but I want to try a few different things before really deciding."

"Grace, going in without a plan. We're definitely headed towards the apocalypse," Alec said in a teasing tone, bumping my shoulder with his.

I held up one finger like a teacher about to clarify a point. "I'm not going in without a plan, I'm just being flexible about my options. I looked it up and the first year of engineering has a lot of the same classes for all disciplines. And dance will keep me in shape so I don't have to worry about the freshman fifteen."

"There's also the perk of being able to transfer to a campus that's closer to here," Em fake-coughed and added, "Leia," before fake-coughing again and finishing with, "hmm?"

I turned my most serious expression on her. "Doubtful but possible, depending on the major I pick, but that's not a reason to change a major, Em."

"Let Em have her fairytale romance fantasy," Kris said with a grin, "Or you know she'll just keep coming up with ideas to make things work for you two." She poked him in the side and he ignored her, adding, "She has a huge packet of train schedules made for us. And I think she already bought tickets for a few musicals in the city."

"He's exaggerating."

"Better be, because everyone knows you only buy tickets the day of from the TKTS booth," Dev said, and Em nodded and pointed at him, mouthing "*see?*" at Kris.

"Anyway," Phoebe piped in, "it still sounds super logical."

"It is," I said with a grin back at her. "But if I decide to switch totally to a dance major, please make sure I wasn't taken over by some alien or something, okay?"

"And," Em said, stretching out the 'a' like an announcer, "she's back." She tossed a huge grin at me and followed that with, "No insulting performing arts majors, because you're got two of us in hearing distance right now." She looked over at Dev, who put on the most hilariously fake-angry face, hamming it up so it was hard for all of us to keep from laughing.

"Pfft, you'll do amazing, since you aren't risk-adverse like me," I shot back with a matching smile, just as someone blew a whistle and teachers called for us to start lining up in alphabetical order. "I'm learning that sometimes the safe way in things isn't always the best, but let me have my somewhat predictable future."

☐Chapter 54

It was already 11 a.m., but after spending most of the night riding roller coasters and eating greasy amusement park food, most of us in the booth looked like we still needed a week's worth of sleep. Except for Leia, who was annoyingly awake as she took her seat next to me in the diner booth, punctuating her, "How was it?" with a super-bright smile at me, Phoebe, and Alec.

"Coffee," Phoebe muttered, holding up her cup before taking a long sip, then added, "I'm never staying up until 3 a.m. ever again unless a book is involved. Books aren't as exhausting as roller coasters."

"Awesome one-hundred-year-old wooden roller coasters

with no lines so we could ride them over and over again," Alec said as he poured almost half the carafe of maple syrup on his stack of pancakes. "Someone text Em and tell her to tell her boyfriend that the student council gets two thumbs up for picking the best place for us to have Project Graduation."

"She's just running late. She'll be here and then you can tell her yourself," Phoebe said, then yawned.

"So, I guess it was good," Leia said in an amused tone.

I held back a laugh and nodded. "It was. I wish it hadn't been PCHS-students-only so you could have come. I know the carousel is your favorite." Collington Park was over a century old and every time we visited, Leia would make a beeline for the carousel, always marveling over the artistry of the carved wooden horses.

"It's okay. The park is open all summer. It's not going anywhere. We can go anytime."

I thrilled a little at the casual "we," but tried to just as casually cut and spear a piece of my cheese omelet, instead. "You're right."

"You'll have to count me out since I'll be in India and then it's Trix's wedding." Phoebe, now looking a little more awake, shook her head and, with a little, almost dreamy smile, said, "Wow, that sounds a little weird to say. I can't believe it's almost here."

Alec nodded. "Right? Sorry, guys, I have to bow out, too. Mom has me painting the garage floor and doing all the stuff I'd been promising to do every summer for the last four years. I'll probably never see the sun."

"I guess it's just you and me, then," Leia said to me, then stole a cherry tomato off my plate.

"I guess so," I said, then grabbed a napkin and pushed all of my cherry tomatoes onto it for her.

Phoebe looked at all of us over the top of her mug, her eyes wide. "I still can't believe that was it. School's over."

"We'll probably never see some of those people ever again," I added.

Alec bumped me with his elbow. "That's a good thing. I'm getting tired of being surrounded by Lamberts," he said with a grin.

"No more late bus or band," Phoebe said.

Leia tilted her head at that comment. "Are you giving up playing flute?"

"Not really, but I'm not doing band anymore. I'll just play for fun. Dev will have enough marching band stuff for both of us." She shrugged, and added, "I love it but we all know I'm never going pro."

"No more disco fries here after Friday night football games," I added, just barely keeping the melancholy out of my tone.

"The diner's going to go broke and close without us here to keep them busy," Alec joked. "And Marranos."

"I can't believe everything's changing so fast," Phoebe said, softly.

"Change sucks, but change is good," Em said, slipping onto the same bench as Alec and Phoebe, forcing Alec to squish against the window. "Sorry I'm late."

I turned slightly to glance at Leia, who, as it turned out, looked over at me at the same time. "I agree," she said, "change is definitely good."

"Some of us just suck a little more at adapting to it, but we're getting better," I said. I had held Leia's hand a million times before, but this time was still tentative and careful as I reached under the table and caught her hand. My heart dropped for a second before she laced her fingers with mine, gave a little squeeze, and aimed a bright smile right at me.

☑

"Can I walk you to your car?" I asked as we stepped out of the diner, feeling a little formal but still unsure of Leia. The hand squeezes and smiles were very good signs and I didn't want to mess anything up.

Leia looked up at me, her smile spreading slowly across her lips until it was blindingly bright. "Sure, I'd like that."

I waved to Phoebe, Em, and Alec through the diner window and then put my hand on the small of Leia's back to guide her down the steps and towards her car. "Forgiven, then?"

She put one finger on lips in a thinking pose for a second, then said, grin never fading, "Maybe."

"You're going to have to swear you'll never turkey dump me because I'm going to be furious if you mess up my GPA."

Leia laughed, and I had to catch her as she tripped on a part of the sidewalk that had been shoved up by a tree root. "Please, you'd survive."

I hunted for the perfect words, the perfect response to

keep our banter going, but nothing good came to mind and I just had to settle for, "I doubt it."

Leia stopped and squinted at me. "You were going through a mental list right there, weren't you?"

I arched an eyebrow at her. "No," I said, dragging out the "o."

"You were." She wrapped her arm around mine and looked up at me. "Did I ever tell you your lists are adorable?"

"Ugh, now I know what Phoebe meant when she said you had a kindergarten teacher talking to a little kid voice," I said, wrinkling my nose.

"I do not." Leia stomped her foot like an angry pixie.

I held back a "you're so cute" comment and instead said, teasingly, "It's such a condescending tone, like you think you're the only adult talking to a bunch of five- and six-year-olds." But just before she could stomp her foot again or cross her arms, I pulled her towards me like a dancer pulling her partner in for a formal dance, and smiled down at her. "But even with that tone, I'm going to miss you."

Leia stepped even closer, bringing us to slow-dance distance, and tilted her head up to catch my eyes with her now serious ones. "You'll survive. We'll survive. Distance makes the heart grow fonder, or something like that."

"True," I said softly.

"We'll just break up during winter break, instead, to preserve your precious GPA."

I bent down and caught her lips mid-laugh, and we sunk into the kiss and each other, familiarity twining with fire.

We broke apart for air and I smirked down at her. "We'll see about that. I already have a list of reasons why we should stay together."

"Oh?" Leia asked, hand reaching up to play with my ponytail.

"One," I gave her a tiny peck on the lips, "You keep me from getting too carried away with my lists."

"Good starting point," she said with a laugh.

"Two." Another kiss. "You're pretty and smart and kind. Probably the kindest person I've ever met. But you don't put up with crap and you don't let anyone else get away with it, either. Three," I kissed her on the nose this time, "you make the absolute best baklava on the planet and since you refuse to give me the recipe, I'm stuck with you if I want any."

"Damn right," she said with a laugh, wrapping her arms around my neck. "You've figured out my secret."

"Four," back to a kiss on the lips, "You make me laugh. Five," a deeper kiss and I grew more serious, looking her straight in the eyes and saying, "You're my best friend and I don't know what I would do without you."

"And six," I pulled her in for an even deeper kiss that left us both breathless. "I love you. I was ridiculous for trying to throw that away. And I will do anything to make sure this—us—survives as long as you still want me to."

Leia's eyes shone, a little watery from what I hoped were happy tears. She reached up and cupped my face, softly running her thumb down the side of my cheek. "I'm willing to try," she said, softly but firmly.

"Good."

"Good."

I copied her, running my own thumb down her cheek, then played with a strand of her hair that had fallen in front of her ear. "So, I hear this one place has great macarons. Would you like to go with me right now to get some, maybe even share a frozen hot chocolate?"

Leia pursed her lips in thought. "Okay, but only if the macarons are rose pistachio flavored. I'm a little hooked on those right now because someone kept leaving boxes of them for me."

"Deal. So, it's a date."

She lit up brighter than the sun. "It's definitely a date."

The End

ACKNOWLEDGMENTS

The most wonderful moments in my career as an engineer were when I heard back from end users—a surgeon or physician—saying a product I worked on or designed was an integral part in saving or improving someone's life. Those of us on the customer-facing part of the team were lucky enough to be in countless surgeries to see the implants or instruments that started out as just doodles or concepts in action. But, as easy as it would have been to open the email, smile, and move on, we always made sure to share the news and the joy with the entire team—from finance to our prototype team and test teams to our manufacturing teams and sites—so everyone knew their contribution touched someone's life, because without everyone, the only thing R&D and marketing would have in our hands would be sketches and a lump of metal or plastic. We were the names and faces the surgeons recognized, but a product is more than a concept and it takes an entire team of skilled people to make it reality. To make a difference.

The most wonderful moments in my career as an author have been hearing from you, the readers, about how a book has touched you or made you laugh when you needed it the most. And one of my favorite parts of being an author is writing the acknowledgements section to thank all the people who made it possible for the books to get into your hands. Books do not happen in a vacuum or appear out of thin air. There is so much behind making a book, both paper and electronic. There are so many hands that touch it and every hand makes it better. It takes a huge team of people, from the author and the team at the publisher, to the printer and people transporting the books or coding the websites, to the booksellers, librarians, teachers, and other readers and bloggers "buzzing" about it, for a book to get into your hands. I'm not going to be able to get everyone in here, but thank you all for all your hard work and support and know that, without all of you, these would just be words in my head. We don't exist alone. My name is on the cover, but this book would be *nothing* without the team that made it happen.

To my amazing editors and the entire team at Spencer Hill Press. To my editors Asja Rehse and Patricia Riley, who saw so much more in Grace's story and in my ability to write it than I realized, and push me, every time, to make better books, books I'm so proud of. To SHP's managing editor, Karen Hughes, who put up with my engineer-fueled need for schedules and details and *at least* one (I may have blocked out others!) complete and total breakdown of confidence in myself and my writing. Thank you for believing in me and in these stories.

To the people who make books readable and beautiful, giving them the polish readers deserve: Thank you to Caroline DeLuca for your magic in copyediting and for putting up with my insistence on regionalisms and my random comma usage. Thank you to PEA's Proofreader Chris Griswold and to beta reader Rebecca June Moore, whose comments also helped me find my path in the story. I have a habit of sending over-the-top requests for interior design in these books—especially this one—and Mark Karis has managed, every time, to make the interiors lovelier than I could even imagine. Thank you so much, Jenny Zamenak, for giving the Ever After series the prettiest set of covers on the planet, especially the wonderful ***pink***-meets-tech for PEA.

To Meredith Maresco, who has the magical ability of knowing when I need heart emojis flung my way. I'm in awe of your creativity and kindness, and I'm lucky to work with such an awesome publicist and friend.

And to Eric Kampmann and the entire, extended SHP team who has made me feel so welcome. Thank you for your support and skill.

We write to allow readers an escape from the everyday world, to provide a mirror or a window, or to help them work through tough times, especially when we write for younger readers. We don't write to hurt, and I am thankful to PEA's sensitivity reader, Candice Montgomery, for your reads of this manuscript, comments, kind words, and guidance towards that goal.

To Carrie Howland, I'm so glad we got to work together on this series. Thank you for being a part of my author journey and supporting me throughout. I still owe you that ice cream!

Thank you, Veronica Bartles, for your friendship, suggestions, and support. Without you, I would have stayed frozen in uncertainty about letting Grace's love of dance and engineering shine through. You've been my lighthouse through some of my largest moments of self-doubt and I am so grateful that you are in my life.

This book wouldn't exist without the engineering professors who sparked my love and curiosity for what would become my "day job." To all of my engineering and product design mentors; HCPs, physicians, and surgeons; coworkers; and, especially, my "day job" managers over the life of this series—Charlie, Matt, Mariel, Kristin, and Alex—you challenge me to be a better engineer, and remind me why I love being a problem solver with CAD and a calculator. Readers will get to see some of your guidance, advice, and skill reflected in Oliver's and Dr. Aubrey's characters. Thank you to the R&Divas, especially Erika, Chris, and Lori, for your constant support.

Just like engineering is a big part of this book, I couldn't do it without an endlessly fed love for writing and craft. Thank you to my friends in Eastern PA SCBWI, especially Kim Briggs and Alison Myers, for being my cheerleaders, supporters, and friends. And thank you to the Highlights Foundation for providing a creative space where I've come back to my roots in making these books and where I always remember why I love to write.

Dance is a big part of Grace and PEA, and though my feet and legs haven't let me take classes in years, and I miss it so much, writing Grace dancing brought me straight back to the studio. To all of my dance teachers and class-mates—especially the Dance Academy and Dance Place Plus teachers and dancers—thank you for helping me to live those magic moments of getting lost in the music.

To my family and extended family, thank you for all the support, love, and (usually dorky, sometimes deep) STEM fueled debates around the dinner table. To Nela and Susie, who have been my partners in STEM dorkiness—I'm lucky I have the best sisters ever. To Dennis and Joey, who routinely put up with getting dragged to their batty sister-in-law's book events—thank you for being there. I'm lucky to have you both in the family.

To Sara, my little dancer, and to Joey, my little writer: I know Joey's "acknowledgements" section will be a million times better than mine and Sara will dance circles around me (and I wouldn't expect anything less). Thank you for being my signing table buddies and writing support team.

Finally, even though I said it in the dedication: thank you, Mom and Dad, for believing in me and supporting me. I love you.

ABOUT THE AUTHOR

Author photo by Rachel McCalley

Isabel Bandeira grew up surrounded by trees and lakes in Southern New Jersey, right on the edge of the Pine Barrens. Her summers were always spent in Portugal, where the cathedrals, castles, and ancient tombs only fed her fairy tale obsession. Between all those influences and her serious glitter addiction, it wasn't a surprise when she started writing stories of her own.

In her free time between writing and her day job as a mechanical engineer who designs and develops medical devices, she reads, dances, figure skates, and knits.

Isabel lives in New Jersey with her little black cat, too many books, and a closetful of vintage hats.

Practically Ever After is Book Three in the popular Ever After series.